THREE TIMES A LADY

EILEEN DREYER

OLIVERHEBERBOOKS

Published by Oliver-Heber Books

0 9 8 7 6 5 4 3 2 1

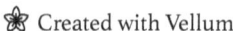 Created with Vellum

1

AUTUMN, 1815

A sensible woman would know when to give up. But then, Phillipa Ellen Alexandra Trentham Knight had never been sensible. Even if she had not been told so since birth, she would know it now. After all, wasn't she standing behind the potted ferns in the Duke of Dorchester's crowded ballroom just so she could catch a glimpse of Beau Drummond? Hadn't she spent most of her life doing much the same thing? Hiding behind ferns and curtains, trees and river rocks, chairs and desks, just to be able to watch Beau Drummond as he went about his day?

This time was different, though. This time she was protecting him, even though he didn't know it. She had sensibly laid down her childhood dreams of a life with Beau a while ago. She had only been able to get passing glimpses of him for the last few years. But her favored lurking position came in handy when she needed to keep him safe.

"Pip, when are you going to give up?" she heard behind her.

Pip didn't bother to turn or drop the gold lorgnette from her eyes. She couldn't afford the distraction right now. Not when Beau needed her. But it was her friend Lizzie Ripton standing behind her, and she could never quite be mad at Lizzie. Lizzie Meant Well.

"This is not what you think," Pip whispered without removing her attention from Beau as he stood across a crowd of swirling dancers conversing with the deadly beautiful Lady Pamela Smythe-Smithe

Pip didn't trust Lady Pamela Smythe-Smithe, and not merely because she had a ridiculous name. Lady Pamela had set her sights on Beau long ago. But worse, tonight she was distracting Beau from what Pip knew was his purpose here. And he didn't even seem to mind. If he did, he would be rubbing at his temple as he did when he was impatient, or tugging at his earlobe, which he still didn't realize was his sign asking somebody to save him from an unpleasant situation. No, Beau was *smiling*.

"Then what is it?" Lizzie asked, her elegant voice patient.

But Pip couldn't tell her. Lizzie was one of her very best friends from their days together at the boarding school they had nicknamed Last Chance Academy. But Lizzie didn't know everything about Pip. She certainly didn't know everything there was to know about Beau.

"What do you think of Pamela the Perfect?" Pip asked instead.

Lizzie did something almost unheard of from her. She snorted. "I think her husband needs to take himself out of the card room long enough to control her. And I'm afraid your Beau is as idiotic as all the other men who have thrown themselves at her dainty little feet."

Maybe her feet were dainty, Lizzie thought sourly. Everything else, though, was built along more voluptuous lines and arranged to highlight them, from the barely contained coils of thick, burnished hair the color of a chestnut horse to the black lace dress that should have made people think of mourning, but somehow didn't, to the perfectly demure diamond and ruby necklace that managed to draw the eye right to her over-sized breasts.

Then there was her face, as sensual and sleek as a cat, with knowing green eyes, porcelain skin, and a mouth that made one think of pillows. Pip was thinking of pillows herself, but more in how she would like to press one over that smirking face.

"You are far prettier than she is," Lizzie said. "She's preda-tory. You're--"

Pip swung around and leveled the lorgnette up at her friend like a weapon. "If you dare say the word elfin, I swear I shall skewer you."

Lizzie grinned down on her. "I would never."

It was Pip's turn to snort. With yellow hair the shape and texture of a dandelion, oversized blue eyes, and the stature of a tweeny, Pip was well-acquainted with her reputation. *Isn't she cute? Don't you expect to find her perched on a lily pad? Isn't she...elfin.* It was enough to make a girl mad as snakes. Espe-cially when the man she loved was making cow eyes at a veri-table siren.

Pamela was sliding her perfectly manicured fingers down Beau's arm, as if petting him, and it made Pip see red. Not because the hussy was acting like a hussy—how else would hussies act, really? —Because Beau—*her* Beau—was smiling like an idiot. And it was the first time she had seen him smile in over a year.

"St. Stephen's sidewhiskers," she blurted out. "Isn't there one man who can think with the correct part of his body?"

She heard Lizzie sputter and couldn't help but grin. One of her greatest pleasures in life was disconcerting Lizzie. Poor Lizzie had been raised the very proper daughter of a duke—the Duke of Dorchester, to be precise. Pip had always consid-ered it one of her own missions in life to loosen Lizzie up a bit.

"Pip, really," her friend cautioned. "You simply cannot go about saying such things."

"Am I wrong?" Pip asked, curling her fingers into her palms to keep from scratching the lovely Pamela's eyes out.

"No. But that is not the point."

"It is precisely the point. Beau is in danger, and yet he continues to dally with that reptile."

"The way I see it," Lizzie disagreed wryly, "the only thing he is in danger of is exhaustion."

Dropping the lorgnette on its ribbon, Pip whipped around to see Lizzie's beautiful blond patrician features go all red.

"Elizabeth Charlotte Warren Dalrymple Ripton," she gasped. Then, abruptly, she grinned. "I'm proud of you. That must be the first even faintly salacious thing I have ever heard you say."

Lizzie's answering grin was weak at best. "You are a bad influence."

Pip giggled. "Finally. Now--" She spun back to consider the couple, "how do we extricate him?"

"We do not. It is none of our business, Pip. And you know he would not thank you."

Pip sighed, her heart aching even more than it usually did in Beau's presence. "He wouldn't thank me even if I brought Theo back."

Beau's little brother Theo. The very best and finest friend Pip had ever had Theo. Lost at the battle of Toulouse Theo, sending Beau into a darkness Pip couldn't seem to pull him from.

"It has been over a year," Lizzie mused. "You would think his grief would ease, at least a little."

"Maybe his grief has. His anger hasn't. He hasn't forgiven me for encouraging Theo to join the Dragoons."

"But Beau bought his colors for him."

"Only after Theo threatened to take the king's shilling and fight as a common soldier."

Battling a surge of grief and guilt, Pip briefly looked away. How could she explain how desperate Theo had been to go? How could anybody know that she would have given anything in her life to have been able to go with him? She knew it was absurd, but she had the most persistent feeling that she could have saved him if she'd been there.

Which was why she felt so compelled to keep an eye on Beau, no matter his animosity toward her. He had no one else who loved him as much as Theo had. Just her.

So she watched him when she could, tried to help him when he had no other choice, and mourned the knowledge that he would never realize that what he really needed in his life was her.

She watched him now, smiling down at Perfect Pamela as if she were a peach tart on his tea tray and could have wept. He was so beautiful to her. Tall, lithe, as elegant and graceful as a stallion, usually as severe as the Spanish grandees who lurked in his mother's family line and made their presence known in his curling black hair and midnight eyes. But when Beau smiled, oh, when he smiled. His midnight eyes gleamed, his temples crinkled, his face eased, and his severely beautiful face lit with a sweetness that Pip once thought reserved only for her.

Now, though, she got only the scowls. The impatience and frustration. Now she paid the double cost for loving Beau and losing Theo.

"Pip," Lizzie said, not moving. "At least dance with someone. You can keep an eye on Beau and help make the evening a success."

Pip turned finally to see genuine concern in her friend's perfect English blue eyes. She understood, because she had known Lizzie for six rather tumultuous years, that Lizzie truly cared. Tall and regal and elegantly blonde as a duke's daughter should be, Lizzie had been trained away from excessive shows of emotion. One had to look deep. But Pip had long since perfected the talent.

So, she gave her friend a quick, tight hug that made Lizzie instinctively stiffen. "Oh, Lizzie, you don't need me to have a success. You and your mother are the best hostesses in the *ton*. Look at the crowd out there. They're dancing and laughing and eating their way through enough lobster patties to feed Liverpool."

And indeed, they were. Dozens of them who'd made the trip from London for the duchess's house party; the cream of the *ton*, chattering like a flock of exotic, multicolored birds caught in a marble and gilt cage. Jewels glittered in the light of chandeliers, fiddles scratched out a country dance that sent the birds flapping and jumping, and the air was redolent with the mix of floral scents, patchouli and sweat. Society at its finest.

"But it isn't the same without you," Lizzie protested, her lovely face scrunched in something approaching misery. "I don't believe you know how much everyone loves you. Why, you're the life of every party."

A happy talent to have when you constantly find yourself foisted on friends and family while your own is a continent away.

"In a moment. I promise." Giving Lizzie another hug, Pip tried to gently push her friend back toward the dance floor. "Go. I'll be fine."

Lizzie sighed, just as Pip thought she would. "You don't mind covering for me later in case anyone asks my whereabouts."

"Of course not. Although it would be far easier if I knew why."

Lizzie's smile this time looked more weary than grateful. "You will soon. Just not yet."

Pip scowled. "All right. By the way. Did I tell you the price for my silence?"

Lizzie froze. "What?"

Pip grinned. "Where did you put up La Smythe-Smithe?"

Lizzie frowned. "Pip...."

"I promise. I shan't hurt her. But I think it's important."

Lizzie looked back to where Beau was now bent to Pamela's ear, her elbow in his hand, her breasts all but leaving dents in his waistcoat. "No frogs in her bed," she demanded.

"No frogs."

"No ghostly apparitions in the middle of the night."

Pip chuckled. "Come now, Liz, you must admit that I was inspired. I will never forget the sight of Lady Barker running down the hall in her shift dropping other people's bracelets as she ran. You never would have had the evidence of her thievery otherwise."

"I was going to search her room."

"She was carrying everything on her person. Well, until she was visited by the ghost of her mother, anyway."

Lizzie sighed again. "The Red Suite."

Pip gave her a big grin. "Appropriate. It looks like a bordello."

Lizzie scowled. "Don't be silly. That was the queen's suite."

Pip giggled. "My, our queen has unexpected depths."

"Not that queen..."

"What about our queen?" they both heard.

Pip almost groaned out loud. Neither of them had noticed that they had been approached by none other than the current queen's granddaughter.

"Your Highness," Pip intoned with Lizzie as both dipped curtsies to the seventeen-year-old heir to the English throne.

Princess Charlotte, plump and pretty and up for every rig and row, waved away the formality. "You both know better than to play up to me. I am *quite* powerless to help better your lots, which means we are all three forced to endure this *excruciatingly* dull party. Not that I blame your dear *maman*, Elizabeth. She throws the most *divine* affairs, and she was *so* kind to make sure the Prince of Wales could not deny her invitation to me. It is simply that the Prince of Wales has burdened me with the most *dreadful* watchers. Only my own dear Mercer has my interests at heart. And you also, I hope."

Pip dreaded having to answer. She really did like the princess, but if she became embroiled in one of Charlotte's escapades, it would go much harder on her than the crown princess. And that was just from the government. She didn't even want to consider what her parents would do.

"We are here to serve," Lizzie assured the princess, but in a tone of voice that dampened expectations.

Charlotte giggled and patted both of them on the shoulder. "It is *quite* good to know that you will be there if I need you. After watching your exhibition this afternoon with bow and arrow, Lady Phillipa, I should insist you carry a bow to protect me at all times. Astonishing display."

Pip gave a quick curtsy. "It was my pleasure, Your Highness."

Much more of a pleasure than constantly having to disabuse people of the notion that she could sing or paint or stitch.

The princess patted her on the arm. "I had heard about your unusual skills, of course. Can't wait to see you on a horse. I understand you could do a turn at Astley's. For now, however, I simply wish to hide out along with you to watch the party." Her attention became riveted on Beau and his partner. "Most *diverting*, is it not? I swear, if my heart were not already given, I would *delight* in spending more time with that delicious Viscount Drummond. Too bad Lady Smythe-Smithe found him first."

"Indeed," was all Pip said, but the princess turned alert

eyes.

"Do you think she is his mistress?" the princess asked.

Pip came within a hair's breadth of cursing at a member of the royal family. Because, of course, that was exactly what Pamela was. Pip had known it for weeks now. Her stomach ached with it.

"I wouldn't know, Your Highness," Lizzie demurred grimly.

The princess just grinned. "Would you like me to have her...*discommoded*?" she asked, leaning close to Pip. "A word to my guard and she can be taken up for a spy."

Pip battled an unholy urge to say yes. After all, it would solve more than one problem. But Pip didn't need Beau finding out that she had lodged a treason charge against his mistress.

"If I could take that under advisement, Your Highness."

Charlotte chuckled. "Well, let me know. I am quite certain that I wouldn't wish that harpy getting her claws into the man *I* love."

Pip sighed. It was hardly a secret that she had been trotting after Beau since the day she had been released from leading strings. She wondered right now how many people were watching her watch him to see how she reacted to his behavior, even though she had deliberately done her best to cut him off from her own heart.

But why would she react, really? He was only lifting La Smythe-Smithe's wrist to deposit a lingering kiss on the tender inside.

Dolt.

"I am quite certain I can think of something that might get his attention," Princess Charlotte offered, obviously amused. "Or I could simply call for her husband..."

Pip swung on her. "No!" Taking a breath, she smiled. "Thank you, Your Highness, but this is a dance I have long since walked away from. I have better things to do than try to convince a grown man he has the taste of a street sweep."

Smiling, the princess gave Pip another condescending pat, which looked fairly ludicrous coming from a seventeen-year-old girl, no matter how royal, considering the fact that Pip had passed her twentieth birthday. "Of course, you have. Although I am certain I cannot imagine why. I will have my Leopold, no matter what anyone says."

Pip wasn't certain how to react. This was the first she had heard of this. "I am certain you will, ma'am."

She didn't even mention the fact that it would do her no good if Leopold didn't agree with her.

Compelled, Pip turned back to Beau, only to realize that he was gone. The pouting Pamela was still there, now scanning the ballroom with avid eyes, but Beau had somehow slipped away while Pip wasn't watching.

Pip couldn't quell a burst of panic. She needed to warn him before he found himself in serious trouble. She had to tell him about the men she'd overheard earlier.

She had been tucked into the shadows on the patio hiding from the unappreciated ardor of a junior Guards officer when she'd caught a gleam of silver hair in the shadows.

"I tell you someone has been sent to look for the plans," another man murmured. "We shall watch for him."

Well, if that didn't bring a girl to a stop, Pip didn't know what would.

"We shall *stop* him," the silver-haired man answered, his voice a distinctive rasp Pip didn't recognize. "I have let it be known that the plans are hidden in the library. If we catch him, we can dispatch him."

"And the real plans?"

"Safe in her bedroom." There was a low chuckle. "I placed them there myself."

Pip had actually stopped breathing. They were speaking of spies. Government spies. And Pip knew perfectly well who the government spy at the party was.

And now he had disappeared before she could warn him.

"Excuse me," she murmured now, giving the princess a last curtsy. "But I must...."

Charlotte chuckled, having seen just what Pip had. "Good hunting."

She had no idea, Pip thought.

"Pip...." Lizzie warned.

Pip dropped a quick kiss on her friend's cheek. "Don't worry."

"That's what you always say." Lizzie's face looked positively lugubrious. "Right before disaster strikes."

A SENSIBLE MAN would have given up long ago. But Beau Drummond couldn't afford to be sensible. He had been sent to this house party to uncover vital information in a plot against the throne, and he couldn't quit until he found it. In the meantime, he was forced to endure yet another pointless house party with a group of perfectly useless people. It was enough to give a man a headache.

Or was that from the stench of patchouli that lingered on his coat sleeve? Good God, what did Pamela think she was doing, marking him like a civet cat?

He scowled, because of course that was exactly what she was trying to do. The only upside to her possessive display was that he knew Pip had been watching. Pip always watched, and he could no longer allow her to. No matter how much it hurt her, he had to warn her away.

It would be so much easier if Pamela could simply intimidate her. After all, how could a tatterdemalion like Pip with her dandelion-puff hair and tiny stature and ever-present spectacles compare with the most sensual woman in the ton? Pip was a gamine. Pamela was a witch. And even Pip should know that

men far preferred the dark magic of a witch to the uncomplicated enthusiasm of an elf. And yet, Pip refused to be shaken
loose.

He took one final look around the room, where couples
spun by in a whir of color and form, their teeth bared, gems
glittering, and chatter deafening. Violins scraped, crystal
glasses tinged like bells and the butler gravely intoned a late-
comer's name. Normal, familiar, and a crashing bore.

Beau had more important things to do, and little time in
which to do them. Standing in the shadowed corridor just long
enough to see Pamela slip her arm through Billy Fielder's, he
turned to go. He saw Pip, of course, tucked in behind the potted
palms, that silly little gold lorgnette raised to her eyes as if that
would make her need for spectacles more romantic. Her hair
was a pale nimbus around her head, untamable and
unarrangeable, and her dress was a burnt orange, simple,
unadorned, and just a bit short at the ankle so that he could see
her tiny feet tapping to the music.

Irrepressible, was Pip. A creature of impulse and emotion.
The very worst kind of person to have in one's life. He was
finished with that nonsense, and the sooner he could convince
her of it the better.

He waited until he saw her turn to answer....bloody hell,
was that Princess Charlotte she was talking to? He almost
groaned out loud. The last thing he needed, the very last, was
to have Pip walking into his investigation, and if she took up
with the princess, that lady would surely put herself in a position to completely muck up his work.

Ah well, he thought, turning back to his purpose. She could
be dealt with later. She wasn't going anywhere, and he had
business that needed doing right now. Before anyone took
notice of his departure. Before anyone asked questions.

Pip's first impulse was to follow him. After all, she knew where he was going and why. She could intercept him. Warn him.

Except that he wouldn't believe her. Not unless she walked in on him in the act of searching for the plans. There was no question it was Beau the men had been talking about. Pip had long since known of Beau's involvement in a group set on protecting the crown. Her own brother Alex was in the same group, who had long since been dubbed Drake's Rakes. And Alex had just been here on much the same mission.

Neither of them knew she knew, of course, even though years ago she had tried to tell Alex. Pip decided that that made her all the more vital to Beau right now. After all, Alex had left the house party along with the other Rakes who had been here, so Beau needed someone to watch his back. And only Pip had seen his enemies make their plans this evening. Only she could protect him from his enemies.

She hoped.

Putting on her most credulous expression, which had always served her well when she wished people to underestimate her, she turned to follow him past the swaths of crimson silk that hung from the chandeliers and camouflaged the corridor.

She had almost made it out of the ballroom when Lizzie's mother, the duchess, stepped in front of her.

"Dearest Pip," she said with a gentle smile, her hand on a short, pudgy gentleman's arm. "I haven't seen you dancing."

Biting back a protest, Pip halted. "Oh, I have been, your grace. But the Princess of Wales wished a word."

"And now Mr. Larson has expressed a desire to make your acquaintance. I am quite certain he would enjoy a boulangère with you."

Blast. The last thing Pip needed. Mr. Larson had the look of a man who would be difficult to shake off. And she simply did not have time.

"When I return if I may, Mr. Larsen," she said. "Right now, I'm afraid I have need of the women's retiring room."

And a man couldn't very well argue with that.

Mr. Larsen's dim brown eyes widened at her solecism. "Oh, yes. Quite. Indeed."

Before the duchess could protest, Pip had slipped past.

Thank heavens Ripton Hall had become something of a second home while her parents were in Russia, because Pip knew it like the back of her hand. Not only did she know exactly where the library was, she knew how to route herself to camouflage her intended destination.

The place was immense, three hundred years of ducal excess built around the cloistered square of a once-proud Cistercian abbey. The public rooms were to the south, with the ballroom on the ground floor and the dining room and card room a floor up, a corridor away from the family rooms and the duke's private library. So it was a quick trip up the stairs and along the corridor, nodding to strolling guests, smiling at well-known footmen as if she were simply heading to the retiring room, which was just around the corner.

She had just turned that corner when several women stepped out of the retiring room. Drat! Since there was no other reason for her to be in the hallway, she smiled and nodded.

"Oh, Pip, dear," one of them trilled, and Pip braced herself for the inevitable venom. "I haven't seen Viscount Drummond dancing with you tonight, have I?"

Pip smiled back just as sweetly. "You have not seen me dancing with him for a year, Susie. Which you would know if you were usually invited to the same parties we are. Your aunt brought you, did she?"

Susie's face grew mottled, and she swept past, pulling her skirts away from Pip's. Which suited Pip perfectly. Just so no one questioned her actions, she entered the retiring room and spent a few moments behind the screen. It was taking too long, was all she kept thinking. She would be too late.

The other women who had shared the room with her left in a chattering group, and Pip reemerged to make the last turn to the library.

There was a light under the closed door. Pip's heart sped up even more. She took one last look down the brightly lit corridor to make certain that no one was paying attention and turned the handle.

She had hoped to see Beau inside, so she could warn him. It would be even better, of course, if he were already gone, but she was honest enough to admit she would be happier if she could be of some help. She eased the door open and slipped through.

Beau was there, all right. He was standing by the desk with folded papers in one hand and a gun pointed right at her heart in the other.

His expression went hard, and he lowered the gun. "What in God's name do you think you're doing?"

"I don't think those papers are real," she said, easing the door closed behind her. She could see that the desk was perfectly tidy and the walls seemingly untouched. She had no idea where he had gotten the papers, but he had obviously hidden his entry. "We have to leave."

"I don't know what you're talking about——"

"The plans, Beau, whatever they are. You cannot take them. They will know it is you looking for them."

He shoved the pistol into a drawer and the papers into his jacket. "I'm not. I've copied—" His head came up, and he was scowling. "What are you talking about?"

But in the end, they didn't have time, because Pip heard it. The voice. That unique raspy whisper, approaching down the hallway.

"I'm telling you someone is in there," it was saying.

Beau had been approaching her, Pip knew, to give her a

piece of his mind. To shove her out of the door and out of his life. She never gave him a chance. Only able to think of one option to explain their presence alone in the library, the minute he got close enough, she grabbed him by the lapels and pulled him to her. Before he could protest or chastise, she pulled his head down and kissed him.

For a moment, he froze. It was enough. She grabbed fistfuls of his jacket and held on as tightly as she could, terrified he would pull away and yell at her before the door opened. Before the spies realized that there wasn't a perfectly logical reason for Beau to be here. Pip kissed him with every ounce of passion in her. She prayed he knew what she was about and would just shut up. Would be distracted enough that he wouldn't waste her effort.

Something went wrong, though. Something dark and hot and shattering.

She had never kissed Beau before. Not like this. He had never let her. And so, she wouldn't know that when their mouths met they would ignite a firestorm. She felt stunned, shaken, as if lightning had struck. She gasped. She thought she gasped. Or it might have been Beau, because suddenly his arms were around her and he had her pushed against the wall, his body pressed against hers, his hands suddenly roving.

His mouth was hot and hungry and demanding, urging hers open until she felt his tongue invade, slick and sleek and sensual against hers. She met him in a dance she had never learned, scrabbling at his chest, his shoulders, his neck, twining her fingers into the thick curls at his collar. Desperate for the touch of him, the taste of him, the hard length of him against her, surrounding her, supporting her when the strength went out of her knees and only his arms held her up against the wall.

She couldn't think. She couldn't remember what she was doing here. She didn't care. She had imagined forever what it would be like in Beau's arms. But she had had no idea. No

earthly clue. She hadn't realized that there would be no tender-
ness between them, no restraint. No patience. Just a terrible
need, a glittering, sweeping heat that fused them, even before
she felt his hand on her breast. Before he dragged the top of her
bodice down far enough to pull his mouth away from hers and
drop it to her nipple.

Pain, pleasure, she wasn't certain exactly, but hot and sweet
rocketed through her. She was gasping, clutching, arching
against him, desperate for the heat of his mouth against her,
the sharp, sweet pain of his teeth scraping her nipple. His hand
sliding down her belly, down between her legs, trailing fire,
terrifying her with the power of his touch.

"Beau....oh, Beau...."

The world would never be the same. Her life, her beliefs,
her dreams had been tumbled askew, forever colored by this
moment, this fierce, frightening compulsion to finish this. To
find out where it all led. To know what it meant that she could
feel something hard and urgent against her belly. Her
Beau, her...

"Oh, dear. Did we interrupt something?"

She was proud of herself. She didn't shriek, even when she
realized that the voice belonged to the ubiquitous Pamela. She
froze instead, her face pressed against Beau's jacket, her bodice
pulled askew, her knees the consistency of pudding.

Beau slowly lifted his head. She could feel his heart
pounding against her chest. She could hear the rasp of his
breath as he strove for control. She desperately struggled for
clarity.

And then, that voice.

"We obviously interrupt."

That voice. That deep, odd rasp. She felt as if she'd been
doused with cold water. Of course. It was why she had come.
Why she had dragged Beau into that kiss in the first place. She
had to make sure that the man with the voice didn't know what

Beau had been doing. Briefly closing her eyes, she lifted a hand to right her bodice, briefly dipping into Beau's jacket on the way by.

"You are *de trop*," Beau warned.

"So we see." There was amusement in the voice.

Pip carefully turned to see who it was.

No one she knew. A middle-aged man with snow white hair and oddly gentle eyes. And behind him among a small gathering, as if to punish Pip for all her sins, Lady Pamela Smythe-Smithe, looking at once arch and condescending.

"Dabbling in the infantry, Beau?" she asked, the fury in her voice barely contained beneath its saccharine tone.

She smells like a whorehouse, was all Pip could think. *And she will do everything she can to ruin me.*

"You both may congratulate us," Beau said, taking a step in front of Pip. "Phillipa has consented to be my bride."

Pip's heart shrank. No. Not like this. Never like this. She must have taken an instinctive step of protest, for suddenly she felt Beau's hand clamp onto her arm. She wasn't going anywhere.

"Excellent," the gentleman said, stepping up to take Beau's hand.

Beau let loose of Pip to shake hands and ended up in a full, quick hug from the man. Pip stared, wondering at it, until she saw the man's eyes flit over the library toward the painting of Ripton Hall that hung behind the desk. The painting Pip knew covered a wall safe.

She swore her heart stopped. Had he been making sure Beau didn't carry papers? St. Peter's pipes, that was close.

"If you would give me a moment with my fiancé," Beau suggested, not moving.

The gentleman beamed. "Of course. We shall see you in the ballroom for the announcement."

And with that, he all but dragged his followers including

Lady Pamela from the room.

Finally allowing herself to breath, Pip turned a smile on Beau. She had saved him after all. He would be so grateful.

One look told the real tale. He looked as cold as death, staring down at her as if he'd seen a slug in his soup. "Did you arrange that?"

She blinked. "What?"

Pip could never remember seeing such disdain in his eyes. "Did you finally run out of patience, Pip? Was that it? Or was this just one of your brilliant spur-of-the-moment ideas to coerce me into marriage?"

Pip felt flummoxed. "But I didn't..."

His expression only grew more disgusted. "Of course, you did. I expected more of you than a cheap trick like this. Was it Pamela? Were you jealous? Or just tired of waiting to get married? Or did you know, finally, that the only way I would ever marry you was to be tricked into it?"

She kept staring. "You think that was what this was all about?"

"Of course. And you finally got what you wanted. Whether you'll be happy with the results is another matter."

For the longest time, she could only stare, the delirium of the past moments disintegrating into cold ashes. She swore a great chasm opened up where her heart had been. She couldn't even draw breath.

And then, blessedly, the rage came, clearing the cobwebs and slipping steel into her spine. "Why yes," she said, her voice at least as cold as his. "I did get what I wanted. But it obviously is not what you think."

"What then?"

Her smile was as grim as death. She shook her head. "Don't worry. You'll know soon enough."

And before Beau could see the tears welling in her eyes, she swept out of the room.

2
_____

Beau would have discovered the answer to Pip's challenge a lot sooner if he hadn't been so completely bowled over. For the longest time after the echoes died from Pip's dramatic exit, Beau couldn't seem to do anything but stand there, his lips still hot, his stomach hotter, and his brains melted right into his shoes.

What had he done?

What had *she* done? Who did she think she was, setting him up like that? Had she arranged to be followed by Pamela and the earl? Did she really want to be ruined? And why in bloody hell had she ever kissed him?

Kiss? That had been no kiss. It had been a whirlwind. A cataclysm. Christ, he was shaking as if he had the ague, and his cock was bone stiff. For Pip. For pugnacious, precocious, provocative Pip.

Pip.

It was incomprehensible. He didn't like sprites or elves or children dressed as fairies. He had certainly never wanted to bed one. But he was sure as hell ready to bed Pip. How could that be? When he thought of her, he thought of that pugnacious little ten-year-old who had insisted on coming on adventures with him and Theo. And yet...

He shoved his hands through his once-carefully styled hair. How had she known? She had to have somehow realized that he would react like this. Planned on it, to the second so they would be caught in a compromising position. She must have been planning this for days. Weeks. And all so she could finally force him into noticing her. No, not noticing her. Marrying her. After all, it was the only possible outcome of her little ploy.

A small voice of reason whispered that that wasn't like Pip. She was many things, but he had never known her to be less than honest. Painfully so, sometimes. Pip might have worked to get her own way, but he'd never known her to be underhanded.

It might have helped if he'd given her a chance to explain. For now, though, he had to convince his cock to surrender so he could be seen in the corridors, otherwise he would never get these papers back to...

He patted his jacket. He patted again, expecting to hear the crinkle. He reached inside, only to find the pocket completely empty. His gut lurched. Someone had lifted those papers from him. Somehow, while he was being compromised, he'd been compromised.

The earl? Inconceivable. He was on the Privy Council, a gentle man with gentle hobbies. Pamela? No. She hadn't come close enough. Not when the evidence of his disloyalty had been so painfully obvious.

Then who?

There was only one option left.

"I'll kill her," he snarled, stalking over to the door. But when he yanked it open, he stalked straight into his Aunt Maude, who had just raised her hand for the knob. The old harridan looked ready to commit murder.

"How *could* you?" she demanded in a voice like Gabriel's horn, which was distinctive coming from a woman the size of a gnome. "Even *you*. I should have known better than to expect you to respect the honor of your family, but when have you ever made us proud? And now, to take up with that little ragbag, and in the duke's own home! Well, I will tell you this. Let her be your mistress. I have no care for that. But you will *not* bring her across the threshold of Delamere."

Again, Beau found himself frozen in place, struggling for control. What was it about tiny women and out-sized personalities? He stared down at the squared-off, suspiciously blond woman who had tormented him as a youth and adult. Fortunately, he had gained far too much experience in subterfuge to let her distract him.

"This may come as a shock to you, aunt," he said, his voice deceptively lazy, "but you have no say in who I bring across the threshold of my home."

He didn't even mention the fact that her relationship to the family she was so protective of was only by marriage. That would just provoke another tantrum and further recriminations from her husband when he showed up to support her.

Beau might as well have turned the old battle-axe to stone, which might be the only thing saving Pip's life. He couldn't remember the last time he had surprised his aunt into silence.

Flashing her a dry smile, he stepped past. "Now, if you don't mind, I need to collect my fiancée. We have an announcement to make."

He imagined his aunt thought he would be crushed by the fact that she pulled her puce skirts away from him as he passed, but in fact, he wasn't. The smile he had donned to annoy her just grew.

"Unfeeling boy," she snapped.

"Indeed, I must be," he said, not bothering to stop. "But if that bothers you, feel free to leave Delamere and return to your own home."

He could hear her sputtering behind him, which only made

his smile grow. Either way, he realized, he won. Either his marriage would finally dislodged his aunt and uncle from Delamere, or his aunt would bedevil Pip into dribbling madness. Suddenly, the future seemed a bit less bleak.

His improved mood lasted until he stepped into the ballroom to be met by sudden, dead silence. In a blink, the buzzing started, accompanied by smiles, winks, and the shaking of more proper heads. The word was out, then. All that was left was to collect Pip and make the deuced announcement, just as she wanted.

Except Pip wasn't in the room. Instead, the duchess approached, her expression betraying nothing.

"I understand we are to congratulate you and our dear Pip," she murmured, setting her hand atop his arm and turning him back toward the corridor.

"Where is she?" he growled.

He got quite a healthy pinch for that solecism. "She has retired briefly with my Elizabeth to freshen up before we call you both forward. I know that you, too, would like to make sure you show the proper enthusiasm for your announcement. Would you need a moment?"

He pulled in a breath, furious as much at himself for being blindsided as with Pip for accomplishing it. Even more furious that his body still threatened to betray his reaction to that damnable kiss. God, and it had to be in front of Pamela of all people.

And here he'd believed his mission here had been accomplished.

"Viscount Drummond?"

Startled, he forced a smile for the duchess. "My apologies, Your Grace. I was merely planning."

She smiled back, as placidly as if they discussed seating arrangements. "Of course. I have the address of the Knight family lawyers who will be able to negotiate the contracts, and of course, her father's direction in St. Petersburg. I am certain you will wish to contact him."

This time Beau's smile was genuine. "An excellent idea, your grace."

Better than excellent. He could delay any action as long as he wanted, blaming the mails to Russia. Given a few weeks, he and Pip could simply decide they didn't suit. And in the meantime, he could get the plans to his superiors.

"And now," the duchess said with another pat, "I imagine the drinks bar in the small saloon might be a nice stop to make while our dear Pip prepares."

Giving the duchess's hand a quick salute, he strode off to find some comfort. Dutch courage.

HIS NEMESIS WAS HAVING troubles of her own.

She might have escaped the consequences of her impulsive act if she could have kept her countenance better. But when she had stalked out of the library, it had been right into Lizzie's mother. And she could tell with one look that the duchess had already heard the news.

"I won't," Pip insisted, red-faced. "That ungrateful cur can whistle his engagement down the wind as far as I'm concerned."

Without a word Pip found herself hustled up into her bedroom to be met by her lady's maid and Lizzie, both of whom were wringing their hands.

Pip was not surprised at all that it was her maid who took the first shot.

Soft brown hands on generous hips, Joyful Matthews turned her great dark eyes on her. "Ya gone and done it now, missy."

Pip usually enjoyed sparring with her maid, but right now

she wanted sympathy. "That odious beast thought I had arranged to be found by his mistress. His *mistress!* Can you believe it? He thinks I deliberately compromised him into marriage. Well, I will tell you this. He can wait until he's stooped and drooling before I accept him."

She spent the diatribe pacing the room as if she could outpace the disaster she had just created.

"But you were found together," Lizzie protested, waving her hand in ineffectual punctuation. "Didn't you?"

Pip spun on her. "Didn't I what? Seek to compromise him into marriage? Plot and scheme to make sure that he would be condemned to life with a woman he obviously loathes? When exactly have you heard me express such a desire, Lizzie? When have I ever done anything that would convince you that I could so betray Beau's trust?"

Lizzie frowned. "Then you didn't wish to compromise him into marriage?"

"Of course not!"

"Well then, what *were* you doing?"

Which brought Pip stumbling to a halt, shocked to silence. She could not tell Lizzie, of course. She couldn't tell anyone. She had never even spoken to Joyful about Beau's clandestine activities, and Joyful had been her maid since she was ten.

"Pip?" Lizzie asked.

"Missy?" Joyful echoed.

But Pip couldn't think how to answer them. She laid a careful hand against her bodice, if only to feel the reassuring crinkle of paper. She had saved Beau from being exposed, possibly killed. But in doing so, it seemed she had backed them both into a trap.

Oh, sweet lord, what was she going to do?

She was briefly saved by the duchess sweeping through the door. "Drummond is going to write to your father for permission," that kind lady announced. "With the time that will take, I anticipate a spring wedding."

Pip swung around, swamped by relief. Yes. If they could wait five months, maybe she could find a way to avoid this disaster. She didn't want to think about how much it hurt that the thing she had always dreamed of would effectively destroy any affection she and Beau had ever shared, much less the more tender feelings she suffered.

She was glad she hadn't seen Beau's expression when the duchess offered this escape. She could not have borne seeing the relief in his eyes.

"Yes," she said, nodding. "I will write father as well, shall I? He can help us sort this all out."

"After we make the formal announcement downstairs," the duchess said. "Drummond is waiting for you. Why don't you tidy up a bit, and find your spectacles? And perhaps pinch a bit of color into your cheeks?"

Pip's smile was half-hearted. "You mean I am not ruddy-faced with humiliation?"

The duchess's smile was indescribably gentle as she lifted a soft hand to Pip's cheek. "You are too much of a lady to allow yourself to resemble a tomato, my dear. Now, come along, do. We are keeping your fiancé waiting."

"And his mistress," Pip muttered as she sat to allow Joyful to rethread the bronze ribbon she had somehow dislodged from her short curls.

Lizzie huffed in surprise. The duchess *tsked*. "You are also too much of a lady to acknowledge that unfortunate situation as well."

"No," Pip demurred with a sad shake of her head as she exchanged her pretty lorgnette for her practical wire-rimmed spectacles. "I don't believe I am. Which is why it is good that my father will undoubtedly intervene. Otherwise, I would end up confronting Beau about that harpy and find myself locked away in Delamere. Or Bedlam, depending on his mood."

"I say you just scratches her eyes out and be done wit' it," Joyful suggested with a sly grin.

"You are not being helpful, my dear," the duchess suggested with her own sly smile. "Now, come along, Pip. Make this right."

Pip's stomach felt sour, and she thought she was developing a headache, but she linked arms with Lizzie and followed the duchess out the door and all the way down the grand staircase to where she could see Beau waiting at the door to the ballroom.

"Oh, no," Lizzie muttered, slowing.

The duchess made an inarticulate sound as she, too, saw who was speaking with Beau. Haranguing Beau, more like it, her pudgy fingers wrapped securely around his arm and three of her guards and Lady Mercer Elphinstone flanking her.

"I haven't been so diverted in *ages*, Drummond. I simply insist you allow me to help. After all, what good is it being the heir to the throne if I cannot even procure a simple special license?"

Pip slowed almost to a halt, her stomach plummeting. Blessed Beatrice's beads. She was sunk.

The duchess, never one for flight, stepped right around Pip and approached the princess.

"Your Highness," she greeted her, dipping a curtsy.

Princess Charlotte turned about, smiling as if she had won a prize. "Oh, cousin," she greeted the duchess, both hands out to her, "the most *romantic* situation, is it not? We knew, of course, of Miss Knight's regard for our dear Drummond, but to see its fruition before our very eyes! I am in *transports*. I *insist* I be allowed to help."

Pip felt as if she were strangling.

"Just your being here at the announcement of our engagement is more than we could hope for, Your Highness," Beau said, looking a bit pale himself. "Is that not right, Pip?"

Pip thought her smile probably resembled a rictus. "Indeed, Your Highness. And when my parents return from St. Petersburg, we would be honored to have you witness our wedding."

The princess waved her off. "Nonsense. There is no reason at all to wait so long. Why, if I could, I would run away with my Leopold this minute. But I am a princess. You are not. And I would dearly love to see you joined to the man of your dreams before my very eyes. For if you must wait, who knows what could interfere?"

Indeed, Pip thought in growing despair. Who knew?

"It is too much," she protested.

"Don't be silly," the princess scoffed. "You have a chaplain, do you not, cousin?"

The duchess gave a half-hearted nod. The princess smiled and clapped her hands. "*Excellent.* The only time the dear Archbishop of Canterbury usually hears from me is when I find myself in a scrape. He would be delighted to hear *good* news from me for a change. All you must do is provide Mercer with your full names and birth dates, and she and a few of my guard can hurry to see it done."

"I must beg you not to put out such an effort," Beau protested, his posture growing increasingly stiff.

"And I," the princess retorted, suddenly every inch a royal princess, "must insist that I do."

It was the duchess who finally admitted the inevitable. "And so it shall be, Your Highness."

Pip had an overwhelming urge to look to Beau for support. For sympathy. She couldn't. She could see too well with her spectacles on, and she was terrified that what she would see was rage, betrayal. Resentment. And a woman should never see such emotions in the eyes of the man she was about to marry.

Marry.

Oh, St. Swithin's scissors, how could this have happened?

And she hadn't even had a chance to explain to Beau about the plans she had lifted.

PIP HELD Beau's hand when the duchess made the announcement. After that, she wasn't allowed within twelve feet of him, not just during the remainder of the ball when she was whirled from one avidly curious guest to the next, but all the next day. It was probably better for her nerves that way, she admitted. She was having trouble enough with the course her life had suddenly taken without having to face Beau's outrage.

But she still needed to tell him what she had heard. She needed to help him find the real plans. She needed to do a bit of searching herself, since she didn't think Beau would believe her about where she was sure the plans had been hidden.

The silver-haired man had said that the plans were in a woman's room. There were a lot of women at the house party; at least twenty. But only one woman had been walking with the silver-haired man when he had discovered her with Beau. Beau's mistress, Lady Pamela.

Perhaps it was no more than wishful thinking. After all, who wouldn't want to face the man she loved with proof that his mistress was an enemy agent? There had to be a certain amount of satisfaction in that. Even if Pip made Beau even more angry at her. It was inevitable, after all, that Beau would be angry at her. Why not gain at least a little satisfaction from it?

She wanted Lady Pamela to be an enemy. She wanted, basely, to know that Beau had made such a mistake in his assessment of his mistress's character. Even in the privacy of her own mind, Pip wanted to be able to gloat that he hadn't merely been so stupid he couldn't see Pip's qualities. He had been so stupid, he had seen qualities in Pamela Smythe-Smithe that simply didn't exist.

But instead of sneaking into Lady Pamela's room to retrieve the real plans or sneak into Beau's room to return the false plans—with an explanation that would exonerate her in his eyes—and humble him in hers—Pip was caught up in emergency wedding preparations. Not only did she have to approve any wedding plans the duchess was hatching with the princess (Pip categorically refused to set doves loose to celebrate the vows. With her luck, she would end up wearing the doves' opinion of the whole business in her hair), she was forced to assess her wardrobe for an appropriate wedding gown and fight back all attempts to style her like a porcelain doll, all frills and lace and orange blossoms. First of all, there were no orange blossoms in November. Second, she would look like a rearing caterpillar in all those flounces. Third, she did not feel celebratory in the least. She decided to settle for solemn.

She finally put her foot down and insisted on a simple white silk gown with a cross-over bodice, puffed sleeves supported by an evergreen ribbon that also appeared in her hem. Her bonnet was white with green lining and one egret feather that brushed her cheek, and her bouquet was to be made up of white roses and holly.

Joyful sniffled as she finished adding the ribbon, her thin fingers dipping at lightning speed as she sewed. "This wasn't the way it was supposed to be," she protested. "What'll happen to us now, Miss Pippin?"

Pip had no idea what would happen to them. So far, the only correspondence she had had with her fiancé was the note he had sent to notify her that the special license had come through with blessings from the Archbishop of Canterbury, blast him. It had been twenty-four hours, and Pip was still sequestered in her room. The wedding was scheduled to take place at ten in the morning in the old manor chapel, which was seeing the cleaning of its life. In fact, if Pip looked out her window, she could see the candles bobbing through the windows of the little church, as if ghosts hovered impatiently waiting to get out.

Which was much the way she felt. She was expected to stay in her room alone, as if she were a penitent preparing for confession, and she had no idea what Beau was up to. She had no idea what he had intended to do about the fake plans, or if he even knew that the real plans were somewhere else. She had read the papers, but they were obviously in code. She had copied them again just in case anything happened to these.

If she had had her schoolmate Fiona Ferguson there right then, she could have made some sense of them. Fiona loved puzzles like this. She had taught Pip quite a lot about codes, but this didn't look to be one of the easier transposition codes they had used at Last Chance to pass information. Pip almost smiled at herself at the idea that people who were so diabolical as to overthrow the British crown would use codes simple enough for schoolgirls.

Still, she wondered what the code hid.

She also needed to find out who the silver-haired man was. In all the excitement, she hadn't had a chance to ask. The only thing she knew for certain was that he was not Perfect Pamela's husband. That unfortunate was a short, rotund, balding nonentity more interested in wagers than his wife. She suspected, however, that the silver-haired man was some kind of lynchpin in the whole mess. She suspected even more strongly that it would be an uphill fight to get anyone to believe her accusations against him.

"Joyful," she said, her attention on the pages, "will you do me a favor?"

Joyful's mother might have chosen her name as a portent. Sadly, it hadn't taken. The Negro woman who had followed Pip around the world, always anticipated the worst. But then, Joyful had experienced the worst, so Pip could hardly blame her. "Depends on what you want me t' do," she said in her sing-song voice.

"Deliver a message to my fiancé."

Joyful shrank into herself. "You want me to go to a white man's room in the middle o' the night, jus' like that?"

"No, I'd rather go myself. But it seems that I am forbidden. It truly is important, Joyful."

She got absolutely no response. Joyfully bent over Pip's dress, focused completely on the tiny stitches she was setting into the hem as if Pip hadn't spoken at all. Pip struggled between laughter and rage. Well, that was it, then. Once Joyful had made up her mind, the Savior himself couldn't change it. She would simply pretend she couldn't hear or see.

Pip got to her feet, tucked the original pages away in her trunk, and folded her copies to stuff them back into her bodice. "All right then," she groused, repositioning them and heading for the door. "I cannot see how I could further disgrace myself. I will go see him."

Joyful came rocketing off the chair, but Pip was already out the door, the pages once again nestled between her breasts. Fortunately, she knew where Beau's room was. Even more fortunately, at this time in the evening the guests were still mostly downstairs enjoying a few hands of whist. The staff, well used to her wanderings over the years, just nodded as she passed. Pip felt her heart rate increase. Her palms felt a bit damp, and she swore a peach pit was lodged in her throat. If she got caught, she would only be compounding the scandal. But then, the sentence for scandal was marriage, and how much more married could she be than she would be in the morning?

The corridor to Beau's room was shadowy and long, with a tall window at the end that reflected back the shadow of Pip creeping towards it. Suddenly, she wanted to giggle. It was ludicrous, really. Or it would have been if the nation weren't at risk. If a certain silver-haired gentleman wasn't plotting against her Beau, not to mention the king.

The silver-haired gentleman. Beau knew him; that had been obvious. Pip wondered how. Where. It could have been anywhere, really. All those places a woman wasn't allowed, where men swapped lies and sipped brandy. She needed to ask Beau who the man was. And what he had been doing with Pamela Smythe-Smithe.

Just before she reached the tall window, she stopped at the last door on the right and raised her hand to softly knock. At first when she heard the woman's voice, she thought she'd conjured it. After all; hadn't she just been thinking of her? No one else had those sultry, throaty tones. Pip looked quickly around, hand still raised, certain to see Beau's mistress slinking down the moonlit hall.

But she wasn't. Pip knew it for certain when she turned back to his door and heard the low rumble of Beau's voice. Then, astonishingly, the throaty chuckle of his mistress. In his room. The night before his wedding.

Pip's first instinct was to shove the door open and confront the dolt. Demand to know what he thought he was doing entertaining a loose woman within hours of marrying Pip. Perhaps beat him to a pulp with his own chamber pot.

She couldn't, of course. It simply wasn't done. Hadn't she seen it time and again during her years in society? Women weren't supposed to acknowledge their rivals. They were forbidden to sully their silly thoughts with suspicions of infidelity. Because even if a man was bedding every guest at the party, a woman had no right to object.

Pip knew that, but couldn't tolerate it. But as she stood there in the hallway, her fists clenched so tightly she knew she would have crescent-shaped cuts in her palms from her nails. Worse than imagining what those two were up to in there would be finding out. She was too much of a coward to risk it.

Fine. Beau could just wait a couple of days more to find out about his precious papers. So, pushing her glasses up her nose, she turned around and walked back the way she'd come.

She had almost reached her room when something else dawned on her. If Lady Pamela was in Beau's room (may her teeth rot and her eyes cross), she was not in her own. And with the card room open, it was a dead certainty her husband wouldn't be. It would be a perfect time to search. And wouldn't that be a lovely revenge on her and Beau both?

Again, Pip seemed to have perfect timing. The women's hall was silent and dim. Pip gently tapped on Lady Pamela's door, still furtively looking around. She wasn't terribly surprised that no one answered. If she were Lady Pamela's maid, and she knew where her mistress would be for a good long time, she would have spent her free time in the kitchens. Taking one more look around, Pip opened the door a crack and slid inside.

She almost betrayed herself with her first breath. Good Gawain's geese, she thought, striving mightily not to cough at the cloud of patchouli she'd stumbled into. How can Beau tolerate the stuff? It was perfectly vile.

As for the room, it was too clean. Not tidy clean. Obsessively organized, fragrance bottles-and-brushes-lined up-on-the-dresser-like-hussars-on-parade clean. Not so much as a fan escaped from its drawer or a closet door left ajar.

Pip grinned. This actually made it much easier to search. If the room had been a mess, it would have been too difficult to put everything back just as it was. And Pip had a strong suspicion that Lady Pamela would have known in a second if her scarves had been touched.

That was where Pip started anyway. If she had been in the mood to be amused, she would have been by the character revealed in this room. Not a sensual seductress with oceans of exotic knick-knacks and faintly salacious miniatures. A precisely regimented perfectionist who probably knew to the inch where everything belonged. Scarves and hats and slippers and muffs and shawls, day dresses and walking dresses, carriage dresses, and formal gowns. A treasury of jewels, all arranged by stone, her favorite evidently being ruby. Not a surprise, Pip thought. Rubies would match her painted lips and set off her dark hair.

For a moment Pip was distracted enough to wonder what her own jewel would be. What would set off her best feature? What *was* her best feature? Her brother Alex said it was her eyes. Her father said it was her laugh. Her mother had tweaked her nose and said all of her, which Pip thought patently unfair, the kind of thing a mother might say when she couldn't think of an actual answer.

Pip gave her head a sharp shake. *Focus*, she thought, setting the bottom tray back into the jewelry case. *You have work to do, and who knows how long Beau will keep the hussy busy?*

Where would someone hide papers? Not Pamela. A man. A man who thought he knew her, but probably didn't at all. Probably thought it was her maid who kept order. Men had no concept of the difference between how a maid tried to keep up with a careless woman and how a rigid woman made certain her maid followed orders. This was definitely the latter.

Pip took another slow look around. Not in any of the usual places, she thought. No false trunk bottoms or locked drawers or portable writing desks. Too easy. But someplace another person could recover them without any trouble. Someplace easy and quick.

Pip carefully ran her hands over the curtain hems. No suspicious crinkle. She patted down cloaks and opened every door she could find. There were no secret cubbies, niches, or rooms. She knew every room in this house, and the Ripton line had evidently passed their history in completely unsuspicious behavior, which would have demanded secret cubbies or rooms. She was running out of ideas.

Finally, Pip's gaze settled on the lovely mahogany four-poster bed with its steps and piles of pillows, its curtains the same lovely dark gold as the window's. She grinned. Too easy. Which might be the point. Taking a final look toward the door, she knelt at the bedside and shoved her hand beneath the mattress.

It took her a good ten minutes crawling about the entire perimeter of the bed, but just as she'd given up, she felt the crinkle of paper at her fingers. Eureka! Holding her breath, she carefully pulled until she succeeded in retrieving the papers that had been hidden there. One look was all it took. They were so similar to the papers she had taken from Beau that she could have mistaken one for the other if she hadn't already studied the others. She could easily substitute the fake plans for the real ones so that no one would realize until too late that the plans had been switched. And if Pip was very lucky, when the traitors discovered the substitution, they would blame Pamela.

Reaching into her bodice, she pulled out the other set and positioned them exactly where she'd found the others. The real plans were then tucked back into her bodice, and she climbed to her feet.

Only to hear footsteps approaching down the hall.

Oh, blast! Her heart suddenly thundering, Pip quickly looked around for a place to hide. Darn the Riptons for their open natures. They simply didn't have the mentality for subterfuge. She finally resorted to the obvious. Dropping back to her knees, she paused and listened. It was pointless climbing all the way under that bed if it wasn't Pamela approaching.

The door latch lifted. Pip scuttled under the bed, praying nobody dropped anything on the floor. She had just managed to get her skirts tucked all the way beneath the bed curtains and her glasses firmly positioned on her nose before the door opened and Pamela swept in, her maid right behind her.

Pip closed her eyes, as if that would help. She swore they could probably hear her heart.

"But my lady..." the maid protested in a guttural accent. Leave it to Pamela to be the only woman of Pip's acquaintance to eschew a French maid for a German one.

"Speak German," the hussy snapped. "We do not wish to be overheard."

Pip grinned to herself. Poor Pamela. She chose the wrong language if she wanted to protect secrets. Pip was not only fluent in French, Spanish, and Italian, but could manage in German, Portuguese, Latin, Russian, Hungarian, and Greek. Theo had always said that a knowledge of languages could only help a soldier do his job. So, Pip had learned them right alongside him, and then used the languages whenever she had been allowed to join her parents abroad.

Besides, she thought, almost snorting out loud. It obviously hadn't occurred to Pamela that the princess down the hall was a dab hand at German herself.

"Check to make sure they're still there," Pamela ordered. "Bobby said it was important."

Pip's heart almost seized. The maid was walking right around to the site Pip had just mined. She was dead; she knew it. She was so paralyzed she couldn't even come up with a reasonable excuse for hiding under Pamela's bed. As if there could be one.

The maid knelt. Pip opened her eyes to see a very nice pair of peach satin slippers stop and face the bed. She held her breath. But the maid didn't bend to reach under the bed. She reached under the mattress with one arm while telling Pamela she was trained for more than retrieval, like a dog.

Pip was fighting between panic and laughter. It just figured.

"You are trained to do what I tell you," Pamela insisted. "Are they..."

The maid backed out and straightened. "Just where he put them. What else do you need from me? I am in sad want of rubber balls to fetch."

Amazingly, Pamela laughed. "I should sell you to the gypsies, Gerta."

"You could try, Pamela."

Pip raised an eyebrow. Odd for a maid-employer relationship. Was Gerta also part of the cabal Beau was helping to stop? It would make sense.

"Well," Pamela said from over by her dresser, "the important work is done. He will retrieve the plans on his way home from the party. Although I am sad that in the end Beau will suffer for his intransigence. It would have been delicious to have him owe me for saving him from a charge of treason. I suppose even death would be preferable to marriage to that mouse."

The maid stepped up behind her mistress. "It is his own fault. He could have had you."

Pamela chuckled. "He will again. It is only a small matter of patience. I give him a month before he is back begging for me."

"Two weeks," the maid countered. "Will you stop in on Thomas tonight, or shall I?"

Pamela sighed. "You do it. I've had enough of men today."

Pip came within Ames aces of correcting the harpy on her assumption. Pip might in the end be forced to give Beau up. She would be damned if she gave him up to this monster.

But then she smiled. At least she knew that Pamela would come out on the short end of this endeavor. Pip had the real plans and Pamela had nothing. Pip would have loved to have been there when the truth came out, but she had other things to do. Like get married in a few hours. If she ever made it out from under Pamela's bed.

In the end it was a close call. Pip waited through Pamela's nightly routine, which

seemed to involve a dozen different kinds of cream, gloves slid onto oily hands, various gems categorized and counted, and the entire spectrum of attires chosen for the next day. Pip supposed she should feel honored. For the wedding, Pamela was going to wear her brightest red, which Pip chose to believe meant she felt threatened by the whole situation. After all, didn't birds wear their brightest plumage to try to steal attention? Pamela evidently needed red to challenge a mouse.

Even finally dousing the candle did not free Pip. Either la Pamela had a guilty conscience or a bad back, for she tossed for what seemed like hours as Pip lay beneath, more and more bedeviled by the dust that lurked in such places.

Finally, though, the room was quiet but for rhythmic breathing. The rest of the house was even quieter, the revelers having long since sought their own beds. Checking her bodice one last time, Pip carefully slipped from beneath the bed and crept to the door. She was once again thankful that the party was at the Riptons', since the staff was conscientious and the door hinges well-oiled. She escaped Pamela's room with no more than a whisper of her gown.

It would be perfect if Joyful had already sought her bed. Pip did not want any recriminations, especially when she felt so triumphant.

Joyful had not sought her bed. Worse, neither had Beau.

"There you are," he greeted her from where he waited in her own armchair he'd dragged by her fire, his legs crossed, his countenance fierce. "Do I need to call some gentleman out even before the wedding?"

3

Pip couldn't help it. She barely got her door closed before she took one considered look at the fury on Beau's continence and the outrage on Joyful's and burst out laughing. Of all the accusations Beau could have made, it had to be that one.

Beau seemed not to be amused. "It is the night before your wedding," he snapped, getting to his feet. "Where the hell have you been? And I will tell you right now, Brat, that this kind of behavior will not be tolerated. Do you hear me?"

She laughed even harder. It seemed she couldn't stop. Waving ineffectually at Beau, she dropped onto her dressing table stool, removed her glasses to wipe her eyes, and set off again. She wasn't quite sure she wasn't becoming hysterical.

"Hush, Missy," Joyful admonished. "Everybody will hear."

Pip waved her off as well. If someone wanted to drop in on her hours before her wedding to find her fiancé glowering at her in her own room chaperoned by her maid, let them. How could that possibly make the situation more ludicrous?

"I would love to know what you find so funny," Beau growled.

She waved at him again. "You."

Joyful silently passed over a lace-edged handkerchief, and Pip mopped at her eyes.

"Oh, Beau," she mourned, shaking her head. "You do know how to put a coda on the most absurd four hours I have ever spent."

For a moment she seemed to have successfully confused him. But never let it be said that her Beau lost his purpose for long. Theo used to say that his big brother would manage to do his estate books in a bordello.

Oh, Theo.

"Well?" Beau demanded, straightening to what Pip had always called his 'head lad' position. "Where have you been? There can be no answer that is acceptable at this time of night. I'd better not hear you were in another guest's bedroom. If you were, I'm warning you. I shall walk off and humiliate you."

That made her laugh all over again. "But I was," she gasped, almost sobbing with the absurdity of this conversation. It was better than howling with outrage at the unfairness of it. "Under Perfect Pamela's bed, as a matter of fact."

Joyful gasped.

Beau snarled."That is not funny."

"No," Pip agreed, giving her eyes a final wipe and reclaiming her glasses so to be able to see Beau clearly. "You are correct. It was not funny at all. Well, except for what she eats when she's alone. I swear I think her maid dragged in an entire steer."

He looked ready to bite. "Pip…"

"It must take so much effort to maintain that 'eats like a bird' myth, don't you think? Fortunately for me, no one expects delicacy from me."

He truly looked angry now, which forced her back to the point. She took in a calming breath.

"Yes, yes. The point is that I had snuck in earlier since I

knew she wouldn't be around, and didn't get out in time, leaving me under her bed during what I must tell you is a most protracted skin care regimen. And the steer, of course."

That brought him to his feet. "You invaded a guest's room while she wasn't there? What made you think she wasn't there?"

She lost her smile. "Oh, Beau, you always do get snarly when you've been caught."

Getting back to her feet, she met his gaze unflinching, even though she stood chin-to-chest. "I knew she wouldn't be in her room because I was at *your* room just before that."

He went rigid. "You weren't...."

Her smile this time was cold as truth. "But I was. I wasn't going to say anything. After all, isn't that what girls are taught? That they have no right to be...*entertaining*...someone not her fiancé the night before her wedding, but that she also has no right to expect the same of her fiancé? But," she said with a shrug, "I find I do not like such hypocrisy. Neither of us may want this marriage, but lying under that bed for the last three hours, I came to the conclusion that we will approach it honestly or you may indeed walk out and humiliate us both. I find I just don't care."

She did, desperately. But he didn't need to know that. At least she had silenced him. He just stood there frozen in place, his features pale and stark-looking. Probably with rage. Pip would deal with that when she had to. Right now, she needed to finish the night's task before she collapsed in a heap.

"Joyful," she said, turning to her maid. "If you wouldn't mind. I need to speak with Lord Drummond alone for a moment."

Joyful glared at her. "It ain't right."

"I promise," she said. "We will do nothing beyond the pale. The way we feel about each other right now, you might return to find us both dead, but we will not be compromised."

With one eloquent glare at Beau, Joyful complied. It occurred to Pip as she waited for her friend to leave that she was feeling calmer than she had for the last twenty-four hours. Was this what it felt to have the upper hand, she wondered. Because for at least these few minutes, she did. It wasn't a familiar feeling. Not at all.

The door clicked shut and Beau turned to her. "Brat..."

She shook her head. "Me first."

Rather than continuing to crane her neck, she walked over and took the other

armchair, waving Beau back down. He looked even more thunderous, but he sat.

"Well?" he demanded. "Why would you act like a sneak thief in another

woman's room? Tell me you weren't planning some kind of petty revenge. I won't have it, Brat."

She sighed, rubbing at the headache that had been building since she'd battled the dust underneath that bed. She'd have to tell the duchess, she was afraid.

First, she had to deal with Beau. "You can finally be done with calling me Brat, I think. By now I hope you know that I have the plans from the library, which you could have asked for any time in the last twenty-four hours. Well..." She gave that little dismissive wave again. "I *had* them."

He looked, if anything, more thunderous. "What do you mean, *had* them?"

"Have a little patience."

"Are you finally going to explain?"

She cocked an eyebrow at him. "Are you finally going to listen?"

He scowled. "This isn't a game, Pip."

She laughed again, a harsh rueful sound. "Considering the fact that this marriage is probably the worst thing that could happen to me, believe me, Beau, I know. I believe I am learning not to be quite so impulsive about my thoughtful gestures."

He straightened, his frown impressive. "What do you mean by that? You've wanted this marriage since you were ten."

"Wanted marriage to a man who will begin our life together resentful of me and only grow more so over the years? Who would have complete control over me, and is already thinking of ways to punish me? How quickly were you thinking of dropping me at Delamere with your aunt and uncle, Beau? Were you going to wait at least a week before taking up with Pamela again? After all, you seemed to not be able to forego her on the night before our wedding."

He looked away. "You don't understand."

"No, I imagine I don't. So let me just answer your questions and we can both find our beds. In a few hours we shall be very busy."

Beau considered her for a moment, his head tilted as if he were gathering input. "You aren't acting at all like yourself."

"Maybe you didn't know me as well as you thought. Although how, I don't know. I have been under your nose since I was three. Now, do you want to know about Pamela?"

"You mean you weren't planting a booby trap for her?"

She considered him for a moment. "You really don't know me, do you?" With a sigh, she reached into her bodice for the papers and held them up. "I was searching for the real plans. The ones you copied in the library were fake. They were left there as a trap to draw out the spy at the house party. That being you, of course. The real plans were left in Pamela's room. I'm not certain who was to pick them up."

"That's absurd."

"It may be. But it is true. I heard two men talking about it out on the balcony earlier in the evening. I tried to catch you alone to warn you, but Pamela was attached like a limpet."

Standing up, she tried to pass over the papers. "By the way, who is the silver-haired man?"

Beaux followed to his feet. "Lord Burke?"

She nodded. "He was the one giving the orders."

That stopped Beaux cold, his hand still inches from the evidence. "Don't be ridiculous, Pip. He's a member of the Privy Council."

"Well, if what I heard is correct, he is also a Lion. Please. Take these blasted plans before I throw them into the fire...oh, and here," she said, striding over to her dresser. "Take my copy of the false papers as well. I have marked them as such. The ones you retrieved are now under Pamela's mattress in place of the real ones. Unless they look very closely, whoever picks them up will think they are the real ones. It might introduce a bit of chaos into things."

He grabbed the papers and then just stared at them. Then with a snap, his head came up. "A Lion? What are you talking about?"

She sat back down again. "I was wondering when you'd catch on to that."

"Yes," he said, clutching that paper as if it posed a new threat. "That."

She shrugged. "I supposed I should begin by telling you that I have known about Drake's Rakes since I was quite young."

It was as if he'd turned to stone. "Of course, you know about Drake's Rakes. We had some of our better entertainments at Delamere when you were at your grandmother's next door."

Pip scowled at him. "Really, Beau. Isn't it a bit late to be protesting your innocence? You are holding plans you were supposed to recover at the behest of Marcus Drake. I. Recovered. Them. I imagine that means I know exactly what Drake's Rakes are."

"What do you think they are?"

"None of you were able to go to war," she said, looking down at her hands. "The heirs who were left behind while their brothers were allowed to fight for king and country."

Theo. Theo had been allowed to go in his bright blood-red uniform, the anticipation in his eyes terrifying. Theo, whose body was lost somewhere in France. But Pip couldn't tell Beau that she knew Theo was the reason he worked so hard for the Rakes and the government. Why he'd tried half a dozen times to enlist since Theo's death, although evidently Horse Guards had recognized a death wish when they saw it. She and Beau hadn't been able to mention Theo's name since the day they had gotten the news.

Pip cleared her throat and began again. "I found out about all of you when I was a little girl. You and Alex gave it away, actually, when you used to whisper in the corners about your plans. You had no idea I was paying attention. But I was always paying attention."

The paper crinkled in his hands. Pip looked up to see a mixture of emotions skim across his eyes; frustration, anger, pain. Ah, she thought. Here is where we should talk about how I once shadowed Theo, how I copied his every move and lesson so I could follow them both into the breach. But we won't. We won't let Theo's shade loose between us, no matter how badly we need to.

How sad that they couldn't even bring the person they both had loved most with them into their marriage.

"In fact," she said, deciding it was far better to get over the hurdle quickly. "You should know that all my friends from Last Chance know. Ever since we found out we were in that godforsaken place because our brothers or fathers are in sensitive positions—like the Rakes. And, well, it has been becoming increasingly difficult to ignore it lately."

Lately being when they had uncovered even more spies in Lizzie Ripton's cellar just four days ago, leading to the exodus of four other rakes to London, leaving the house party sadly unbalanced at dinner and Beau in charge of their original mission when he showed up later. Which Pip had just accomplished.

"What do you all think you know?" he asked.

"I told you. Marcus Drake collected all you restless, frustrated oldest sons to do what you could here to support your siblings. And then to pull the teeth of the Lions before they tried to topple the throne. For some reason your Pamela and Lord Burke decided to lure you out of the shadows this week. Although how they didn't know the place was swarming with Rakes, I do not know."

For the longest moment he just stared at her. Then he lifted the papers as if presenting evidence. "What did you think?" he demanded. "That by pilfering these from that group you could act out your childhood fantasies?"

"The Lions, Beau. You know their name. I know their name. And no. I thought I could save you from being murdered by giving you another reason for being in the library with the plans. And then I finished the job of getting the actual plans and replaced them with the fakes, because I was in a position to do it. You can thank me any time you want."

She got up then and walked to the door, suddenly so tired she wanted nothing more than to cover her head and disappear. "And now I need to call my maid back in so I can change for bed. I hear I have an appointment in the morning I shouldn't miss."

Looking a bit as if he'd been kicked in the head, Beau slipped the plans into his inside pocket. "No one else can know about this," he warned.

She almost laughed again. "St. Stella's suspenders, Beau. You really do think I'm still ten, don't you? Go on. You have an appointment as well."

He approached her as if she were feral. She turned the knob and paused. "One more thing," she said.

"What?"

She looked up at him, so she could make sure he heard her. "I had a lot of time to think while I was listening to Pamela snore."

"She doesn't--"

She silenced him with a look. "I fear that I realized something else tonight. Whatever you expected from this marriage, you'd better expect it with my participation. I cannot be a complacent bystander. Whatever we do, whatever decisions we make, I will be involved."

His jaw worked like it did when he ground his teeth. She was positive if anything called for it, it was her challenge.

"We'll have enough time to work that out later," he said.

"No," she said equably. "We won't. If you cannot take my decision into account, leave before dawn. I will take responsibility, say I changed my mind."

He raised an imperious eyebrow. "And exactly who do you expect to believe that?"

She sighed. "Beau, I have spent my life on the fringes of everyone else's families. Even my own. I think I have finally grown tired of it. Make your choice. I'll know the answer if you show up tomorrow."

"Listen, Brat," he retorted, leaning over her. "You don't know me well if you think I will back out now. I shall see you in the morning."

She nodded and opened the door.

"And since I recovered your state secrets for you," she added. "You can probably stop calling me Brat."

She actually got a quick grin for that. "Not on your life."

After checking the hall to find no one but Joyful waiting, she shooed him out and shooed her maid in. And then, knowing that she had settled exactly nothing with her fiancé, she let Joyful help her ready for her last night as a single woman.

She just wished she felt more hopeful about what was to come.

FOR A VERY LONG FEW moments Beau made it no farther than the hallway outside Pip's door. First, by dint of the threat in her maid's eyes.

"You don't deserve my girl," she said softly enough not to be overheard, her deep brown eyes somehow glacial. "You better know that."

Actually, he did know that. It didn't change anything though.

Still, he felt bad. Even after the maid swept through the door and closed it behind her, he just stood there, hands clenched, the words he should have said to Pip lodged in his throat.

He should have thanked her. He should have praised her. He should have told her never to do that again, since he still didn't think she had any idea what she was up against. But this had been classic Pip, acting before she considered consequences.

He should have anticipated this, really. Pip had never been a slow child. And she had trailed Theo and him around like a faithful spaniel until the two of them went off to school. Then to put her in that school where every other student seemed to be a Rake sibling or daughter. It was inevitable she would suss out secrets.

After all, it had been her passion. She and Theo had played Round Table, except she had refused to be the helpless maiden. She was Gawain to Theo's Galahad. Littlejohn to Theo's Robin Hood. Restless, inquisitive, determined Pip, who had spent so much time as their shadow that Beau found himself looking for her in the sunlight.

And he was going to marry her. He still couldn't comprehend the enormity of what was about to happen. He couldn't come to grips with the upheaval he was about to suffer in his life. And not just by having a wife. Having *that* wife. Having Pip. He supposed she was right. He couldn't very well call her Brat anymore.

And that wasn't even the worst. How would he overcome his cataclysmic reaction to her? Catastrophic, more like. In a matter of hours, he'd gone from an effective, reasonable, unemotional investigator into a distracted, frustrated, confused, aroused—he tried, but there was simply no denying his physical reaction to his brother's best friend—fool. Even after only a few minutes of talking to her, not even touching her, he was beset by a new and very unsettling arousal.

It was why he'd been so surly, he knew. He'd gone from all but taking Pip against a wall like a two-bit whore to being given the church's official blessing to do just that. Which only made him harder.

He really should apologize to her for his behavior. He'd had an excuse, of course. After all, even though her intentions were good, she'd still backed him into a marriage he didn't want. With a woman who affected him in ways he had never expected. Or needed. Certainly not wanted. Not from Pip.

Not from the girl Theo was supposed to marry.

He could still feel her soft skin in his hands, smell the clean lavender scent of her hair, hear the surprising little whimpers he seemed to have elicited. He was hard all over again just thinking about it.

And he couldn't be. It would make him the worst kind of thief.

But Theo isn't coming back, the devil on his shoulder whispered. *Why is it so wrong to want a marriage with her, even a little?*

Because he could still see the love in Theo's eyes when he'd waved her goodbye the last time. He could still hear his brother lament that he couldn't take her along with him.

"She'd be the perfect person to follow the drum," Theo had confided in him. "After all, she's prepared her whole life for it."

"You've prepared her," Beau had corrected him. "You've so taken up her time with your horses and tactics and war games that if she hadn't gone away to school, she wouldn't even know how to curtsy."

Theo, damnably optimistic Theo, who had been so unforgivably excited about going to war, had laughed. "Pip couldn't care less about that nonsense."

"She will when she goes to find a husband."

Theo had laughed. "Tell you what," he said with a clap on the back. "If nobody else has the sense to marry her, I'll step up. Wouldn't mind at all eating over her campfire. Or teaching her children how to ride and shoot half as well as she does."

Well, Theo would never have the chance now. And as fate would have it, it would fall to Beau after all.

He would be the one with the right to wake that lithe, sweet body, the one to teach her what pleasure was. He would be the one to hold her children in his arms.

It simply wasn't right.

Rubbing at the headache that had been brewing behind his eyes since Pamela had slipped into his room hours ago, he willed his body into obedience and turned to return to his room. He would get no sleep this night. He still had to make sure Pip wasn't mistaken about these plans. Then he had to get the plans off to Drake before anybody knew he even had them. As soon as he could after everyone showed up at the little stone church out back in the morning to see him get married.

It was going to be a long day.

And he still had to apologize.

4

―――――――

Pip imagined other girls dreamed of their wedding day, planned it down to the last tossed flower petal and champagne sip. She hadn't. Not because she had never expected to get married. But she had never expected the wedding ceremony to be the focus of her life. She had spent her daydreaming hours working out how she would make Beau's life easier for him, how she would bring him laughter and spontaneity and comfort. How she would love him back to life after Theo's death.

She should have known better than to risk her own happiness on a fantasy. Bringing Beau back from the darkness that surrounded him would have been hard enough if he had chosen to marry her himself. Now it would be all but impossible. Which meant that she would have to wade around in the morass of his guilt and grief as well as her own for years to come.

Was it a wonder she hadn't bothered planning her own wedding? Besides, the Duchess had had quite enough fun planning it for her, with mostly unhelpful suggestions from the princess. Pip figured that if she could make it through the ceremony, they would be in ecstasy, and she would be past all the fuss.

Still, it seemed that the wedding couldn't be accomplished without her participation. Nodding and smiling didn't seem to be enough. So, she had sat through fittings and hair stylings and menu decisions, flower planningand seating arrangements for the wedding breakfast. The only thing she was saved from was invitations, since they wouldn't have time to ask anyone not already at the house party.

But that wasn't the worst of it. That came with the morning, dim and chilly and threatening rain. Joyful, with her lugubrious expression, helped Pip into her newly beribboned dress and fluffed her short curly hair like down in a pillow before tucking it up under her new bonnet. Pip was content after that to just sit before her mirror wondering what in the name of St. Monica she was supposed to do with this marriage now.

Which was where the duchess found her. With a quick rap on the door, Lizzie's mother swept into the room with the elegance of a swan, her attire flawless in Bishop's blue and her hair swept up like golden silk. She was smiling, her dear blue eyes twinkling. But then, the duchess was always smiling. Every time Pip had ever found herself deposited on the Riptons' doorstep as the handy alternative to her grandparents when she wasn't allowed on the more delicate diplomatic trips, the duchess had greeted her with a gentle smile and open arms.

Just like now.

Pip got to her feet, shorter than the duchess by several inches, and surrendered to that generous embrace.

Closing her eyes, Pip inhaled the scent of lilacs, the duchess's particular scent, a scent that comforted her. "I didn't mean to cause you such a fuss," she apologized, wishing she could stay safe here with just the duchess and her lilac scent and smile.

"Of course, you didn't, my dear. Can we sit a moment?"

They sat. Joyful took one look at the arrangement and retreated like a tide.

"I know I am being unpardonably tardy," the duchess said, her eyes expressing anxiety she would never allow in her posture. "But I did want to tell you that if this marriage is too onerous, we can call it off. We would be glad to have you stay here for a while until the news dies down. I hope you consider this as much your home as Knight's Rest."

For the first time since this disaster unfolded, Pip fought tears. Leave it to the duchess. Pip leaned forward and briefly took the duchess's hand in hers. There was so much she wanted to say, but she knew it would make this lovely woman terribly uncomfortable. So, she would tell Lizzie later and let her pass it along, all of the love Pip felt for this most kind lady she had always considered her second mother.

"Thank you," she said instead, sitting back. "It is more than kind to offer to entangle your family in my problems. But Beau reminded me that not one person would believe that after all these years of trotting after him like his faithful spaniel, I'd suddenly run shy. They would be certain that it was Beau who backed out." She smiled, even though there was no humor. "I find I cannot do that to a man who is one of the most honorable gentlemen I have ever known."

"You seem quite sure. You don't think he will...er, punish you for your actions?"

Pip's smile was a bit sad. "No. Not in the normal way. He will do his best to simply pretend I don't exist for a bit."

"Even though you did him such a favor?"

For a moment Pip could only stare at her. "I...."

Lizzie's mother had quite an impish smile on her when called for. "Do you imagine you are the only one who knows exactly what goes on with the men around here? Why do you think Lizzie was at the Academy with you?"

Pip blinked a couple of times. "The late duke? He was a…"

Again, the duchess smiled, although this time tinged with sadness. "Let us just say that he had a position of some delicacy, which put our girls in a vulnerable position. Thus, they all went to the academy with you. My assumption about this current peccadillo is that you prevented our Beau from being caught out in some clandestine work."

Pip blinked. "Life gets more and more interesting by the day," she admitted.

She got a pat on the hand for that. "If Drummond in any way tries to punish you for this marriage," the duchess insisted, "you come to me. I would be more than happy to set him straight."

Pip patted the duchess's hand. "Oh, I think I can handle Beau."

She didn't, actually. But she couldn't bear to have him suffer anymore for her own actions, no matter how well intended. And successful.

"You do love him, then," the duchess said, her voice thick with memories. She had loved her duke as well, even through his final terrible problems.

Pip's smile grew too obviously wistful. "I'm afraid so. Unfortunately, the person we both loved most in the world stands right between us. Beau will never forgive me for supporting Theo's desire to purchase colors."

The duchess nodded. "I know. I'm afraid that you have some work ahead of you if you plan on making this marriage a living thing, Pip."

This time Pip almost lost her battle against the tears. "I am greatly afraid I lost that battle before it ever began."

The duchess squeezed Pip's hand and reached up to brush back an errant curl from Pip's forehead. "Nonsense. I have never known you to falter in the face of a challenge, little Pip. In fact, I would have said that you thrive on them. Don't you think this one is worth the effort?"

Pip looked into those gentle blue eyes and wondered how to hope. "I don't know," was all she could admit.

"Well, my dear," the duchess said. "It seems to me you have two options. Either work on this marriage or consign it to the dustbin. I must tell you from my experience with many ton marriages, the second option makes for very long, very lonely years." For a minute her eyes grew distant and sad. "From my own experience, the hard work to attain the first is well worth it."

For a moment, Pip was too moved to speak. "The situations are a little different," she finally protested.

"Not so much. Our marriage was arranged. Yours is...urged. But still, he chose to announce it to an audience."

How funny, Pip thought. It occurred to her at that very moment that as much as she'd dreamed of it, she had never actually expected Beau to choose her. No one chose her; not really. Maybe for an entertaining dinner partner, or a comfortable house guest. But even her family had a bad habit of misplacing her when they weren't paying attention. She had learned not to expect more.

Was there an option? Could the duchess be right, that a real marriage was possible after all? If it was possible, she could do no less than try.

She must have been unconsciously nodding, because the duchess began to smile.

"All right then," she said, and then, oddly, looked away. And hemmed and hawed a bit, gazing over the bedroom Pip had been assigned back when she was a scruffy girl of ten and been allowed to decorate in hand-painted Japanese wallpaper, cherry red bed curtains and spring green chairs.

"We shall miss you here," the duchess softly said.

Which was when Pip really understood just how much her

life was about to change. She would no longer have the comfort of a familiar bedroom here. No longer be able to see the staff as friends and the Riptons as family. She would have a new family now. A new home. It would be her task to turn Delamere from a rigid mortuary into a home. She actually looked forward to that. She had always loved the old place.

She just wished she could say the same about Beau's aunt and uncle.

"Where are you going after the wedding?" the duchess asked.

Pip blinked. She blinked again. "I have no idea."

The duchess smiled. "Well, I'm certain Drummond does. He is such an organized man. And a gentleman." She nodded to herself, smoothing her hands over her skirt. "A real gentleman."

Her hesitation was making Pip nervous. "I have always thought so."

The duchess nodded again. "Pip, your mother would have this talk with you right now...."

Pip almost bounced to her feet, suddenly understanding. "Oh. Oh, no...I mean...."

She could think of nothing more embarrassing than having the duchess instruct her on the matters between a man and a woman. Especially if the man was to be Beau. *Especially* after that scene the other night, which was still producing odd aftershocks.

"My mother *did*," Pip insisted. "Instruct us. While we were in Vienna. There were so many foreign gentlemen, you see, and so much entertaining. She thought...well, she thought we girls should be...er, enlightened."

It was the duchess's turn to blink. "Oh. Oh, well, that is good. But...did she tell you that with the right man, this time can be...wonderful?"

If only Pip had seen no more than the wistful expression on

the duchess's face when thinking of her late husband, she would have understood. Her own mother had positively beamed when she had spoken of what it meant to make love with the man you loved. Not something Pip wanted to hear about her own father, no matter how much she loved him. But reassuring in its own way.

"Mama felt we girls should be completely prepared as we went out into the world." Pip smiled. "You know how she loathes forced ignorance. Mary Wollstonecraft was our primer."

"Oh, good," the duchess said with another series of nods. She sounded quite relieved, which made Pip even more relieved. "Just remember that. It is a wonderful adventure, Pip, with the man you love. I couldn't be happier that you will enjoy that adventure with Beau Drummond." Her smile grew impish. "Once you convince him of the wisdom of it, of course."

Pip smiled back at her, wishing she were as sanguine. Perhaps if Beau had come to her on his own rather than been dragged into the declaration by bad timing.

"Well," the duchess said, getting to her feet. "Are we ready?"

Pip followed along, once again smoothing out her dress.

"Is it truly all right that Lizzie's great uncle Philbert gives you away?" the duchess asked, reaching over to straighten that errant curl on Pip's forehead again. "I would wait until we had some more men return from their little London jaunt—at least your brother--but the princess insists we not wait. She is putting off her departure until after the wedding breakfast."

Pip finally did smile. "Who am I to gainsay the heir to the throne, ma'am? I adore Uncle Philbert and would be honored to have him walk me."

Uncle Philbert was an amateur natural scientist and could as easily pull a lizard out of his pocket as a handkerchief. Over the years Uncle Philbert had spent long summer evenings tromping over the nearby downs with the children in search of wildlife and nests. It had been one of the real charms of Pip's visits.

But now she had outgrown her time here. The idea suddenly became unbearable. This little room on the second floor of Ripton Hall had become the closest thing she likened to home. And she didn't even have her mother or sisters here to accompany her on.

Before the duchess could open the door, Pip reached out and pulled her into her arms, hugging her tightly. Again, the words that would convey her love and gratitude and grief became clogged in her throat. All she could manage was a teary, "Thank you."

And somehow, the duchess understood. For a long moment the two of them stood together, the duchess patting Pip on the back and humming, something she'd done since Pip had been young, an atonal resonance that seemed to weave comfort around a person. Pip knew as she heard it that it was the duchess's way of easing Pip away from the last of her childhood.

It was time to move on. There was a man downstairs waiting to marry her. And no matter what came of the marriage, she could not insult him by refusing to appear. Besides, she didn't want to give Uncle Philbert any cause to fret.

Pulling back, she swiped at the tears that had escaped to her cheeks and smiled at the woman who had mothered her just as much as her own. "'If it were done when 'tis done, then 'twere well it were done quickly.'"

The duchess chuckled and waited for Pip to collect her gloves before slipping her arm through Pip's and leading the way to Pip's future.

BEAU HAD NO BEST MAN. The other Rakes who had been at the house party had all retreated to London before he'd even gotten there, leaving him to babysit the Princess of Wales and collect the plans. He had never considered having anyone else but one of the Rakes stand up with him. Well, not since Theo had died anyway. But Theo wasn't here either. He lived nowhere but the never-ending ache in Beau's chest. The flush of resentment he couldn't control every time he saw Pip.

Beau swore he would work on easing that. But right now, standing in the vestry beside the plain altar in the Gothic gray stone chapel with its clear glass windows awash in morning light, he had to stand up alone. And then he had to figure out how to run out on Pip within minutes of the marriage to deliver the plans to Whitehall.

Assassination. The Lions were going to murder Wellington. They had tried once already, and Beau had been told the next attempt was called out amid the coded messages he kept protected in his inside pocket. He couldn't make them out: from what he'd heard, he needed a cipher, the identity of which a whole separate section of the Rakes had been working on. He could tell, though, that what Pip had said was true. The messages differed by just a bit. A date, possibly, a name, a site. Just enough to throw pursuers off the track. And both signed with no more than a Tudor Rose, which for some reason had become the symbol for the Lions.

Drake needed to know. Beau needed to deliver this message in person. It was too dangerous to entrust to anyone else. But he had to escape the house party without Pamela or Lord Burke being any the wiser, and without Pip being blamed.

Lord Burke. Beau shook his head. He would have loved to scoff at Pip's allegation. After all, Burke was welcome every-where, a quiet, genial man with a mind of a mathematician. But Beau had to admit that it had been most odd that he'd been the one to accompany Pamela when she had discovered Beau with

Pip. And Beau couldn't ignore the quick, hard hug Burke had bestowed. From anyone else it might not have meant anything. But Burke was not a hugger. Could he have been checking to see if Beau had snuck the plans into his coat? If Burke really was a member of the Lions, that might be even more important information than the message itself.

Beau kept wanting to check his watch. He didn't have time to wait around for Pip to primp and posture her way to the altar. He had more important business to attend to.

"Nerves from the bridegroom?" a soft voice asked behind him.

He turned to see the ducal chaplain arrive in white surplice and stole, girded for battle. A severely handsome man, Dr. Borden was more scholar than shepherd. But he had fit the old duke to a thumb. Beau liked him.

He smiled. "Never know when my bride will manage to be on time," he said.

He wouldn't know either how she would react when he dragged her off. How could either of them explain when he pushed her into a carriage and tore out of the estate before the wedding breakfast was over.

First, though, he had to get married. Devil take it.

And apologize. That.

Maybe he could wait on that until he got back.

Every member of the house party crowded the pews in the small chapel. Who, after all, would risk missing the scandal of the season, if only so they could take it back to spread like manure around town, manufactured concern dripping like honey from their words, honey that ended up tasting like venom. Poor Pip. She was the one who would suffer. He'd get ribald jokes and slaps on the back. Knowing winks and settled bets in Whites. He and Pip had been on those books for a while now, even though her name was never really mentioned, as was gentlemanly. Just "Drummond's shadow."

Where the deuce *was* she, his shadow?

"No best man?" the vicar asked, his attention still out over the guests.

"Not time to collect him. Uncle Philbert is happy to stand in if necessary. Rather tidy, since he's walking the bride down the aisle as well."

The vicar nodded. "Yes, I understand most of her family are in the wilds of St. Petersburg."

Beau wasn't exactly sure he would call St. Petersburg the 'wilds', but otherwise perfectly true.

It was chilly in the chapel with its seven-hundred-year-old stone floor laid down when the Hall had been an Abbey back in Henry II's day. That probably didn't fully account for the cold clamminess in Beau's palms. Neither did it diminish the heavy scent of the lilies that had been brought in from the duke's succession houses to bracket the altar. Beau loathed that smell. There had been lilies at Theo's memorial, cloying reminders of mortality. If he didn't think he would distress the duchess, he'd toss every one through the newly cleaned windows.

"I'll tell you something I have never admitted to another soul," Dr. Borden whispered, stroking the Book of Common Prayer he held at the ready.

Beau looked over to see a look of real discomfort on the gentle face. He was about to beg the man not to tell him, not to make this moment worse, when the chaplain smiled. "I loathe the smell of those lilies. Very unecclesiastical of me, I'm sure. But they remind me..."

"Of funerals."

The chaplain shook his head. "No. No, indeed. But when I was a lad they were a favorite of a certain rather overstrict...*bishop*?"

The sudden shock on the man's face caused Beau to turn.

There really was a bishop walking up the side aisle. Mitered, crosiered and robed to the gleaming teeth, he looked to be a man on a mission. And following in his wake, strolling as if he were late to the opera, Marcus Drake himself.

"What is he doing here?" Beau and Dr. Borden asked in awed tandem.

"Hopefully relieving me of my duty," Beau responded, his eye on the smiling head of the Rakes, who looked as if he had dressed that morning specifically to attend a wedding a hundred-twenty miles from his home.

The vicar started. "You cannot back out now!"

Beau could smile. "No, no. Not that duty. Something else I had queued up right after."

Every person in the chapel craned to see the short procession. Beau couldn't blame them. Then there was a glad cry, and the bishop stopped in his tracks and gave a courtly bow.

The Princess of Wales was on her feet chattering at him as if they had met at a tea.

"Ah," Dr. Borden said.

Beau turned back to see the chaplain nodding.

"Bishop Fisher is the Preceptor of the Princess Royal. She must have called on him to officiate."

He looked inordinately relieved, but Beau didn't have time to ask why. At that moment Drake stepped into the vestry, his every move unhurried. "I hear you are in need of a best man," he said with a slow smile.

Beau shook his hand. "I don't understand."

"Cousin John was having dinner with me at White's when word reached him that the princess was desirous that he marry her dear friends Miss Phillipa Knight and Beaufort, Viscount Drummond. Since I knew that most of your friends were at that moment in London, I decided that I would accompany the bishop on his mission of mercy. After all, old son, I've had a bet on this match since the bride was fifteen."

Beau glared at his erstwhile superior. "Not funny."

"She is well?"

"Didn't you see her?"

"Not a hair. Can't wait to hear the tale."

"It's quite a story," Beau said, half an eye on the chaplain who had moved to the door to let the bishop in.

"I imagine it is."

Which was as far as they got, since at that moment, Bishop Fisher strode through the door with a patient smile and a hand out for his ring to be kissed by the chaplain.

"You are satisfied with the particulars, Peter?" he asked his compatriot.

"I am, my lord," the older man said.

The bishop nodded, evidently satisfied as well. Nobody asked if *he* was satisfied, Beau thought blackly. As if he'd heard him, Drake clapped him on the back. "Time to face your future, my lad."

Beau scowled. "Your lad is two years older than you are."

"But still a wide-eyed boy when it comes to the ladies, or we all wouldn't be joining in this odd little dance."

Beau scowled even more fiercely. "We are not all joining in anything. Only me."

"And her."

Beau was about to turn for a retort when Drake took him by the arm and led him in to stand before the altar. Beau didn't see anything at the back of the church, but the organist hit a resounding chord, and everyone in the chapel quieted.

Beau took up his position before the step, Drake to his side. The bishop, solemn-faced and awash in dignity, handed off his staff to the chaplain, who stood to the side like a server and took up his place of prominence. In the front row the Princess of Wales was beaming as if it were her own wedding. Beau took notice and then forgot she was even there. Because the back door was no longer empty.

The Duchess of Dorchester's Uncle Philbert was a man with bristling gray hair, the most wonderful laugh lines, and very possibly a salamander in his morning suit pocket. Looking nervous enough for his own wedding, he yanked at his coat and stuck out his elbow. Which was when Beau simply lost his breath.

She should not have been breathtaking. She was a tiny thing, her shape sleek rather than voluptuous, which he'd always thought he preferred. Her dress was simple, a soft white silk lined at bodice and hem with spring green ribbons. Rather than a circle of flowers or lace veil, she wore a simple bonnet lined in matching green fabric, within which her hair seemed to glow. It was the morning sun, he realized, finding her through the back windows. Nothing special.

Yet he couldn't take his eyes off her. And not because she had those huge blue eyes or that kissable mouth he could still somehow taste from the other night. Not her heart-shaped face or her uptilted little nose that should have made her look like a child playing dress-up.

Her expression. He supposed he'd expected her to look frightened, sad, anxious. Her expressive little face betrayed none of these. What her face showed—what her posture and lifted chin and preternaturally calm eyes showed— was the mien of a warrior. Pip was not meeting her doom. She was commanding her fate. She was demanding his respect and offering her partnership, no matter what he expected. Or wanted.

He fought the unholy urge to grin. His body fought the unholier urge to just grab her, run out the door and find somewhere to stake his claim.

"I always thought Boadicea was taller," he heard beside him.

He did smile, then, and thought her posture eased a fraction. "No," he told Drake, who looked more than a bit smitten himself. "I think she is just this size."

And then he stepped up to meet her.

————

5

"**D**early beloved..."

What was a bishop doing at her wedding? Pip wondered. What was Marcus Drake doing here? And why in heaven's name had the duchess insisted on stuffing the altar with those dreadful lilies? Pip hadn't been able to tolerate the smell of those things since the day of Theo's memorial. It was an omen, she decided, her commitment faltering a bit. A warning that she should raise her hand right now and put Beau out of his misery before she had to suffer it the rest of her life.

"...and therefore, is not by any to be enterprised, nor taken in hand, unadvisedly, lightly, or wantonly to satisfy men's carnal lusts and appetites..."

Pip swallowed. Did they have to mention carnal lusts? Standing this close to Beau, her hand in his, she could smell the citrus of his soap, the starch on his crisp linen shirt. She recognized the essence that was Beau. She had first discovered it her fourteenth summer, when she realized that the attraction that drew her to her best friend's brother had metamorphosed into something more powerful, more primal. Something that drew her like magnets to iron and set her body to humming in a way that disturbed her.

It still disturbed her, even more knowing what it meant, and that he resented the same attraction to her.

"...Secondly, it was ordained for a remedy against sin, and to avoid fornication..."

There he went again, she thought, wondering why she had never noticed how many times the marriage rite talked about lust. She didn't want to know about lust right now. She was having trouble enough attending to dignity and control.

She wanted to think more about the Duchess's words than the bishop's. Was there a way to make her marriage succeed? Could she win Beau over? Could she ever get him to forgive her for encouraging Theo to follow the only dream he'd ever had?

"...Therefore, if any man can show any just cause, why they may not lawfully be joined together, let him now speak, or else hereafter forever hold his peace."

Pip swore that every person in the chapel held their breath, even the bishop. Beau, blast him, turned just enough so she could see him raise an eyebrow. It wasn't funny. But if she wasn't careful, she'd burst out laughing.

She also swore the pause lasted quite a bit longer than any other service she had attended.

She was just about to remind the bishop that they still had half a ceremony to get through when he nodded, bent back to his book as if he didn't know the blasted ceremony by heart—and if he didn't, how did he ever make Bishop?—and moved on to the various promises.

Would they notice if she didn't promise to obey? There was only so much a girl should be forced to surrender; her money; her autonomy, her children, her dreams...well, all right, it was only *her* dreams. Other women weren't being forced into wedlock. Her mother was living her dream of traveling the world, helping her father in his diplomatic missions. Her older sister Georgina had her country squire husband and rosy-cheeked babes she'd dreamed of since she'd considered Pip her own baby doll. Several of her friends.

But none of them had been forced into marriage by a royal princess.

"...Wilt thou love her, comfort her, honor, and keep her in sickness and in health; and, forsaking all others, keep thee only unto her, so long as ye both shall live?"

Pip snapped to attention. They had gotten to the important part. She chanced a look up at Beau to see that he looked perfectly serious when he said, "I will," as if she hadn't over-heard him only ten hours earlier cavorting with a blowsy, round-heeled doxy.

She wanted so badly to say something, to snort or offer him that wryly lifted eyebrow back. But it was too late. She had had her chance at "speak now" and hadn't.

"...Wilt thou obey him, and serve him, love, honor, and keep him in sickness and in health; and, forsaking all other, keep thee only unto him, so long as ye both shall live?"

She couldn't help it. It slipped out before she could think of it. "As much as he will me."

The Bishop stiffened as if she had blasphemed, which she probably had. Behind her there were a few gasps and titters, and what sounded suspiciously like the Duchess's chuckle. The Bishop turned to Beau, as if he needed Beau's permission to move on.

And Beau, the traitor, was grinning. Of course, he was. "That should be fine," he assured the bishop. "I know what she means."

"But it's not..."

"It's as close as we're going to get from her."

"Good that you realize that," she muttered.

He pinched her finger.

It took the bishop a moment to get back on track. Thomas a'Becket's backside, Pip thought, you would think by the time you reached bishop you would be a bit adaptable. He cleared his throat portentously and resettled the Book of Common Prayer in his hands. Pip did notice that just beyond him Dr. Borden was struggling to keep a calm face. But then, Pip had attended her share of services with Dr. Borden. And argued scripture with him over many a cup of tea.

"I, Beaufort William Villiers Francis..."

Pip giggled.

Beau lifted an eyebrow again.

She shrugged. "It occurs to me that I've never heard all your names. Were your parents truly never that angry at you?"

The bishop wasn't entertained, but Beau grinned, and Pip felt triumph. It was the first time she could remember him lighting up like this since Theo had died. No matter what people would say about her behavior, it would be worth it. She had gotten Beau to smile. At least for a moment.

"Never," he said. "I was a perfect child. Your entire name, however, I do know. Which I will prove if you will allow me to finish."

She beamed at him. "Please do."

"I, Beaufort William Villiers Francis," he said with an arch look, "take you, Philippa Ellen Alexandra Trentham—"

"You don't need to gloat."

The bishop finally lost his patience. "Do you both wish to finish your vows before you bicker?"

"Oh, we're not bickering," Pip assured him. "That's much louder."

It was Beau's turn to clear his throat. "Take you to my wedded wife, to have and to hold from this day forward, for better for worse, for richer, for poorer, in sickness and in health, to love and to cherish, till death us do part, according to God's holy ordinance; and thereto I plight thee my troth."

The words almost made Pip weep. Oh, if only it would be true. But promises made under duress weren't as binding, even for Beau. It wasn't the same for her. She had known from the time she had decided to marry Beau when she was twelve that if she ever got to make a vow to him, she would live it with her whole heart.

She should have been sadder when she spoke. She couldn't be, even knowing what she was walking into.

"I, Phillipa Ellen Alexandra Trentham, take thee, Beaufort William Villiers Francis, to my wedded husband, to have and to hold from this day forward, for better for worse, for richer for poorer, in sickness and in health, to love, cherish, and honor, till death us do part, according to God's holy ordinance; and thereto I give thee my troth."

This time the bishop evidently chose to ignore the breach and called for the ring.

When Pip saw the ring, she gasped. An old circle of gold adorned with only a square cut sapphire bracketed by two baguette diamonds. It was familiar to her. She looked up, tears in her eyes, to see that the duchess was just as emotional. The ring had been the duchess's mother's, one Pip had seen on the duchess's right hand for years.

She opened her mouth to protest, but the duchess shook her head, and Pip knew that she would hurt that wonderful woman if she turned down this most precious gift.

"Well," she whispered to Beau, "I didn't give you much time to get something else."

Beau hushed her. "She insisted."

So, Pip smiled. And she smiled for the rest of the ceremony until Beau finally bent to drop a fleeting kiss on the lips that did no more than frustrate her and turned her back down the aisle.

"Time to face the lions," he murmured as he laid her hand on his arm.

"Don't be silly," she retorted, her smile feeling more like a rictus. "Lions are far kinder."

IT TOOK Beau two hours to catch Drake alone. First it had been the princess, then Lord Burke, and then every person there making certain they had a chance to collect their own tidbit to carry back to the autumn season. Since the duchess had been the one to arrange the wedding breakfast, Beau was never without a glass in his hand as he danced his way through one uncomfortable encounter after another.

Separated from his wife by an ever-changing parade of guests, he answered a thousand questions with nonsense— where will you take your bridal trip? He didn't know, as he hadn't had time to plan, although the continent looked much more inviting, didn't it? How long had you planned this little surprise? If he told them, it wouldn't have been a surprise.

He even found himself exchanging cool looks with his Uncle Edward.

"I assume this means we should begin counting months," his uncle snapped, effectively catching Beau's attention. "I cannot think of another reason for this travesty."

Knowing it would infuriate the old tartar, Beau took a languid sip of champagne. "Thank you for your best wishes, uncle. I knew I could count on you to be a gentleman. As I told Aunt Maude, if this situation distresses you, feel free to escape the outrage back to your own home. We would certainly understand."

Evidently some outrage was too great for words, because Uncle Edward simply spun on his heel and stalked away, leaving Beau behind with a surprising thought.

Should we start counting months? How odd. The thought saddened him. He did not want children with Pip. He did not want a real life with her. He wanted a little peace and the freedom to do his work and the chance to forget the conspiracy the two of them had entered into that had sent Theo to his death. But still, he suddenly wondered if Pip did want children. She had never really talked about it. Not that he would have listened.

He came within ames ace of making the fatal mistake of asking her. The guests had risen from the table after excellent food and a cake sculpted like the kind of flowers Beau preferred —the kind that didn't smell of funerals— and were now cluttering up the Great Hall. The duchess was patting Pip on the shoulder, and Pip was showing off the ring to one of the Duchess's friends. She looked so bright and carefree, as if this were any party. Her laughter rang out clear and melodic. Not the suppressed titters of the debutante, but whole-hearted enjoyment so few people conveyed.

It was Pip's special gift, her relentless joy. No matter how bad things got, she could dredge up a smile and a kind word and seem as if nothing mattered more than that moment or the person she was talking to.

Watching her now, Beau simply couldn't understand how he'd so lost control the other night. One simply didn't ravage a sprite. One didn't want to toss everyone out of the way to get back to her to finish what they'd started. For a perilously long moment, he did nothing but stare at her as she charmed everyone around her. For just that long, he found himself clutching his glass of champagne as if it were a lifeline.

Well, at least he could give her Delamere. She did love the old place. Maybe she wouldn't mind being left there for a while as he finished his work. God knew it would be safer all around that way.

"Have you ever thought of diplomatic work?" Beau heard in his ear.

Startling, he turned to find Drake standing next to him watching Pip as she described something mostly with her hands.

"What? Why?"

Drake grinned with a nod toward Pip. "You couldn't do better than having Pip for a wife. She'd be perfect."

Drake stared at his friend, wondering if he'd suddenly run mad. But Drake, as ever, was the perfectly groomed English gentleman, from the top of his scrupulously arranged blonde locks to his gleaming shoes, his expression serene. Beau turned to look at Pip, and then back again.

"Pip," he said and pointed. "*That* Pip. The Pip who cannot define the word discretion. The Pip who would rather shoot than sing. The Pip who is such a pattern card that her parents refused to take her to St. Petersburg."

"The Pip whose father didn't want her forced into marriage with the Russian princeling who was hounding him for her hand."

Now Beau stared back at his wife.

His *wife*. He wasn't sure whether the shiver that swept down his spine was dread or fear. Or something else entirely.

"A Russian princeling."

Drake nodded, sipping at his champagne. "She refused him after hearing him order some of his serfs off their land. Pip has very particular ideas about those things."

Beau knew that too well. He had once had to physically pull her away from a neighboring squire who had taken a riding crop to a groom. She had been ten at the time.

"How do you know that?" he asked.

Drake was watching Pip as well now. "I told you. I was in Vienna at the Peace Talks at the same time the Knights were. So was the prince. And his cousin who threatened to duel him over her. And the Italian Count who wanted her to have his babies. And an entire cadre of people who looked for her at every party."

Beau briefly closed his eyes, not certain if he felt more unnerved by her success among the most sophisticated of men or, damn it, jealous that they had captured her smiles.

No. Definitely not that. It would be far too uncomfortable. "Excellent. So, I want a wife who would cause an international incident the minute we stepped out of the country."

"You might want a wife who can work a room like an ambassador, speaks eight languages and counts most of her parents' contemporaries as honorary aunts and uncles, rather as you can see with the Countess Lieven over there."

Countess Lieven, who was even then hugging Pip like a long-lost niece. Countess Lieven, who hugged no person. The two of them were chattering in French and once again assessing Pip's ring.

Drake grinned at Beau. Amused at his discomfort, Beau was certain. "I'm telling you, she is a natural. I'm surprised you haven't noticed before."

"I have spent very few diplomatic balls in the same room with Pip."

Drake's grin was unapologetic. "I'm just saying that you might want to make the effort to look closer. She can be a real asset."

Suddenly Beau understood. His stomach dropped. "No."

Drake didn't react by a twitch.

"I said no. You are not dragging her into your plots and schemes."

"I think she would enjoy it immensely."

"She would get herself killed. Worse, she'd get *me* killed. No."

"And did she get herself killed recovering those plans?"

Drake was stunned into silence. He resisted the urge to look around for eavesdroppers, even knowing that Drake would never be so careless as to say anything incriminating near witnesses. But both Burke and Pamela were at far corners of the room. "Did she tell you?"

"Try not to be ridiculous. She would never do anything to endanger you."

They both looked over to where Pip was now commiserating in German with Princess Charlotte and her lady-in-waiting, Lady Mercer Elphinstone.

"The duchess told me," Drake said, lifting his glass of champagne for a sip.

Beau rubbed at the bridge of his nose. "How does *she* know?"

"Because the duke, until his unfortunate illness--"

"He went mad, Drake."

Drake frowned. "Spectacularly."

Running through the House of Lords screaming about invaders. From Shropshire. It had been a horrific end to a good man.

"We both know that he was working with the Home Office," Beau said.

"Which is another lesson you should undoubtedly take to heart. No man keeps that kind of secret from his wife."

Beau snorted. "Too late for that anyway."

"From what I hear. What *did* you find?"

"What did *she* find, you mean. You can collect it after the wedding breakfast."

"That dangerous?"

He shrugged. "I don't know, do I? The whole thing is in code."

Drake nodded as if Beau had just shared an anecdote from Whites. "A timely thing. I believe we might be in the process of cracking the damn thing."

"That isn't all. She also uncovered a rather unexpected feline."

"And that would be?"

"Burke."

This time Drake admitted surprise, whipping his head around to stare at Beau. "White-haired, genial, best-friends-with-the-Prince Burke?"

Beau took a sip of champagne. "The very same. Not just friends with the prince, evidently, but my own Pamela Smythe-Smythe, who waylaid me last night in my room, ostensibly to enjoy a last ride. Except later I realized she was spending a lot of time wandering aimlessly around."

"Looking for something."

"I would say so. The difficulty for her was that Pip was ahead of her. Pip evidently heard Burke talking and sussed out a plot to identify and...er, *take care* of whichever Rake had been sent to retrieve the plans—that being me—by making a fake set available while the real ones were tucked in Pamela's rooms. Pip lifted the fake plans right off me during that...er, compromising moment."

Drake gave a soft whistle.

"I haven't decided whether 'take care' meant compromise, implicate, or just eliminate."

"Glad we didn't have to find out. You have them?"

"I do now. After Pip got hold of the false plans, she evidently took the opportunity while Pamela was with me to sneak into her room to search for the real ones."

And got stuck under Pamela's bed. The more Beau thought about it, the funnier it seemed. Only Pip, he thought with a shake of his head. And to be able to squeeze out of that dilemma only to run smack into him.

"Pip put me in possession of both real and fake plans, with copies of the fakes left behind."

By the time he finished telling Drake, his leader was

shaking his head. "That is what I'm trying to tell you. Resourceful, is our Pip. She'd be a natural."

He wasn't going to argue this. Just the idea gave him the shakes.

"No."

Dropping her off at Delamere was looking more and more provident.

"You'll stay here a few days more anyway?" Drake asked, not even looking at Beau. "Since our suspected predators will not leave yet."

"I do have business to attend to, you know."

"Next week. For now, you are the only one available. The rest are taken up with the last contretemps."

Beau intended to tell Drake no. He needed to get Pip somewhere safe so he could go over the reports on the security for more than one at-risk prince. He was in the process of turning to do just that when he was intercepted.

"My dear Drummond," the duchess called, approaching at a fast clip.

Blast.

He bowed. "Your Grace."

She smiled that Mona Lisa smile of hers and took him by the arm. "You'll excuse him for a moment, won't you, Lord Drake?"

Drake made his own bow. "Anything for you, ma'am."

She patted his arm on the way by as if he were a schoolboy again. "Such good sense."

"Have you managed to pass off the plans?" she murmured as soon as she had Beau moving again, seemingly aimlessly circling the floor.

"Not yet. Although I am relieved to see Drake here."

"Me as well. It will keep you from haring off to London before the breakfast is even over and humiliating my dear Pippin."

Their eyes met, a wealth of understanding passing between them.

"Exactly why I was relieved as well," Beau conceded.

If it had been anyone but the duchess, Beau would have sworn she snorted. "I know you have not had a chance to discuss settlements," she said with another pat to his arm. "I have the address of Pip's family lawyers. I am confident you and they will make certain our Pip is protected."

It was pointless to even nod. Besides, she wasn't waiting for it.

"In the meantime," she said, looking around, always on alert around her guests. "You must go somewhere this evening. Together. No one gets married and then simply stays at a house party."

"Even your house party?"

Her smile was luminous. "Even mine."

He should be working out a place to take Pip where they could be alone. Somewhere he could still monitor the house party. The problem was, he didn't want to be alone with Pip. It would just complicate matters. It would make resisting that strange and terrible attraction all the harder.

"Well," he mused as they walked along nodding to people. "I cannot take her to Delamere right now."

"And subject her to your relatives? I think not. You *are* going to encourage them to move on, aren't you, my dear?"

He finally grinned. "I might just leave that to Pip. She has been threatening action since she was twelve."

The duchess grinned right back. "Please do alert me when she does. I should love to watch."

He gave her a polite nod. "This is not my neighborhood. Do you have a suggestion? I must stay in some proximity."

Her smile was beatific. "If you wouldn't mind, our Dower House has stood empty since my Aunt Eleanor passed away. It lies just about a mile away in a lovely copse of trees. My staff is very fond of Pip and might have already begun removing holland covers and stocking the pantry."

Coming to a stop, Beau bent to the duchess's lifted hand and kissed the air just above it. "Your price is far above rubies, Your Grace."

The duchess seemed to consider a moment. "It is, is it not?" She patted his hand. "All I hope is that you not rush into any decisions."

Beau blinked. "I believe we just did."

"Not that. One that will irrevocably set the path for your marriage."

For the first time Beau saw real vulnerability in the eyes of the most elegant woman he'd ever known.

"Do not waste your future on past regrets," she said.

Beau almost turned away. She didn't know. How could she? She hadn't been there to hear Pip urging Theo to do whatever he could to follow the drum. She wasn't there when the Dragoon appeared at the door to Delamere.

The duchess gave his arm another pat. "Please," she said, a wealth of emotion in her voice. "Talk to each other. Find a way through. She loves you, you know."

He sighed. "I know."

It didn't matter. He didn't think it did, anyway.

But how could he douse that kind light in the duchess's eyes? "I'll try."

She gave a brisk nod and one more pat. "In that case, you should begin to collect your wife."

Beau lifted an eyebrow. "Begin?"

The duchess just smiled back. "If you do not know how long it takes your wife to say her goodbyes by now, you are woefully unobservant. The coach will be at the door in thirty minutes."

He gave her a little bow.

She didn't move. "And Drummond," she said, and he knew

the entire tenor of this visit had changed. "Since her grandparents died, I have acted in loco parentis for Pip when her own parents are unavailable. I consider her one of my own, which makes her very precious to me."

She said not one word of threat, but Beau heard it. The warning from Pip's maid might have been more impressive, but Beau knew perfectly well that this threat was far more serious.

"I shall do my best," was all he could think to say.

It must have been enough. The duchess smiled and patted his cheek before walking off, leaving Beau to wonder exactly what he was supposed to achieve.

PIP WAS EXHAUSTED. It wasn't just the fact that she hadn't slept in the last few days. It wasn't even that she was suddenly and irrevocably married, or that as many people who had sincerely wished her well, an almost equal number were looking forward to some sort of scandal. It was that they didn't have to look far for the scandal. Perfect Pamela had taken up position just at the edge of Pip's line of sight. Draped in slithery crimson and moving with the sensual aggression of a python, every so often she made it a point to look on Beau with a secretive smile and then turn to Pip with patently false sympathy.

Whether it was supposed to be for Pip or for Beau's benefit, Pip couldn't exactly tell. She suspected it didn't matter. The point was to get the other guests to watch Pamela's antics. And they did. With relish. And Pip had to spend much of her time pretending to be oblivious not only to the act going on in the corner, but the heads swiveling back and forth.

Oh, if she could only reveal what she really thought, that Perfect Pamela was positively pathetic. That she might have been Beau's very public mistress, but her reign was over. Pip had not realized until now quite how possessive a woman she was. Not only would she not allow poaching on her preserves, but she would publicly punish whosoever attempted it.

She made a tactical move to lift her champagne glass for a sip to hide the grin she couldn't help. Perfect Pamela was also making her positively alliterative. That was crime enough in and of itself.

"Oh dear," Lizzie said alongside her. "It seems mother is putting the fear of God into your husband."

Pip carefully turned so her interest wasn't noted. And she smiled even more. Lizzie was right. The duchess had a hand on Beau's arm and was smiling in a way any of her children— including Pip—would recognize. And if Beau was smart, he would do whatever it was she wanted him to.

"His aunt could take some lessons from her in persuasion," Pip admitted to her friend. "Your mother could terrify Wellington."

Lizzie grinned. "Oh, she has. She has."

"How delightful," she heard behind her.

Blast! Pamela had snuck up on them. Lizzie stiffened. It took all her control, but Pip didn't so much as twitch.

"I congratulate you," Pamela purred, coming into her line of sight.

"Don't be silly," Pip retorted easily. "It is the groom you congratulate. You give the bride best wishes."

All right, so maybe she was not so controlled, when she gave the word *wife* just a bit more emphasis.

Of course, she was dealing with a professional.

"In that case," Pamela said with a cat-in-the-cream smile. "I do. Give you best wishes for what you face, knowing that Beau would never have married you unless you'd forced him into it."

Pip tilted her head a bit. "I'll ask him later," she said. "I shall also remind him that I have never grown lax in protecting that which—or whom—I cherish."

"That is very true," Lizzie piped up with a bright nod, as if she didn't hear the undercurrents. "You should have seen her in boarding school when one of the teachers tried to hurt a younger student." She grinned in reminiscence. "That woman couldn't walk for a week."

Pamela made a perfect *moue*. "Violence is crass."

"But effective," Lizzie and Pip said in unison, just as they had when they chased the teacher from the school grounds.

Pip threaded her arm through Lizzie's, astonished at Lizzie's blatant defense. "My brother Alex taught all of the girls in my form how to defend ourselves from...predators."

Pamela's laugh was just a mite strained. "How dear. Let me know if the fantasy comforts you."

Because Pip's luck had been steadily waning, that was of course the moment Beau strolled up. "Brat, the duchess has just reminded us that it is time to go."

And blast it if she didn't blush. He would pay for that later, she swore.

As for Pamela, she just laughed, strolled by Beau with a slow stroke down his arm and murmured, "Brat. How perfect."

Later no one would be able to say exactly how it happened, but suddenly from one step to the next Pamela shrieked and pitched forward, flat on her face, her dress floating up to betray legs that weren't as sleek as one would assume, her champagne glass shattering spectacularly on the marble floor.

Everyone stopped to look, of course. Beau spun to glare at Pip until he realized that she had been completely out of reach of the woman. The only person close enough to have tripped La Smythe-Smithe, was Lizzie. Lady Elizabeth Ripton, daughter of the Duchess of Dorchester, who at that moment was watching her daughter walk towards her, seemingly unaware of the havoc she'd left behind.

"Oh, dear," Pip murmured. "How unfortunate."

A footman was running toward Pamela along with half the males in the room. Beau made to turn after them when Pip caught his eye. She didn't say a word. But there was no question that if he laid a hand on Pamela Smythe-Smithe in order to help her up, there would be bloody retribution when they were alone. He waited just too long to help Pamela up, leaving it to the other men.

The first salvo in their marriage had been fired.

6

They were sent off in splendid style. Of course, they had to wait for Princess Charlotte to make her regal exit in the state coach, followed by her entourage and surrounded by her mounted guards, looking for all the world like the procession to the opening of Parliament. Even before that they had to withstand the self-congratulatory best wishes from the princess, who was not shy about claiming credit for her favorite wedding of the year which she couldn't *wait* to trumpet to all and sundry.

But finally, the princess's train disappeared in a cloud of dust, and it was Beau and Pip's turn. The duchess lent them the crested ducal coach and added two outriders. A second coach carried luggage and servants. The house staff right up to the butler and housekeeper who had lined up down the stairs for the princess refused to leave, smiling for Pip as if she had been a daughter of the house. Clustered in the drive, the house party guests waved them off as if they were bound for a voyage.

Lizzie serenely smiled, as she would. The duchess had her arm around her two younger daughters as they waved madly at the girl who had occupied the Chinese bedroom off and on all these years even as they argued over who would inherit it.

Inside the coach, the occupants sat as stiffly as if they were on a tumbril on the way to the guillotine. The stately line of ash trees along the drive were turning gold and crimson and yellow, and the sky was an unusually sharp shade of cobalt, but neither paid particular attention.

For Pip's part, she felt dislocated, as if she had just been dropped into empty air. Her life had changed utterly, and she hadn't had time to know how. It had been all right when they still had all the other people to buffer them. But now she was irrevocably alone with the man who'd been forced to marry her, and the silence was deafening.

Not that she hadn't suffered sudden dislocations before. There was nothing like learning the week before your parents would leave for a new diplomatic post that they had arranged for her stay with friends instead. She should be used to it by now.

But this dislocation separated her completely from everything she knew and had assumed. This one put her under the control of someone who really didn't want to be with her, which had never happened before. Someone she had once desperately wished for. Someone with whom she had long dreamed of sharing a trip just like this one.

She'd always thought she would be overwhelmed with joy.

She was terrified.

And it didn't help that the man she was closed in with didn't merely set off that old hum in her, but a new seething restlessness born of a more immediate memory. Blast him.

They were turning onto the Dorchester Road, and suddenly she couldn't bear the silence another moment. Well, she thought, taking a calming breath that did not calm her at all. Might as well begin as she meant to go on.

"So," she said in the brightest voice she could muster. "What now?"

Seated across from her, Beau startled as if he'd been half asleep. "What now what?"

She shrugged. "What are our plans? Do we *have* plans? Is there to be a bride trip, or will we settle into our life? If so, will we be going to London next or Delamere? And if we go to Delamere, may I have the pleasure of putting your aunt and uncle on a coach?"

"I haven't decided, although I would appreciate a bit more patience for my aunt and uncle. They cared for Delamere while I was taken up with government."

She frowned. "They have been fighting you for control since your fourteenth birthday."

The day his parents had died and he had become Viscount. The day his aunt and uncle had descended on him and taken over Delamere. The day Pip had found Beau crying in the stables and sat with him. Simply sat with him, knowing there were no words big enough for what he faced.

"They took good care of it, no matter how well you like them," he said.

Pip's opinion differed, but she chose discretion over disagreement. At least for now.

"You'll be taking over once and for all, though, won't you?" she asked.

She did not want to begin her married life having to wrestle that house from his Aunt Maude.

He sighed. "I can't even think that far ahead until I finish my work here."

"Then we aren't going there now?"

He shook his head.

She nodded back. "Well, at least it should be a comfort to know that I can help you there when we do. I make a brilliant estate agent."

He looked truly confused. "What do you mean?"

It occurred to her that no one had had time to apprise Beau of his windfall. She made it a point to smile. "Just that it might please you to know that I do not come to you empty-handed. Besides my bright mind and charming personality—and dowry, of course—you will gain my grandparents' acres across the road from Delamere. Their estate agent Mr. Clark has been keeping it in good heart for me...well, for you."

"How do you know?"

"I have made it a point to work with him over the years to keep it healthy. After all, it would have been mine if I hadn't married by my thirtieth birthday."

Now he looked positively flummoxed. "You? Why you? Hasn't your father or brother seen to it?"

She laughed. "Father is brilliant in the fields of diplomacy and governance. Not mangel-wurzels. I seem to be far more suited to the task."

Poor Beau. He had no idea what to do with this revelation. "I don't suppose you have found the same kind of affinity for piano. Or embroidery, like a normal wife. Watercolors? Charades?"

She grinned. "Heavens, no. And as you well remember, no one wants to hear me sing. I have a rooster on the estate who makes far more pleasing sounds. I have decided instead to focus on those skills at which I do excel."

He shook his head, but there was a bit of a gleam in his eyes. "Heaven help us all."

The carriage trundled along. An uncomfortable silence once again stretched between them.

"And now?" she finally asked, plucking at her gloves. "You decided where we are going?"

"I did."

She looked up to find that he'd turned to watch out the

window and waited. And waited. "Please do not play this game with me, Beau."

It had been hard enough making it through the wedding breakfast, fending off personal questions and smiling, always smiling as if the wedding were an uncomplicated joy instead of the disaster she was beginning to fear. But if Beau was going to make this even more difficult, she might just stop the coach and get out, no matter what anybody said.

They couldn't be more disappointed in her anyway. Oh, they might have smiled and acted happy for her—well, except for Perfect Pamela, and truthfully Pamela's spite made Pip smile—but Pip suspected that since most of the witnesses to her abrupt wedding would never know the real reason for her ruin, they would assume all the wrong things and either scorn her or pity her. What else could it be after Beau's exhibition with the Perfect Pamela only moments before the fatal discovery? And with everything else suddenly on her plate, Pip was simply not in the mood for that.

Maybe it was better she and Beau were getting away for a bit somewhere no one knew her. The two of them might be able to wrestle this marriage to the ground out of sight of an audience before it overwhelmed them. At least agree on terms and conditions. Immediate terms and conditions. They could work on long-range expectations later when the shock had dimmed a bit.

"Beau?" she nudged. "A destination?"

He finally looked over at her, but in the shadowy coach, she couldn't quite catch his expression. "The duchess reminded me that the other guests would expect us to leave," he said.

Pip nodded. "I imagine it would look odd if we simply moved luggage around."

"They would also expect that we would wish for privacy, I imagine."

She almost didn't answer. "I imagine they would."

Would you? She wanted to ask. *Wouldn't you like to see where that kiss might have led us?*

She knew where it had left *her*. She was still beset by that shattering jolt of surprise, the flood of heat and wonder, the astonishing hunger that seemed to have overtaken her from nothing more than a man's hands on her. One particular man's hands. Blast him again.

It had frightened her. It had astonished her. And like a persistent itch, it still sparked along her nerve endings to the point of destroying her patience.

Tonight was her wedding night. As opposed to most girls of her acquaintance, she knew exactly what would happen. If it happened. If Beau could overcome his resentment long enough to consummate this marriage. She knew Beau would never intentionally hurt her, no matter how he felt. But she suspected that by not touching her at all, he would hurt her worse.

Should she ask him? Did she want to face the definite rejection and begin dealing with it? Or did she still want to pointlessly hope?

Evidently, she wanted to hope. Losing the courage to put the question to the test, she spent a few moments watching autumn approach outside her window as they trundled down the road, the heat in her chest and belly and limbs refusing to ease.

"Will someone be bringing our horses along?" she asked. "I'd rather not leave Macha behind. She pines."

She finally got his attention. He frowned. "Is that what you named your horse?"

She made sure to grin. "After the Irish warrior goddess? Why yes. I think it fits. Not only is my girl fierce, but the goddess Macha is also known as Macha Mong Ruad, of the red hair. And my Macha shines like a copper penny. I can't wait to show her to you."

He sighed, as if accepting an unpleasant truth. Pip refused to cater to him.

"I've also seen your fine fellow," she said. "He looks as if he might give Macha a worthy race. What is his name?"

She almost couldn't hear his answer. "Ares."

She heard it well enough and couldn't help laughing. "Nothing whimsical about naming your horse after the male god of war, certainly."

His expression was pained. "I bought him from Packton. His daughter named the horse."

"And you can't change his name?"

Beau actually ducked his head. "He won't respond."

She couldn't quite wipe the grin from her face. "I need to meet this girl. If for no other reason, to hire her as a groom."

"You do not."

"She certainly knows her horses, if she knew to name him after the god of war. It so matches his owner."

She got quite a scowl for that, even though there was a suspicious cant to the corner of Beau's mouth. "We'll race them," he conceded. "See who's the more godlike."

And blast it if he didn't warm her heart to the point she wanted to plant a kiss on his cheek. "I look forward to it."

Before she could do something inadvisable, he turned back to his window.

"Did you manage to hand off the plans?" she asked.

"Drake will meet me later so we can talk."

She drew a breath. "You can talk, or will the person who actually heard the conspiracy and recovered the plans be invited?"

"What we need to discuss would not be appropriate in front of you."

The last thing she needed at this point was to be patronized. Briefly glaring at the back of his head, she returned to her own view. "Then it must be the breadth of Pamela's skills you intend to discuss. I don't know. I think I could learn something from that, don't you? If we ever were to make use of them, anyway. I should hate to disappoint."

Well, that answered that question. She guessed she'd ended up asking after all.

Beau's response was a surprised bark of laughter. "Good God, Pip. Even for you that was outrageous."

Oh, well. She'd walked right up to the cliff. She might as well jump. "Was it, though? Or should we clear the air with a bit of honesty? She thinks you'll be back at her dainty feet within weeks, you know."

She finally got a reaction out of him, although she was quite certain it wasn't the one she wanted. His head whipped around, and she thought he stopped breathing. "Where did you hear that?"

Not *don't be ridiculous* or *how can you think that.*

All she could do was flash him a big, false smile. "It is illuminating what one can hear from underneath a bed."

He didn't even bother to answer her; just turned back toward the window.

He was so close; I-can-smell-your-cologne close. Sharing his warmth close, whether he wanted to or not. Whether *she* wanted to. She couldn't help feeding on it like sunlight, like air filling her lungs. It only fed the old hum until she could almost hear it.

"Did you know?" she asked, even knowing she was pushing him away. "That she was part of this, I mean. Were you at least suspicious?"

His glower was impressive. "Were *you*?"

"Not until she showed up with the gray-haired man."

She didn't think it was the moment to tell him she hadn't thought Perfect Pamela smart enough for espionage.

"Lord Burke, you mean."

She nodded again. "Him."

There was a pause. "You cannot be mistaken about him? There are several gray-haired men at the party."

She shook her head. "There are no others with that particular voice. All raspy and quiet. I came looking for you because I heard that voice out on the balcony threatening to 'take care' of the person who went after the plans. I had to assume that did not mean offer him brandy and a cigar."

"And you assumed they meant me."

She shrugged. "All of the other Rakes at the party had already left."

"Did you recognize the man he was talking to?"

"I didn't see him," she said, shaking her head. "And he did not sound as distinctive. Is Lord Burke's first name Robert?"

He went as still as one could in a moving carriage. "No. Why?"

"Because Pamela mentioned someone named Bobby told her the message was important. *Did* you suspect her?"

There was another pause, a longer one. "Yes."

Could she ask this? Did she really want to know whether he had deliberately approached Pamela to glean information? If he had, it would mean he would go to uncomfortable lengths—uncomfortable for her, at least—to literally seduce information from a suspect. If he had not, then didn't it suggest that he didn't care whether his mistress was an enemy spy?

If she asked, would he give her an answer that would push her even farther away? If he answered, did she really want to hear it?

"Do you think she suspected you, too?"

"Hopefully not after the scene in the library."

She nodded. It was all she could think to do.

She was about to deliberately change the subject to something else—anything else—when the carriage slowed to make a turn. A familiar turn.

As if things couldn't get worse.

"Where are we going?" she asked, leaning forward.

It was a smaller lane that looked as if it disappeared into a stand of oak. A stand of oak where Pip and Lizzie had picked bluebells back in the day. A stand of oaks that was part of the Ripton Hall land.

Beau didn't bother to answer, since once they turned one more corner they saw the tidy little brick Queen Anne Dower House tucked in at the edge of the trees.

It had always seemed like a dollhouse to Pip, a place where little girls shared high tea with Lizzie's eccentric aunt who had written lurid stories with ghosts and pirates.

The house had been closed up since her death several years ago. It seemed that it was open again. Billings, the first footman, and Mrs. Webb the undercook from the big house stood on the stairs along with two maids and two footmen.

Oh, St. Agnes's ankles, not here. Not where everyone knew her down to the date she had lost her last baby tooth. She had just started to feel as if she could breathe again.

"Why *here*?" she demanded frantically.

Beau frowned, seeming bemused. "Because the duchess offered it. I told you. I didn't have time to make other arrangements."

"No. You said the duchess suggested we go away. Not where we were going. I thought we would at least get as far as a village or two over where we could have some privacy!"

The frown deepened. "I also told you Drake would be meeting me. This is a convenient place. Don't enact a tragedy, Pip. You know perfectly well this is all for show."

She felt that statement kick her in the chest. Tears stung the back of her throat. "For people who know me better than my parents do."

He studied her a moment. "What exactly don't you want them to know? I suspect they already know the nature of the marriage, as any house servant would."

"That you loathe me."

"That I *what*?"

She waved an impatient hand, wishing she knew how to say what she needed to. "I know we can't pretend that this was a long-standing understanding..."

He scowled again. "A little hard to do, considering how many witnesses enjoyed that little drama."

"Could you at least pretend that this marriage is not the very last thing you'd wish inflicted on you?"

That seemed to stun him to complete silence. Before Pip could at least urge him to consider the idea, the carriage reached the circle driveway and pulled up before the front steps where the staff waited, smiling. Pip felt as if she were smothering. She smiled anyway.

And then one of the grooms was holding the coach door open and holding out a hand to help her out. Pip drew a deep breath and did her best to appear delighted for the staff.

"Billings," she greeted them. "Mrs. Webb. Did you perform a miracle for us?"

Mrs. Webb dipped a curtsy. Billings, too young yet to appear formidable, bowed, grinning. Pip imagined she would grin too if she had been given the opportunity to practice her butling skills in such a safe place.

"Were the duchess's idea," Mrs. Webb said, plump hands tucked under her flour-dusted apron. "'I want a comfortable little hideaway for our Pip,' says she and sends Billings and me straight off. She even gave us leave to make your favorite dishes. Hope you like it, my lady." Abruptly, she chuckled and shook her head. "Imagine that. Calling our little imp my lady."

Imagine that indeed, Pip thought, her stomach clenching. She'd been addressed as such at the breakfast, of course. But somehow it seemed real for the first time on the lips of the delighted Mrs. Webb. She wished it tasted so good on hers.

"Welcome, my lord," Billings said with a precise bow as

Beau stepped out onto the raked shell drive. "I hope you'll find your stay all that is pleasant."

"I'm sure we will, uh…"

"Billings," Pip offered. "And this is Mrs. Webb, and Mary and Patsy, Mike and Cam from the big house, and Hawkins from the stables." Suddenly, she was the one to giggle. "Rather reversed, isn't it? Usually, it is the lady who receives the introductions."

"A pleasure to meet you all," Beau said without noticeable reaction. "If you could show us to our rooms in a few moments. But first, I need to speak to Lady Drummond in the parlor. And I expect Lord Drake to stop by. If you could provide refreshments until I can attend him."

"Tea for you and Lady Drummond?" Mrs. Web asked.

Beau looked about as if expecting it to show up. "In our suite when Lady Drummond goes up, I'm sure."

A bit of the light went out of the servants' eyes, but they moved as if choreographed to see to Beau's requests. For Pip's part, she had not thought her stomach could get tighter. But the signs were not good for her escaping humiliation before her friends from the big house. Especially when Beau made it up two steps before remembering to turn and take her arm.

All she could do when she made it into the house was remove her bonnet and pelisse and hand them off to Billings, smooth down her skirts, and lead the way into the South Parlor.

Mrs. Webb and the girls had done a good job cleaning up an unused space, but the salon was still decorated for a quirky septuagenarian. Pip had never needed to notice it before. It just was. But now she saw the faded gold chairs and lumpy mud brown settee. She saw the ornate little French desk in the corner that had once been buried in manuscript pages and the empty parrot cage by the window that had been occupied by a bright-feathered denizen with a breathtaking store of sea curses. A fire flickered in the uninspired fireplace, and the air was redolent with the scents of lavender, beeswax and burning wood. It should have felt homey. It felt like a punishment.

"Not even tea, then?" she asked as he shut the door behind them. "What have I done this time?"

Beau turned on her. "Please be seated, Pip."

She noted that he didn't move in a way to indicate he would follow her lead. "I don't think so," she said, stiffening her spine. "I have far enough to look up to you as it is. What is it you have to say before we could even reach the privacy of our rooms, where it might not look so particular?"

He looked around, frowning. "Particular? I don't understand."

She rubbed at the fresh headache that had just bloomed behind her eyes. "We might speak of anything in our rooms, Beau. Plans, schedules, a discussion of the people we visited with at the wedding breakfast. No one would have thought to comment. But this smacks of a punishment that should not be witnessed."

"Don't be..." He looked around again. "I just didn't want people around."

"Then you wait until our unpacking is done and suggest Joyful and your valet take some early dinner. You do sensitive work for the government, Beau. You should be familiar with the niceties of appearance. Newly married people don't march into a parlor like an executioner on the way to the scaffold. They smile and hold hands until they are alone. *Then* they can scowl at each other to their heart's content."

Now he was pacing. "This isn't the Paris Peace Talks, for heaven's sake."

No. It wasn't. It was the foot upon which her marriage would take its first step. At least the public side of her marriage.

She ended up sitting down after all. She simply didn't know what else to do. "What is it you wanted to tell me, Beau?"

How could you feel defeated before you'd even spent a day with your new spouse? Especially after so briefly feeling things were improving.

Beau shoved a hand through his hair, which told Pip everything about his state of mind. Beau never presented himself as anything other than fully put together. Seeing his hair disordered did something to her insides.

"I know you didn't want this marriage," she said, deciding that she wasn't in the mood for uncomfortably dancing around each other. "I didn't either, for the very reason that it would make you unhappy." *And thereby make me unhappy.* "But I would appreciate it if we could at least act as the friends we used to be."

His expression was unreadable. His hair was still distracting Pip. All she wanted to do was smooth it back again where he was sure to believe it belonged.

She'd spent a childhood wanting to rumple his hair into disorder, to throw him off his perfect stride. But Theo had done that for him, and Pip found that she didn't like it after all. Especially since this surprise marriage had disordered him even more.

He dropped into the other armchair as if someone had taken his knees out. "I'm sorry," he said, hands clenched on his knees. "I wanted to talk. I just wanted some privacy. We've been surrounded by people since this whole thing began. Not exactly an optimum place to decide where we go from here."

"I want to talk, too," she said, grieving for his distress. "But could we do it after we've eaten Mrs. Webb's special dinner? I did not eat much at the breakfast. Telling a raft of such clankers as I did this afternoon tends to disrupt the peace of a stomach."

He actually offered her a wry grin. "We should at least compare notes on exactly which clankers we both told."

She smiled back, no matter what her stomach still felt like.

"My favorite was the long-standing familial understanding that had been disrupted by an unnamed misunderstanding."

An eyebrow went north. "Was the misunderstanding blond and...er..."

"Overripe? No. That was the punishment. You should be glad I'm so forgiving."

He nodded, looking marginally more relaxed. "We can compare notes at dinner."

"How about after Drake leaves again? Then we'll know where you are in the investigation and what still needs to be done."

He scowled. "Pip...."

She climbed to her own feet, which wasn't nearly as impressive as Beau doing it. "You said he is coming by. Let us tackle one problem at a time, shall we?"

And before he could argue, she walked to the door. Her hand on the knob, she paused. "One thing we'll settle right now, though. I would appreciate your not calling me Brat in front of your ex-lovers."

Standing back up, he tilted his head. "Even when you're acting like a brat?"

She scowled. "Don't be absurd. I never act like a brat. An original, maybe. A diamond." She shrugged. "I would even allow a charming eccentric."

"And is that what I should call you?"

She nodded graciously. "I will accept being addressed as beloved, sweetheart, goddess, and my passionate delight. You can save Brat for when I inevitably beat you in billiards." She flashed him a bright smile.

He choked on his own laughter. "You're going to be every bit as difficult as I'd imagined."

"Yes," she said with a definite nod. "I am."

He took a step closer and reached over to push her glasses up her nose. "Forewarned, is that right?" Without waiting for a reply, he dropped a kiss on her forehead. "And just so you know, Brat. I don't loathe you."

It wasn't exactly a vow of undying love, Pip thought, but for now she would hold on to her small joy.

In the end, though, she could only hold on for a moment, because before she could turn back to open the door, somebody was scratching on it. Pip opened it to find Billings standing stiffly outside.

"My apologies, my lady," he said. "But Lord Drake is in the library for Lord Drummond."

Beau briefly laid a hand against her back on the way by, inciting another smile, a small ray of hope. Until he spoke.

"Why don't you get some rest, my dear?" he asked. "Lord Drake and I have some business to attend to."

And she heard it. That tone of voice. The dismissal she had spent her life hearing. *Be a good girl and stay out of the way. Keep yourself busy while we do the important things. Don't you have somewhere to be?* Once again dismissed, discarded, dispensable.

Suddenly her future yawned ahead of her, vast and empty, once again spending her time trying to find someplace to belong. Someplace to call home, rather than the various places she had simply resided. Without purpose, without purchase, always standing just a bit outside the warm confines of her loving family. Any loving family.

For the longest time, she stood there where she had always been, left behind while others lived vivid lives. Caught on the wrong side of a closed door with no way through.

Billings was showing Beau into the library with a flourish, and Pip stood alone, where she had always been. Except with Theo.

But Theo was gone. And Pip had a sudden suspicion that Theo would be disappointed in her right now. He would have grinned at her, goading her out of her isolation. "After all the work I've put into you?" he'd demand with a sly grin. "Don't waste it on fitting in. You were never supposed to."

She so missed him. She always would, deep in those places that became loud in the silence. But Theo wasn't here to push her forward. She had to do it herself. She had to decide what she deserved and then take it.

She had to decide how to fight for her marriage. And to do that, she had to construct some self-respect.

Billings was turning back toward her when she marched up to him. "Announce me, please," she said.

There was a certain satisfaction in seeing the shock on the faces of the two men lounging in the library when she strode through the door Billings was about to close.

7

Both men jumped to their feet as if spring-loaded, the brandy in their hands sloshing around in the glass. Pip sailed in like a very small ship of the line.

"No tea, thank you, Billings," she said. "I can see the gentlemen have their brandy. I imagine they won't mind sharing a bit."Billings backed out of the room faster than a pastor in a bordello. Giving her glasses a little push, Pip waved both men back into their seats, matching brown leather armchairs situated in front of the best fire she'd seen in the house. Before either man could interfere, Pip grabbed the chair that fronted Eleanor's 'household accounts' desk and dragged it over to a spot facing them. Then, imperiously, she sat. Smiling as if he'd just sat down to a Drury Lane farce, Drake took a moment to splash a bit of brandy into a snifter before turning back to Pip. Taking a look at the amount, she just lifted an eyebrow. He smiled wider and added an inch or two before handing it over.

"Thank you," she acknowledged, taking a sip and ignoring the fire in Beau's eyes."Now, then," she chirped with a bright smile as if presiding over a tea tray. "What are we discussing?"

Beau was grinding his teeth. Drake couldn't seem to stop smiling.

Pip took a moment to peruse the room where she'd spent so much time as a girl. "I do love it in here," she said, taking a sip. "Lizzie and I used to spend an inordinate amount of time here writing stories, just like Aunt Eleanor. Mine usually involved knights and dragons." She didn't feel the need to tell them she had played the part of the knight.

The room was the definition of cozy. The bookshelves might have been a bit sparse—Aunt Eleanor considered classics boring and anything that didn't help her write her books superfluous—but they were well-cared-for mahogany and carried a few vases with the last of the garden flowers. Brightly designed Persian rugs littered the dark wood floor, and overstuffed furniture cluttered up the rugs.

Pip shook her head. "I never could have come up with anything like what we have experienced the last few days, though. I don't have the imagination."

"I thought you were going up to take a rest," Beau growled, sitting forward.

She flashed a bright smile. "I find I am not weary."

"Then you should simply be happy to accept that you are not part of this conversation, just as I said. You just vowed to obey me, madam."

She once again lifted a single eyebrow, although she knew her glasses dimmed the effect. "Ah, but in fact, Beau, I did not. I did, however, warn you that I will not be shoved aside. Besides, don't you think national security trumps personal preference?"

"You wish to help us with national security?" Drake asked, leaning back and crossing his leg as if at his club.

"Why, yes," Pip said with a bright smile. "I do."

"No, you do not," Beau insisted, now on his feet. "I don't want you anywhere near this."

"But I already am," Pip countered gently, "near this."

"She truly is," Drake drawled, swirling his brandy a bit. "Ever since she overheard that conversation."

Pip tilted her head. "Beau already told you about that?"

He nodded.

Beau ran his hand through his hair again. "Pip, no. I told you. It isn't safe."

"Neither is riding horses. But I do that."

"And quite well," Drake said with a placid smile.

Beau slammed his drink on the cabinet. "This is different, and you know it!"

She so wanted to lay her hand against his cheek, just to comfort him a bit. "And I am very careful."

"Really? Hiding under an enemy's bed is careful?"

"I did not get caught. And I can share information you cannot, Beau. Impressions, observations, conclusions. I can also bring information about what the women know. As opposed to you, I have access to women when we are separated from our menfolk. I can tell you, a lot goes on in salons and retiring rooms."

"You don't belong in this investigation, Pip," he insisted, and suddenly Pip knew they were coming to the crux of the problem.

"I do, and you know it, Beau."

He was on his feet. "I won't put you in a position where you might be hurt!"

"It isn't your decision, my dear."

Suddenly, he looked frantic. "It damn well is! And I won't have you mixed up in this. I won't have you end up like..."

He abruptly cut himself off, his face suddenly red, his knuckles white around his glass.

And Pip knew she could no longer be polite. "Theo? You think that my helping you would be the same as sending me to war?"

Finally, she couldn't stand it anymore. This was not a

conversation they should be having in front of witnesses. It belonged between them. But she needed Beau to understand that he wasn't responsible for every wrong in the world. But neither was she. So, she followed him to her feet to see the stark horror in his eyes.

"That wasn't your choice to make either," she said very quietly.

He didn't answer. He just glared at her. Tears crowded the back of Pip's throat to think of her beloved Beau's grief, exacerbated by the venom from his aunt and uncle. Discounted by Theo, who had only seen what he was missing.

"He would have gone anyway," she said, holding onto her glass like her last lifeline to keep her from finally doing what she'd so badly wanted to and holding him. Knowing he would never let her. "You could not have stopped him, Beau. I couldn't have stopped him. You gave him the best chance you could have."

He jerked back as if she'd slapped him, his features tortured. "You want to get involved?" he snapped. "Fine." He downed the rest of his drink and slammed it back down on the cabinet. "You talk to Drake. I'm going for a walk."

And without another word, he slammed out of the room.

For a long moment Pip could only stand where she was, frozen in place. "Well," she finally said, knowing her voice was choked with tears as she sank back down into her chair. "That went well."

Drake set down his glass. "I should follow him."

Pip considered Drake's slight frown and shook her head. "No. He needs to walk it off for a bit. There is plenty of estate to stomp across."

He offered a wry smile. "What if he should run across one of the house party guests? Won't it look bad on his wedding day to be walking off a tantrum?"

Pip scowled. "You really believe this marriage could look

worse? Unless he regales them with the tale of me underneath Perfect Pamela's bed, I sincerely doubt anyone could think it more ludicrous." Taking another sip of her brandy, she sighed. "No. Leave him be. He has always been one to walk off a problem."

"You consider yourself a problem, do you?"

She did her best not to sigh. "I spoke of Theo. We do not speak of Theo. Ever. Even though he desperately needs to."

"You know him pretty well."

She used that eyebrow trick again. "I have known him since I was three."

And loved him since I was twelve, she thought in some despair.

"So," she said, settling back into the straight-back Sheraton chair as if she could make it more comfortable and giving her glasses another shove. "What is it you would like to know?"

BEAU KNEW HE'D OVERREACTED. But the minute Pip brought up Theo he lost all reason and knew he couldn't stay there. If he had, he was afraid he would have said something inexcusable. He would have vilified her for something that wasn't her fault.

He knew damn well Theo would have gone no matter what. He'd known when he finally gave in and bought his brother his colors. He'd known when he saw that sweet, fierce pride in his brother's eyes the first time he'd donned the scarlet of the Dragoons. He knew with the same awful despair he'd felt sending that brother he had watched over for eleven years into the carnage of war.

He knew it wasn't her fault. He knew she mourned Theo as much as he did. But she was inextricably entangled in his guilt and regret and rage over Theo's death. His brother lay somewhere in France, and the girl his brother had loved belonged to Beau.

It wasn't right. It simply wasn't right. And she shouldn't be caught up in Rake work, no matter what.

Maybe, Beau thought, striding past the small Dower House stables and off beyond the oak woods, there was something he could do. Maybe he could prevent worse happening to her. Lock her away in Delamere. Lock her away in the Antipodes. He would use this walk to come up with something.

For fifteen minutes he wandered aimlessly over the acres painted in autumnal sleep trying to think of a way to protect Pip from her own impetuousness. From his irrational resentment. From the danger he still felt lurking in a house party. From his emotions that had been on a wild swing since the moment he had first walked in the door and seen her. They kept coming close to amity between them. But the path was still too rocky, the pitfalls subtle and hidden to too easily stumbled over.

He wanted peace. He wanted vengeance for Theo. He wanted the pain to end. And just by being Pip, she complicated all of it.

As if to punctuate the need and his own failure, when he was returning to the Dower House fifteen minutes later, he caught sight of a horse and rider heading out to the pastureland above the estate. One look, even though he shouldn't have been close enough to identify her, and he knew it was his wife bent over that magnificent bay hunter urging her on. And damn if she wasn't riding astride in breeches, the little devil.

If it had been any other rider, he would have been terrified. But he'd known since she was ten that Pip was an exceptional rider, a horsewoman in her very bones. He knew that whereas he walked off conflict, she rode.

He saw her now, her hair glowing like a nimbus around her head, her body fluid and elegant, and he was quite forcefully reminded that this was who Pip was. Who she *should* be. Unfettered and courageous, not constrained by expectations, restraints, social norms.

He stood still out in the middle of the back garden watching her streak away and remembering the explosions that lithe, sweet body had set off in his own. From one minute to the next, he was rock hard and hungry, and he knew better. Because it couldn't come to anything, not really. Not if he wanted to protect her. And he did.

Pip deserved better than to survive life with him, with his aunt and uncle who would never come to appreciate her. She deserved a real family. And he had none to give. If only he knew how to protect that rare life, that singular light that animated her from within. If only he knew how to protect her from what he had become.

And then, as if to emphasize how delicate the situation was right now, he caught sight of movement by the old stand of oaks. A man. Not a servant. He was too well-dressed. But not someone Beau recognized from the house party. Medium sized, medium build, medium color. Eminently forgettable. The kind of watcher that set off alarm bells in Beau's head.

For a moment, the man stood still, his attention on the horse and rider that had just disappeared over the hill. Then he simply turned around and walked off in the direction of the manor house.

Beau's first thought was that the man knew about Pip's discoveries. That he would hurt her. He had obviously been waiting there and was leaving upon seeing her. But if he'd wanted to attack her, he had the perfect opportunity. Instead, he walked away. As if maybe, he was assessing her place in the scheme of things.

Maybe Beau had been playing this game too long, but he couldn't help thinking that someone might be assessing his wife for her importance to him. For her value as a threat. A hostage.

Bloody hell. Now what did he do?

Turning on his heel, he strode back to the Dower House. He could worry about Pip's future later. Right now, he was very afraid he had to worry about her immediate safety.

BEAU FEARED that by the time he walked back into the house, Drake would have been long since back at the party—or back in London. Instead, he found him where he'd left him, casually reading one of the books from the shelves—the history of the Plantagenets, the best he could see—and sipping at his brandy, leg crossed, looking lazy and unmoved, as if the most important thing he had to do was relax for an autumn afternoon.

Catching sight of a rather windblown Beau, Drake lifted his head and offered a mild smile. "She said you'd be back in exactly thirty minutes." Flipping open his watch, he nodded. "On the nose."

Beau didn't bother to answer. He just refilled his half-drunk brandy and began to pace. "Do you know where she is now, my new wife? Riding that mad horse of hers like she was at Newmarket. Evidently, stealing vital information from enemies isn't quite exciting enough for her, which I should have anticipated. I may find myself forced to lock her in her room."

Drake tilted his head in consideration. "For a man only a few hours married, don't you think you're a bit harsh on your wife?"

Beau looked out the window, but for the moment there was nothing to see but bare trees and rolling green fields. "Not if it keeps her safe. Someone besides me was watching her ride. Someone who looked just a bit too...forgettable. Someone not from the party."

Drake closed his book. "You think he waited outside on the off chance he would see your wife?"

"I don't know. He did seem very interested in her. Is it too unbelievable to think that someone is searching out my vulnerabilities? Or that they never bought the scene in the library? What if they suspect Pip?"

Sighing, Drake rubbed at the bridge of his nose. "Why could this not all be simple? I cannot put off my trip to London to help. What would you want me to do?"

Beau shook his head. "Talk to the duchess. She will know which of her staff to trust. I would far rather take Pip away from here somewhere safe. Maybe Canada."

"Not until I can get someone else down here to replace you."

Beau sighed. "I'm too afraid of that bad habit she has of getting involved."

"Then maybe we should completely fill her in."

"No!" Beau stopped in his tracks. "I will tell her enough to convince her to cooperate. Beyond that, she could be a liability."

She could be in more danger.

Drake considered Beau for a moment. "Are you certain about that? What if she is an asset? She has a very sharp mind, does Pip. And we need all the sharp minds we can get."

Beau couldn't help a sharp laugh. "Have you ever wondered why she never plays cards? She is incapable of hiding her emotions. You know she has a good winning hand almost before she does. She would give the game away."

"Not very kind to her."

"But safer. She cannot be connected with us in any way. If it gets to the point where I think it would protect her more to tell her, I will."

Drake scowled. "Which means, never. Do you think she could be in danger now? Should we go after her?"

Beau shook his head. "No. That wasn't the impression I got. He was just...watching. I will sit her down when she gets back and figure a way to keep her safe."

Drake nodded and took hold of the decanter. "Sit down, then. We have other business to attend to before I leave."

Beau took one last look out the window and reclaimed his chair. Drake filled his glass again.

"She should be back soon anyway," Drake said. "She suspected you would be more comfortable without her for the rest of the discussion and made a polite retreat."

"And that discussion would be?"

"Whether you would rather keep an eye on Burke or Pamela."

Beau's laugh was dry as duty. "Pamela? After being married a sum total of twelve hours? You don't know Pip very well if you think she'll put up with that. And if this little farce is going to cost me my life, I would much rather not have it happen at the hands of my wife. Or her friends. Or the duchess. Or her servants, who all seem smitten with my wife."

Drake grinned. "The butler *did* seem rather proprietary."

"You don't think a search of Burke's financial records will tell the tale?"

"Of possible misbehavior, yes. Of whom he is in contact with, who he is abetting, no." Drake paused to take a thoughtful sip of his brandy. "You might more easily earn Burke's confidences if you vocally mourn his catching you in flagrante delicto."

Beau didn't even think about it. "No."

"Even for the security of the nation?"

"Even for the security of the Archangel Michael. You know perfectly well Pamela would hear of it and spread my perfidy far and wide. And no matter how I feel about Pip right now, humiliating her is not an option."

"You feel so strongly about her?"

"I feel so strongly about not having my wife poison my tea. Unless we can find an acceptable solution, we will be connected for a very long time."

Drake's eyes widened. "An acceptable solution? You're thinking of setting her aside?"

Beau took a considered look at the fireplace. "If I think it might keep her safer. Especially if someone imagines that she is important to me."

"You don't think you should tell her why?"

"Again, no. Not unless I have no other choice."

For a long moment Drake studied him. Then, sighing, he shook his head. "I think you're asking for more trouble than you're preventing."

Beau picked up his half-finished brandy and finished it. "She'll come to understand. Besides, she doesn't really want me. Not the me I am now. Hell, *I* don't particularly like the me I am now."

For a long moment Drake held his silence. Then he reached over and refilled Beau's glass. "Don't you think you might have benefited from reaching this conclusion earlier?"

"Don't you have to be getting certain vital information back to London?" Beau retorted.

"I do. But I needed to make certain I was bringing back the correct information."

Beau shrugged. "You have the coded message, which if I am correct, gives the instructions to instigate another attempt on Wellington's life. You have Burke and Pamela as definitive participants. I'd call it a full weekend."

"And we have Bobby or Robert, whoever that is."

Beau peered at his friend. "You have some ideas."

"I might. I also got some information I thought I would double check with you. Do you know Lady Smith-Smythe's dresser? Someone named Gerta who calls Lady Smith-Smythe by her first name."

That definitely got Beau's attention. "That gray nonentity? What about her?"

Drake smiled. "Evidently, she isn't so gray behind the scenes. Pip noticed a bit of odd interplay while eavesdropping from beneath the bed. As if the woman might be a co-conspirator rather than an employee? Pip says she addresses Lady Pamela by her first name in a way that denotes equality rather than subservience."

Beau took a moment to consider his various exchanges with Pamela's cipher of a maid. Always in the background, never quite defined by her actions. A lot of bobbing and nodding, which looked a bit off-balanced on a woman of her size.

In the end, all he could do was shake his head. "I would be surprised. Perhaps Pip misinterpreted it." The minute he spoke, he shook his head. "Although, who would be a more effective aide? I certainly make use of my man Sullins to check behind the scenes."

Drake nodded. "We've long since known how well staff is able to gather information we cannot. It is why Diccan's Household Army is so effective."

The myriad maids, housekeepers, butlers, grooms, bootboys, maids, footmen and cooks across Europe their cohort Diccan Hilliard employed to great effect.

"It sounds less like Diccan's people than a major player assuming a role," Drake mused. "Do you know how we can find out? Oh, and she's evidently German."

"No, she isn't," Beau automatically disagreed. "She's...Dutch."

Honestly, he thought. Perhaps not. She would not be the only one to play about with accents.

"In that case," he said. "If you cannot insert anyone into that household, I hope you enjoy spending time with Perfect Pamela. Otherwise, Pip will think she should pose as a scullery maid and turn the cook."

"Maybe she should," Drake scowled. "She learned more in twenty minutes than we did the entire week."

"I don't care."

"I do. I need all the resourceful people I can get. Our Pip is just that."

"Not *our* Pip," Beau disagreed as he finished his brandy and stood. "*My* Pip, for my sins. Please do me a kindness and never reveal to her how vital all of this is. I would never hear the end of it."

"That's if you stay married."

"If we *what?*"

They both whipped around to find Pip standing in the doorway, looking thunderous.

8

Hands on hips, feet braced, she was still in her breeches and boots, tapping her crop against her hip. From the condition of her hair, she hadn't even stopped long enough to apply a brush. It made her look like a sprite. An angry sprite. The kind that flung curses and caused flowers to wither.

"How long have you been standing there?" Beau demanded, rising along with Drake.

Waving them back down, she stepped in and closed the door. Only Drake sat. At least Beau knew better than to cede ground.

"As in, what did you hear we didn't want you to know?" she asked, voice dangerously silky. "I imagine 'if you are still married' would be quite enough, but I also heard the part about my learning more in twenty minutes than you all did in a week. And yes, Lord Drake, thank you. I *am* resourceful." Turning, she leveled that glare on Beau. "But let us focus on the first part right now. Not remain married? Is there yet another plan afoot no one apprised me of?"

For the first time Beau felt a flush of guilt. "Why did you

come so soon? I thought you meant to give me time alone with Drake."

She didn't budge. "I remembered something else from my foray into Pamela's room, which we can address after you answer my question."

Beau sincerely yearned for another good swallow of brandy. Or whiskey. Or hemlock. "It is something we can discuss later, Pip."

"If Drake already knows about it, I think we can discuss it whenever we want."

He straightened to his full height, as if that had ever intimidated Pip. "We will discuss it later. Alone. As befits a subject pertinent only to the two of us. Now, what did you have to tell Drake? He needs to get to London. As you well know, he has vital information to deliver."

For a minute he didn't think she would back down. Absurdly, it made him feel both angry and just a little proud of her courage. Finally, though, he saw her shoulders sag just a bit. He saw the light of combat in her eyes fade just enough.

"Thomas," she said, turning to Drake. "There is someone at the house party right now named Thomas who either Pamela or Gerta needed to see last night." Huffing a bit, she shook her head. "Lord, was it only last night? I feel as if I have been circling this dance for weeks. I admit I was a bit distracted by some of the previous conversations about how long it would take Beau to return to Lady Pamela's bed. I didn't really remember the bit after that until a few minutes ago. But I know that Lord Burke is not a Thomas. Whoever it is, they were deciding who was going last night to see this person. I suspect it was to give a report of some kind. Of course, they could just be....er, sharing him. I have never been privy to those kinds of arrangements, so I couldn't give an informed opinion."

Beau was astonished to see a flush of pink on her cheeks. It seemed his Pip wasn't impervious to suggestive behavior. For that brief moment, he was swamped by the urge to show her something to really make her blush. For another long moment, he battled his body's predictable reaction and ended up sitting back down to protect his dignity. Lord, what was happening to him? In those glasses, with that hair, she looked like a fairy tale creature. And suddenly he could not stop thinking of her in his arms. In his bed.

That deserved another swallow of brandy.

"Thomas," Drake mused, leaning his head back a bit. "No, not Burke. But close. Burke's valet is a Thomas. And his secretary, Mr. Thomas March." He shrugged. "A rather handsome man, but on the far side of sixty. And very fastidious."

Pip managed a grin. "Then it is a good thing I am on my honeymoon. I'm not certain I could keep a straight face if I saw him and couldn't help but think of his possible predilections."

Finishing off his drink, Drake set down his snifter and rose, straightening any minor creases in his attire he might have caused by sitting. "Well, my friends, if either of you remember anything else, send a messenger. I shall be in London saving the nation and suffering at *ton* events. And if you need any support, Nate Adams seems to be in the vicinity. Leave a message for him at a charming little thieves' ken appropriately called the Lion and Bandit."

"Adams?" Beau echoed, frowning. "Can't he take over here?"

Beau didn't know Adams as well as the other Rakes. His efforts were rumored to be to the darker side of intelligence gathering.

Drake shook his head. "He is otherwise engaged. Evidently, I am not senior enough to know his purpose. I was just given the information since we seem to have a dearth of Rakes down here. If you cannot wait for him, I believe you can rely on the duchess's staff for support. I will inform her. And after your charming interlude here, I would like you to visit London. We need to get the group together to compare notes."

"You're going, then?" Beau asked.

Drake's smile was almost sweet. "Yes. Which means you two can get back to discussing marriage. Remember, Lady Drummond. If you need to hide a body, I might know someone."

Pip bestowed her second grin on him. "I hope there is no time limit on that offer."

Instead of answering, he bent to kiss her cheek on the way by. "Don't see me out. I know the way. Shall I tell the butler as I pass that dinner will be delayed?"

"No," Beau said.

Pip shrugged. "I can discuss difficult subjects over the soup."

In the end, dinner was delayed after all. Drake had no sooner closed the door behind him on the way out than Pip turned back to Beau, her stomach in knots.

"Do you want to explain what that was all about?" she demanded, hands clenched at her waist as if that could keep them from trembling. Or, come to think of it, striking out.

Beau looked at the closed door with some yearning. "It would be better if we waited until after dinner, just like you suggested."

"I won't be able to eat my dinner if I don't know what is happening. I gave you a way out of this marriage much earlier this morning. If you do not want to be in it, why did you not take me up on the offer?"

"It would have been dishonorable to leave you at the altar, Pip."

"Less dishonorable than setting me aside now?"

"Not setting you aside. Giving us both the time to have more choices. Giving you a chance to be happy with someone who... who truly wishes to marry."

The worst part was, Pip knew, was that he thought he would be doing her a favor as much as himself. Instead, in the end, he would ruin her. And it had nothing to do with society. "Who wishes to marry *me*, you mean. On what grounds are you thinking of doing this?"

He raked his hand through his hair. "The most obvious would be lack of consortium."

"Not lack of consortium," she retorted, flailing again to find her footing. "It must be lack of ability. Are you ready to prove *that?*"

He moved as if he was going to grab her by the arms but stopped at the last moment. "I'm trying to give you the life you deserve. Can't you see that?"

"And you believe marriage to you won't provide that for me."

"No!"

Well, she thought, feeling as if she were physically shriveling. She should know better than to ask questions like that by now. She nodded. "I see. And when did you make this profound discovery? You don't think you could have done it *before* I stood up before some of the biggest gossips on the *ton*, not to mention Princess Charlotte, and said vows?"

"While I was walking. When I saw you riding your Macha. I haven't seen you look that happy since your come-out. You deserve more happiness than I can give you, Pip. We should at least give ourselves the chance to make a different decision than one forced on us by circumstance. We can certainly manage to withstand five days without consummating the marriage in order to offer us that chance. After that we can see what course is available. Because if we do consummate it, then there is no chance in hell we'll free ourselves."

Something was off. She couldn't put her finger on it, but Beau sounded wrong. It wasn't that she didn't believe him. It was that this decision had come much too suddenly.

If only he didn't sound so certain.

"Five days?" she asked.

"After that we shall need to be in London, and we won't be sequestered in a small house with nothing else to do."

"And even after what happened the other night you believe I can safely remain...untouched?"

"Of course. What could compel us to act otherwise?"

HE SHOULD HAVE KNOWN BETTER. He did, but only after he heard the words leave his mouth. His words weren't the reassurance he meant them to be. They were a challenge. And damn it if she didn't tilt her head just so. Damn if her great blue eyes and luscious body wrapped in naught but linen blouse and buckskin breeches, didn't set his cock to standing upright in response. Dammit if she didn't see it before he could do anything about it and drop her crop on a chair before stalking toward him. Damn it if she didn't scowl at him, daring him to deny his reaction, before she reached up, grabbed his lapels, and pulled him right down to her.

And that quickly lightning struck. Again. Whirlwinds, cataclysms, raging rivers of lust and need. Her mouth was open to him and before he could give it a second thought, he ravaged it, tilting his own head to better meet her tongue-to-tongue. And damn if she didn't participate, if she didn't all but growl with hunger. She reached her arms up to wrap her fingers in his hair, and he reached down to wrap his hands around her bottom and lift her against the wall. For an eternity he could think of nothing but the cushion of her breasts, the silk of her mouth, the heat of her body where he pressed against it, tormenting himself, tormenting her. Breaking every promise he had ever made just to be able to drop his mouth to her throat and feast on the throb of her pulse at its base. And now he was the one growling.

He pulled one hand away and caught hold of her breast, her small, firm breast that fit so perfectly in his hand. He slipped his fingers beneath her blouse, pulling open a button, just so he could torment himself with the sound of her whimpers as he rolled her nipple between finger and thumb. So, he could imagine it in his mouth where he could torment her with teeth and tongue.

Dear God, she smelled like summer, like a breeze through the trees, like wildflowers and sunlight. She tasted like honey and, he swore, the cinnamon cakes they had served at break-fast. Suddenly he craved cinnamon like air, like, damn it, sunlight after a long night.

He couldn't stop. She didn't ask him to. She did her own exploring, small hands pulling at his shirt and climbing his chest, sweeping down to his buttocks and setting off another firestorm. Sweet God, she wrapped her legs around him so that he could feel the close heat of her, so he could imagine himself buried deep inside her. His cock strained towards her, aching with impatience. His heart thundered in his chest, and he knew she could feel that, too.

He ran his hand up the inside of her thigh and hated those breeches, because he couldn't simply push them up to her waist and open her to his exploration. To his invasion. He came so close to taking her right there against the wall, just like before. He suspected the breeches were the only barrier that protected her from him, even as she scrabbled at his cravat, as he bent to finally take her nipple in his mouth, even through the material. Hungry, so hungry.

It was the sudden noise that abruptly yanked him to the surface. A clatter out in the corridor as if someone had dropped something. As if, he suspected, they did it on purpose to let them know they weren't alone. He might as well have had a bucket of water dumped over his head. Gasping, he pulled back, set her down as if that alone could resurrect his sanity, both of them panting as if they had run miles.

"So...you think we can...keep safely away...from...each other," she panted, eyes so wide he swore he could see to the bottom like a lake, glasses perilously askew. Not thinking, he pushed them into place and thought abstractedly that she wouldn't be Pip without those benighted glasses, and that somehow those were just another thing about her that lit a short fuse.

"I'm—"

"If you say sorry," she all but growled in a strained little voice, pushing away from him, "I will have your guts for garters."

He couldn't move. He couldn't step away or move closer. His body was still raging for completion. He was shaking with the effort not to pull those breeches off her and finish what they had started. It only made it worse that he could see the same hunger in her eyes. Thank God, then, for the breeches, or he would have ruined everything.

"You cannot say," she said, still sounding breathless as she blinked up at him, "that we aren't...*attracted* to each other."

He dragged the last of his discipline around him and fought to take even one step away from her. She had drained him of his sense, his focus. His purpose. All he wanted was to lift her back into his arms and shut out the world. Forget Theo, forget the Rakes, forget the danger Pip might be in because she had been in the wrong place at the wrong time.

"This is not helping," he said. "This is not the time to let ourselves be overwhelmed."

She pulled her head back and scowled at him. "Our wedding night?"

Good God, she was right. It was. It seemed they had been

caught in this mess for a week. Beau felt as if he would shake apart, but he took a deliberate step back, which only returned him to imminent danger. Deuce take it, she was tousled and soft, her breasts full and her lips plumped from kissing and her hair a tangled mess. No one looking at her could believe she had been doing anything but being pleasured. He needed to get away from her.

He needed to eat the damned dinner the duchess's staff had cooked.

"Yes," he said, still struggling to control his breathing. "On our wedding night. I truly am trying to do the best here, for both of us."

"Then both of us might need to be consulted on the matter," she retorted.

"You can't really want this marriage," he insisted. "Not with me. Not like this."

For the briefest moment, her expression betrayed a horrible loss. "And then what else do I have? A lifetime importuning friends and waiting for my family to remember where I am?"

"I cannot imagine you allowing yourself to languish for long. Talk to Drake. He said he thought you would be an asset in diplomatic circles."

She smiled, but it was not amused. "Not without a husband, I wouldn't," she said. "Without a husband, I cannot see that I would be an asset to anyone. Women are not given that option."

He opened his mouth to argue, but he couldn't. She was right, of course. It was just that this was not the direction he needed the conversation to take. This was not the time to reassure Pip that of course her future had purpose, even without him as her husband. Especially without him as her husband.

"Please," he said, "at least for now until we settle the mess here. We need to stay apart."

For a moment she just looked at him, as if there was too much that needed to be said. It wasn't the time, though. She must see that. Taking a great breath, she shook her head and stepped away. "I will stay apart if you will."

For some reason that did not relieve him. "I don't see why we cannot maintain a respectful distance if we want. I mean, the house isn't that small."

Why then did she smile? And why did that smile seem so fatalistic?

He found out five minutes later when they went upstairs to prepare for dinner.

"What do you mean only one bedroom?!" he shouted.

9

———————

"It is a dower house, Beau," Pip explained as patiently as she could from the bedroom doorway as he strode up and down the little hall throwing doors open on the way by. Well, two doors. The previous duke had installed a lovely bathing chamber with a bathtub for his aunt in one old bedroom and made the other into a kind of office she had never used, being happier working in the library surrounded by shelves. "Used for dowagers and maiden aunts who tend not to bring anyone with them except a companion. Lizzie's aunt wanted nothing to do with companions."

"That is absurd!" he snapped, whirling around on her.

She instinctively took a step back. She couldn't remember ever seeing Beau this furious, this desperate. He suddenly reminded her of a trapped animal who was ready to gnaw his leg off to get free.

But then, if he was feeling even a bit as upended as she did by that kiss in the library, she could hardly blame him. She undoubtedly should never have given in to the temptation to remind him of what he would be forfeiting. She still felt as if her bones had melted like lava, incinerating every inch of her, but especially her brain. All she could think was that she wanted to drag him down and do it again. And again. She wanted to know where his hand would have gone if she hadn't been wearing breeches, which had made perfect sense climbing onto a horse, but not all but climbing her husband.

She wasn't sure exactly what she'd been thinking except to prove that he wasn't anywhere nearly as unmoved as he wanted her to believe. For heaven sakes, all one had to do was look at the fit of his breeches to know the truth of that. Couldn't he at least give them a chance?

Oh, lord, she shouldn't keep looking at them. It would only get her into more trouble. And she knew from his mad pacing that he wouldn't thank her for pressing him.

He was glaring at her as if she had planned the whole fiasco, which spoke volumes of how he saw her. It had only been three days, and she was already exhausted by the mood swings, the accusations, the anger and obviously, now, the desperation to be quit of her. It mixed so well with the seething desire Beau had unleashed not ten minutes earlier. She could barely breathe, much less think. And he expected her to show some sense about this. She was not at all sure she could.

"It is quite pointless to harangue me about it," she finally said, hearing the useless tears crowd her throat. "Staying here was not my idea. If you had thought to inform me, I could have told you all about the accommodations here, and we could have found somewhere else. As it is, we don't have time to argue about it right now. We are expected to enjoy a lovely dinner, courtesy of the duchess's very loyal staff, who are right now undoubtedly listening to you make yourself very clear about being rid of me."

And blast if Beau didn't drag both his hands through his hair, which would have given Sullins heart failure. "I'm trying to protect you, dammit!"

She sighed. "You forgot to ask whether I sought protection. In fact, you forgot to ask what I wanted at all."

His head came up and he stared at her, his expression betraying so many emotions, none of them positive. Frustration, fury, defensiveness, regret. Oh, definitely regret, Pip saw, which made her feel so much better.

"I'm sorry, Pip," he said. "I truly am. But I want you to have a choice. I still think this offers you your best chance at a good life."

And blast if she didn't believe he meant it.

"Tell me the truth," she demanded. "Is it that you cannot tolerate the idea of spending your life with me, or that you believe I will not be able to tolerate life with you?"

And couldn't he at least have had the decency to demand this conversation before that performance that morning?

He went back to torturing his hair. "I believe you have a romantic idea of what our marriage would be like, left over from when you were a little girl. And I know I am not the same man I was back then."

She could hardly argue with him about that.

"Could we not at least try to negotiate our way to an agreeable solution? Countless other couples have done it over the centuries."

The bottomless grief in his dear brown eyes all but brought her to her knees. "I just don't know, Pip. A few days would at least give us time to better think things through."

She had so many answers to that plea, none of which he would understand or believe. She almost made the mistake of telling him she would make him love her. But he was right. That was twelve-year-old Pip talking. Adult Pip had had too many dreams die of neglect to believe that kind of fairy tale.

But she didn't want to simply give up!

"There is something else," he said, dropping his voice so he wasn't overheard. "We need to do it for your safety."

She was so tempted to laugh. "Beau..."

But he wasn't watching her. He was looking into the room the old duke had transformed into a study. Without another word, he took her arm, pulled her in and sat her down on one of the chairs.

"Did you see that a man was watching you ride today?" he asked, seating himself in the other. "A man who was definitely not part of the house party?"

She blinked. "No. Why?"

He leaned forward, elbows on knees. "He was focused on you; nobody else. What if someone believes you are important to me? What if they think they can get to me through you?"

She scowled at him. "It didn't occur to you he might have simply thought I look quite attractive on a horse? I do, you know."

He was not about to be pacified. "That was not the type of attention he was paying."

"Might you be a victim of an overactive protective instinct? They don't even know you're a Rake. We fooled them."

"Are you sure? From what I've heard, I missed quite a melee here with your brother hauling away not only spies, but several others, including the young duke. And yet, at least Burke, Pamela and evidently Thomas are still lingering. Why would that be?"

"The message." Even before she said it, she saw the flaw. "But they have that. At least they think they do."

She had no other answer. All she knew was that she had begun to hope that maybe she could find a place of amity with her husband, a slow beginning that could eventually bear fruit. All she knew was that she didn't want to hear that her marriage was once again some kind of leverage that in the end would destroy her, no matter how it turned out. All she knew was that she was so tired of being tossed around like a shuttlecock. She wanted some peace. She wanted a home that was hers. She wanted...

She looked at the expression on Beau's face and knew it was pointless to want even that much. At least right now.

"I wasn't even going to tell you this much," he said, looking sincerely sorry. "But you will not listen. There is a plot to assassinate every person between Princess Charlotte and the throne, and if you do not take this seriously, we won't have the chance to stop it."

"And if you had shared any of this a bit earlier," she said as calmly as she could, her hands fisted and her chest burning with frustration and grief, "I might have better understood. As it is, we should hope that no one in this house is disloyal, or you have given us all away."

"I had to take the chance. This is not a game, Pip. There is a lot at stake."

"So, you are saying that in order to protect me by making it seem we are not...content together, we need to maintain a certain distance at least until we get to London."

He sighed, she thought with relief. "Yes. Exactly."

She nodded, still wondering if this was simply a ruse by Beau to keep her at arm's length. But he was right. If there really was a man, and he was really situated to assess Beau's vulnerability, then the last thing she wanted to do was put Beau in danger. More danger.

"Fine," she said, standing back up. "We shall play your game. I shall do everything I can to put a distance between the two of us for now, although I demand the right to change your mind once we're out of this mess. But for now, I imagine that means that I will prepare for dinner in my room. If you would like to use the bathing room, please do. There are several rooms you can use to sleep that are not mine. After everything, I find myself disinterested in giving up the bed. And you evidently have no interest in sharing it."

And without another word, she whirled around and stalked across the hall into her own room. She had just taken hold of the latch when she heard Beau follow her.

"One more thing, Pip," he said, and he was using what Theo used to call his voice of authority.

She stopped but didn't turn.

"You must promise me that you won't go looking for trouble. You will stay out of this investigation."

She took a breath. "You should have included that in the wedding vows."

"I mean it, Pip. I cannot concentrate if I'm constantly worried about you rushing off into disaster because you think you're involved in one of Theo's games."

"One of these days, Beau," she said without turning, "you are going to learn how to say 'thank you for your help, Pip.'"

"I mean it. We won't be so lucky next time."

"I'll try."

"Promise."

"I promise I'll try."

And then before he could continue the argument, she opened the door to her room. The last thing she heard as she slammed the door behind her was a frustrated "Pip...."

Pip hadn't even drawn breath before Joyful stepped out of the dressing room, a handkerchief in her hand. Of course, she had heard every word. Of course, she also knew how Pip had always felt about Beau.

"Wash your face," she said, handing over the handkerchief for the tears that made Pip even angrier than Beau's rejection. "Don' let that man see he upsets you. He don' deserve to know. Somethin' to remember, though. He wouldn't be so upset he didn't feel so strong." Her deep brown eyes were unflinching as she very deliberately set her hands on her hips. "About you."

"He's going to set me aside." And take away what purpose she'd thought she had discovered in her life.

Joyful just shrugged. "We'll see."

And then she just walked back into the dressing room to pull out the dress they had chosen for dinner, a delicious emerald sarcenet with a soft gold net overlay and gold acanthas leaf embroidery around the low neckline and hem. Pip loved that dress. It made her feel worthy of Beau's attention.

Not today. Today she knew better.

For a long moment Pip just stood by the door and listened to the silence out in the hall and wished she had never come to this house party. She wished she had someone she could talk to, just to set straight every confusing twist in her life in the last few days. Just to roundly vilify her brand-new husband where it was safe, where Perfect Pamela would not hear of it, where she could scream like a banshee.

Tomorrow she could get in touch with Lizzie. Tonight, she had only herself and her maid.

She had felt so good, so briefly. She and Macha had torn over the hills like furies, tossing up clods of dirt, the wind whipping through hair, the thick autumn clouds matching her mood. She had run fast before the turmoil back in that little house and thought for just a moment she had run free of it there where no one could catch her. Not traitors, not Rakes, not Beau. She could believe for those moments she had had Macha in her hands, that she might be able to gain control of her life. She was a married woman. She was married to the man she had long dreamed to be hers. She was smart and strong and determined. Surely, she could find a way to navigate this marriage. Surely, she would finally have a place to call her own.

She should have known better.

And then she had remembered that last bit of conversation from the night before and turned Macha back just in time to hear Beau's real plan. The clunch. The dunderhead.

The coward.

She sighed, knowing that was one accusation too many.

Beau was not a coward. He was heartsore, and she was the reminder he couldn't escape. And in his own dunderheaded way, he really was trying to protect her. So, she walked over to wash her face and hands and change into the lovely emerald gown and drag a comb through the hair tangled by the wind so that she at least looked presentable before the staff. She knew it wouldn't matter if she looked presentable to her husband. He was probably still outside the door casting aspersions on her good character because she had failed to warn him about the limitations of the honeymoon house he had failed to tell her about. Oh, dinner ought to be delightful.

BEAU STOOD in the hallway for long minutes just staring at the shut bedroom door trying to understand why he was so angry at Pip. No, he admitted. He was angry at himself. None of this was her fault. He had no right to inflict the kind of turmoil he had just seen in those honest blue eyes. He had hurt her without meaning to. He had pushed her away instead of holding her up. Instead of saying thank you for your help, Pip.

He needed to explain his reasoning better. He had to make her understand that she would be better off without the anchor he would become. The ghost, more accurately. She deserved a husband, not a man obsessed with vengeance. Not a shell whose real heart lay in the soil of France. He had to make her see that.

Funny thing about that. Just the thought of pushing her away ignited a new, deep, sharp pain in his chest, as if someone had snuck up on him and shoved a knife deep into him, deep enough to drain out what life force was left to him. Deep enough so that he suspected he wouldn't survive it.

It was for her own good, he insisted to himself, standing

stock still in the middle of the scarred old floor waiting for Pip to emerge from her room. It wasn't that he didn't have the courage to face the possibility of losing her like Theo.

And that quickly he managed a rueful grin, though even that hurt, at the thought of her unflinching declaration that put him quite in his place. In the servants' quarters, no doubt. God, if only he were the man she needed. If only he still had any life left in him.

If only he had the gall to try another kiss and see where it led.

He couldn't believe it. Just the thought made him have to readjust his trousers yet again. He shook his head. The next five days were going to be a lot more difficult than they should have been.

He was just about to tap on the door when it opened, and he was facing Pip's maid, the scowling woman who stood nearly as tall as he did. This time, though, she said not a word. Just took a hard look at him, another down at his betraying trousers, shook her head, and strode by him. He would have said something, except just then Pip followed her out the door, her demeanor composed and polite. And damn it, if just her restraint, her great blue eyes and body lusciously revealed in that emerald green and gold gown didn't set his cock to stirring in response all over again. Dammit if she didn't see it before he could do anything about it. Damn it if she didn't scowl at him as well, daring him to deny his reaction, daring him to forget what had happened just minutes before.

"Shall I meet you in the parlor?" she asked in deliberately even tones. "There is hot water in the pitcher." She took another considered look back down to where his trousers still betrayed his arousal. "There is cold water in the bathing room."

All he could do was nod. He couldn't even manage to remind her that she had once again started things with that kiss. It didn't matter, really. It would have taken another half a minute for him to act himself.

All he could do right now was stand there watching as she nodded and turned for the stairs.

"Remember," he said before she could leave. "It isn't enough that we know we haven't been intimate. Everyone must. We must have witnesses if we are to pull this off. I am determined to keep you safe while we see to things."

"In that case," she said, "I recommend the couch in the library. It isn't long enough for you, but it has leather cushions."

"It will be my penance to pay."

She tilted her head, those owl eyes of hers sparking behind her lenses. "I would have had something more in the line of fire and brimstone in mind. But I suppose I can settle for your being uncomfortable and sleepless."

He managed a smile. "That's my girl. I would also ask for a boon."

She lifted that one eyebrow.

Beau took a breath. "Truce? Until we escape the confines of the Dower House, anyway? Until we are away from both fond spies and foes, I would rather not give them a show."

For a long moment Pip just watched him, to the point he began to feel like a scrubby schoolboy being assessed by a stern nanny. Considering the fact that this nanny only came up to his chest, the image almost made him smile again. Almost. He could still see the hurt in her eyes, and he had never wanted that.

"Joyful will have the key to the bathing room so I am not surprised in my bath," she allowed. "You get to ask her for it when you need to make your ablutions. Stumbling over you while either of us is *en dishabille* will not help your cause."

"Agreed."

Finally, with a regal dignity he never would have anticipated from his Pip, she nodded once and simply walked on by, her skirts swaying nicely with her step, the silk whispering of seduction. He should not have watched. It was not part of any truce he knew. But he couldn't help himself. And then he had to resettle his trousers yet again as he walked into the room to wash.

10

It ended up being a good thing that Pip did not make that promise. She would have had to break it by the next night.

She didn't seek out trouble. In fact, she tried her best to abide by Beau's restrictions, at least for now. She began by meeting him in the little brown salon where they shared a silent sherry before following Billings into the dining room.

Pip imagined the dinner was just as lovely as Mrs. Webb had promised. She bestowed lavish compliments course by course, since she knew how much effort the staff had put into the meal, into making the house as welcoming as possible for Pip and Beau on short notice. She even smiled at young Billings as he poured more wine with each course. She didn't taste a thing. Her head was swimming, though, even as she and Beau discussed innocuous subjects like the house party, the weather, and the horses they planned to take out for a friendly race in the morning.

And then, because she couldn't leave well enough alone, Pip asked Beau about his activities the last few years.

His eyebrows went up. "My activities?"

She nodded as she served herself some cheese and nuts. "Yes. I mean, of course we know what we see in the newspapers. Faithful member of the House of Lords, reliable representative for government business, irresistible guest and impeccable dance partner at various house parties. I understand that Lady A. P., I believe, threatened to sell certain bedroom secrets to the press if you didn't invite her to the victory celebrations." She chuckled. "I'm almost sad you were such a gentleman, although I also understand she looks quite dashing, especially with her new sapphire and diamond bracelet."

Leave it to Beau to not be amused by his own peccadillos.

"Please tell me you had better things to do than read gossip sheets."

She smiled. "Well, we haven't seen very much of each other in the last few years. I had to keep up with my friends some-how. I understand, by the way, that you were in Vienna after we were. It's such a lovely city."

"And I understand you made a name for yourself with Russian wastrels."

Pip couldn't help it. She laughed. "Ivan could be labeled many things. A wastrel was not one of them. Dimitri, on the other hand, had some difficulty taking no for an answer. Fortu-nately, my brother Alex was kind enough to teach the girls at Last Chance Academy a few useful...shall we say, defensive moves. It was after he first helped us evict the original Miss Chase and replace her with our lovely Miss Schroeder. Miss Schroeder was far more practical about what a girl needed to learn to succeed."

He frowned at her. "Is that a story, or a warning?"

Her smile was beatific. "Well, I mean, I already knew the basics from when we were children. But it never hurts to brush up on technique."

"When we were children?" he retorted. "I never taught you that."

"No," she said, completely losing her smile. "You didn't."

But evidently that subject was back off the table.

And then, inevitably, dinner was over, and instead of sitting with the port, Beau ushered Pip into the salon where her after-dinner options were reading about the Plantagenets or staring out the window.

"Probably the time you wish you had taken up needlework," Beau said with a wry smile.

Walking over to the window where all she could see was darkness and darker shadows, she shook her head. "Not even then. My needlework would inevitably look like a brightly colored mouse nest. There is no one I would torture by demanding they praise my efforts." She tilted her head, considering. "Well. There may be one person." Then she turned to consider Beau. "Maybe two. Perhaps I'll ask Lizzie to send some of her extra thread down."

He checked his watch. "Would you rather play cards?"

"Not with someone who knows all my facial expressions."

She got a chuckle for that. "Perhaps we could find you a mask."

Pip gave him a grudging smile. "Even that doesn't work. I am hopeless at it."

"Chess?"

That did get her interest. "That just might serve."

She turned around to see him pulling out the ivory set Lizzie's aunt had cherished. It was nice to see it again and remember the evenings the old woman had beat her nieces—and their guest—to flinders with a delighted cackle and a demand for her winnings. Hairpins and orange slices.

By the time Aunt had passed on, Pip had begun to beat her.

She didn't beat Beau, but she gave him a good game, which seemed to surprise him.

"I suppose I never expected strategy from you."

She scowled. "I am not ten anymore, Beau."

"Another?" he asked, setting the pieces back up.

But Pip had had enough for one day. It was time to make an orderly retreat to her lonely bed and try not to dream of those minutes in the salon that evening.

"Thank you," she said, gathering her shawl and slipping her shoes back on from where they had somehow ended up beneath her chair. "But I believe it is time to say my good nights. It has been an eventful few days."

"Meet me at the stables at seven for a ride?" Beau asked.

She thought about that for a minute. "Any other day I would say yes. But I believe I will be sleeping in late tomorrow and enjoying chocolate in bed. Try me again at about ten."

"Could you manage to wear a riding habit this time?"

Pip scowled at him. "I never took you for a prude, Beau."

"We aren't the only people in the area."

"The people in this area know me quite well and have seen me ride in breeches any number of times these last ten years."

"Just humor me. Maybe your reputation can stand it, but I don't think mine can."

She was forced to grin, even still so conflicted about everything. "Tomorrow at ten."

THEY RODE. If Pip had been a gothic heroine, she would have arrived red-eyed and drawn after her night spent all too alone. Unfortunately, Pip was not romantic at all. She had slept soundly, mostly, she thought, from all the wine she had imbibed that day. And when she rose, she withstood the strong urge to pull out the breeches and slipped into her royal blue riding habit instead. It was more cumbersome, having to carry her skirt everywhere until she got into the saddle, but she had to admit that she looked quite nice in it. From the brief spark in

Beau's eyes when he saw her settling her matching shako hat, she had to believe he agreed.

The ride itself was lovely. Pip's Macha was a lovely, tireless filly, but Beau's Ares was a ghostly grey powerhouse. For the hour they were out, she and Beau were in the closest to perfect harmony they had ever been. But then, when Pip was on a horse, it was almost impossible for her to be angry at anyone.

That lasted until they once again came within sight of the Dower House, and she saw the man. Almost a shadow, medium sized, color, impression. Just as Beau had described him. And just as Beau had said, she knew instinctively there was something wrong with his being there. But he wandered off back toward the manor house before they could approach.

"You're sure you didn't hire him just to unnerve me?" she asked as they rubbed down their horses a few minutes later in the little four-stall stable behind the Dower House.

He flashed a brief grin. "I didn't think of it in time. I'd like for you to stay at the house. I'm going to check in with Nate Adams. See if he has had his eye on any of this."

"Is he another Rake?"

Beau shrugged. "Something like that."

"I was thinking of going into the village with Lizzie. Certainly, that cannot seem in any way threatening or suspicious."

He paused a moment. "Fine. Just bring along a groom."

They did, Hall's groom Clancy, a banty Irishman with a legendary way with horses and far less successful one with humans. He liked Lizzie, though. He liked Pip even better, since she was one of the few people his stallion Boru, a delinquent with an aversion to most people, didn't bite. He also liked how Pip had named her own horse.

Lizzie, of course, rode a perfectly mannered white Arabian named Alabaster, who carried her like a rare gift and refused to consort with Boru as Macha did, prancing like a deb at

Almack's and flipping her mane. It made the ride into the village enough of a challenge that it took some minutes to realize that the street was quiet for the middle of the afternoon.

"Is there a market day somewhere else today?" Pip asked.

"Not that I know of," Clancy said, looking around.

"I hope the inn is open for a bit of tea," Pip said. "I worked up a thirst on my girl this morning. I suspect she would like a bit of pampering herself."

The inn was open. Young Charlie McKay appeared from the stables to take their horses with an ungainly head bob and a big smile. Charlie loved his horses, which was good. A bad fall as a child ensured he would be nothing more than a groom his whole life. Clancy followed the boy into the barn as Pip and Lizzie turned into the White Horse Inn, which they had been going to for tea since they had been teens. Pip opened the door to see three unknown men sipping pints in the smtaproom as Mr. Thorn stood wiping down the bar. He gave a stiff nod as the men took a disinterested look at the newcomers. Before Lizzie or Pip could say anything, Mrs. Thorn appeared through the kitchen door.

"Oh, Miss Pip," she said, her hands clutched in her apron. "I'm so sorry. We're having some trouble with the stove. Man's fixin' it right now. But I'm that afraid there'll be no tea this afternoon."

In all the times she had come to stay at Ripton Hall, Pip could never remember there being a reason for Mrs. Thorn to fail the feeding of everyone who walked through her door. Worse, the taut woman would never have ignored Lizzie in greeting them. Mrs. Thorn maintained a very rigid etiquette around the people she called her betters. She would have addressed Lizzie first as Lady Elizabeth and dipped a quick, smiling curtsy. The hair on the back of Pip's neck stood on end. Something was terribly wrong.

"I'm so sorry to hear that, Mrs. Thorn," she said before Lizzie could speak. "Is there anyone we can send to help?"

The smile she got was closer to a rictus. "Oh, no. We'll do fine, but thank you for asking. I hope we'll be able to see to you in a day or two right enough."

Pip nodded and slipped her arm through Lizzie's. "Then you can expect us. Where to next, Lizzie?"

But before Lizzie could answer, Pip had her guided out the door.

"What was that all about?" Lizzie demanded sotto voce as they stepped out onto the still-quiet street.

Pip did her best to look around without seeming to. "I don't know."

"Should we gather the horses or stop somewhere else and see what is going on?"

"The Martin's," Pip said, turning toward the little mercantile where they had spent hours picking out ribbons, cloth, and buttons.

The little bell jangled over the door as they stepped inside of the cluttered, comfortable store that carried any number of items from ribbons to flour to pots and pans. The store bore the comforting scents of coffee and honey and welcomed visitors with a familiar creaking floor.

"Mrs. Martin," Pip greeted the owner's wife who was standing behind the counter, clutching it. "How is your supply of ribbons today?"

"I..."

Pip met her gaze and held it as she approached the counter. "What is the matter?" she asked softly. "Can we help?"

Her expression never changed. "Oh, Miss Pip, you need to go back up the Hall as soon as can be. There are bad dealings here."

Pip patted her hand and wandered about after Lizzie,

picking up this and that so that they looked normal from outside, if anyone was watching.

"What dealings?" she asked, comparing a spool of ribbon with one Lizzie held.

Mrs. Martin all but groaned. "Oh, miss, you can't be involved in this. Go home."

Lizzie picked out a bright green ribbon and took it over to the desk. "This, I think," she said out loud, then spoke softly. "You might as well tell me, Mrs. Martin. I am not leaving 'til you do. Maybe we can help."

Mrs. Martin took the ribbon with trembling hands. "We never had trouble like this before. Not once when it was our own gentlemen come up from Chesil Beach. Used the old tunnels and never bothered a soul, lest they wanted to help. Left behind a bit of brandy and such for those whose land they crossed. Hid everything away here until it was safe to move on. We never even saw them go."

Smugglers, of course. Pip was amazed that this was the first she had heard about it. Not that smuggling wasn't a fine old tradition along the coast. But the locals had evidently kept their secret to themselves.

"And now?"

Mrs. Martin took an unsteady breath, her lined face pale and taut. "They came last night, snuck up through the tunnel. They're storing everything in the cellar right now. They told us to stay away, and we are. They have the Evans boy just to make sure."

"What tunnel? What cellar?"

"The tunnel up to the estate."

Both Pip and Lizzie froze. "You mean the Fairy Steps up to the manor house?" Lizzie demanded.

Everyone in the area knew about those steps that descended to a tunnel that came out in the manor's chapel.

Pip put her hand over Lizzie's to settle her.

Mrs. Martin shook her head. "No, my lady. Your aunt's old house."

Now Pip stopped breathing. "The *Dower House*?"

Mrs. Martin nodded. "Second cellar. It's what our boys allus used to use. Safe as houses there 'til they needed to move it on."

"And nobody from the manor knew?" Lizzie asked.

Finally, Mrs. Martin managed a smile. "Your aunt knew. That was enough."

Pip couldn't help but grin. "No wonder her stories about smugglers were so realistic. But what about now?"

"Don't know 'em, do we? Somehow got word on the tunnels hereabout and decided to use them. First showed up yesterday. They're bad men, miss. Charlie McKay says he saw crates of rifles being taken down and heard 'em say there was somebody nearby to get further directions from. We're hopin' they didn't pay attention to him, him bein' slow and all."

"When this is over, make sure he knows he is a hero."

Mrs. Martin managed a fleeting smile. "He's a good boy, is Charlie. But you, miss, my lady. You need to stay far away from there."

"But Pip is staying in the Dower House," Lizzie protested. "With her new husband."

"And I've heard nothing in the cellar. Nor has the staff said anything."

Mrs. Martin looked at Pip as if she were already dead. "Second cellar, ma'am. The one the gentlemen have been using since forever. Can't generally hear it from upstairs."

Suddenly, what Mrs. Martin said resonated. "Someone nearby to instruct them. Do you know who it might be?"

Mrs. Martin, her attention on the front window, shook her head.

Pip stood where she was for a long moment, almost afraid to breathe. It could be nothing more than a coincidence. But could this be why Lord Burke and Pamela and whoever

Thomas was still remained up at the party? Were they waiting to contact these smugglers? Could *this* be what the watcher was waiting for? Not her but contact with the smugglers. She had to admit that the Dower House cellars would have been the perfect place to hide contraband. No one had gone near it except to clean in years.

Guns. Insurrection, which would certainly follow on the heels of the assassinations Beau talked of. And if they had brought in guns, what else might they be hiding under the little Dower House? And how could she safely find out?

St Stephens' socks, if she hadn't seen the tension in the village, she would have suspected that she was making mountains out of molehills. But this was not a molehill. And something had to be done.

"Where do they have Robbie Evans, Mrs. Martin? Do you know?"

Mrs. Martin handed off the ribbon. "Down with the guns."

"Where does the tunnel exit?"

"The steep slope just south of the Bridport road. It's marked by a lone willow."

"Can it be caved in?"

Her eyes widened. "Never thought. Better ask yer man."

Pip passed across her shillings. "There were three men in the inn tap room I did not recognize. I assume they're part of this. How many others?"

"I don't know. Four, I think. Some went back to the ship, and that's gone, my man says."

Her hands filled with ribbon selections, Lizzie suddenly straightened. "Ship? What ship?"

"A lugger, my lady." She shrugged. "Too typical to point out."

Luggers were smuggling vessels, of course.

"No name?" Lizzie asked.

"No'm. Didn't expect any. Came and went tidy like from the east."

From the east where there were so many good ports and smaller coves.

Lizzie just stood there, frozen. Pip was beginning to be worried.

"Lizzie?"

That quickly her friend came back to life, offering a rueful smile. "Nothing. I'm sorry."

Pip would ask later. She turned instead to Mrs. Martin. "They plan to move the guns tonight?"

"I think so. Said that if we all stay out of their way, Robbie'll be back tomorrow or next day."

Pip nodded, her brain whirling. "Do you know where the Lion and Bandit is, Mrs. Martin?"

Mrs. Martin scrunched up her placid face. "That place? What could you want there?"

"Help. My husband—" Lord, she thought. She had just said that as if it were true. "—was meeting someone there. We need to get word to him."

"They're watching everyone here, miss."

She nodded. "They're watching the manor as well. And by now they know that somebody is staying in the Dower House."

"It's over to Abbotsbury, miss...I guess it is Missus now, though. Isn't it? My Lady."

Pip smiled and patted the older woman's hand. "I hope I'm always Miss Pip to you, Mrs. Martin."

"I do wish you well, Miss Pip."

Pip shared her best smile. "Thank you, Mrs. Martin."

"Pip," Lizzie protested. "You aren't thinking of getting involved? Let them go. Let them get far away from here so all our people are safe."

"I don't think I can, Liz. I need to reach Beau to find out what we should do and get our staff somewhere safe." She looked over at Mrs. Martin. "I don't suppose there are any other tunnels about?"

That earned her a brief grin. "Afraid not. Just those two."

Pip nodded. "All right. I know I can trust you not to say a word. We shall do our best to get young Robbie Evans back." Although how, she didn't know. "How far to the Lion and Bandit?"

"Maybe two miles east on the coast."

Pip nodded. "Thank you. Now, if you don't mind, Lizzie will buy that lovely orange ribbon she has been clutching, and we will be on our way. Nobody needs to know what we said."

Every instinct Pip had screamed at her to run for the inn and the stables. She didn't know who was watching her, though, so after Lizzie made her exchange, she and Pip stopped into the little lending library for a few minutes and said hello to the blacksmith as they passed his forge, all the while discussing the upcoming Christmas festivities.

When they finally did make it back to the inn stables, it was to find Charlie McKay and Clancy bringing the horses out.

"Figured you'd be back this way about now," Clancy said laconically.

If Pip hadn't been looking close she wouldn't have seen the slow wink he gave her. So he'd been talking to Charlie while she and Lizzie had been touring the shops.

"I wanted to be home by teatime," she said. "I have no idea if Beau will be back from his friend's, but I'd like to be ready."

"Oh, newlyweds," Lizzie said, with a sly smile. "Too long apart already?"

"That is an entirely different discussion for another day, Liz." Stepping up onto the mounting block, she gathered all that useless material in her hands and climbed into the saddle. "Thank you, Charlie. Tell you mother hello for me."

Charlie yanked his cap off and grinned. "I will, miss. Missus. Yer ladyship."

She smiled. "Miss Pip, Charlie. The rest just gets too complicated."

The young man beamed as if she had granted him a boon.

Clancy helped Lizzie mount before climbing onto Boru and turning them all out of the inn yard, the hooves setting up a clattering that echoed around the cobbled yard.

"You aren't gonna let this be, Miss Pip," Clancy said quietly. "Are ya?"

"I'm afraid I cannot, Clancy. We're being watched, though, even at the Dower House. So we have to figure out how to get everyone to safety and have Beau get us help. And guns. We will need guns."

The little man bestowed a big grin on her. "You've been biding your time 'til this yer entire life, haven't you?"

And Pip, who was too often honest, smiled back. "I imagine I have. Now let us go save the country."

And off they rode.

11

W hen Pip and Theo had imagined scenarios like this, the capture of the criminals had been easy. Pip would be brilliant and calm. Theo showed up just in time to protect her. There would be all manner of weapons and spirited horses available, and Pip and Theo—and sometimes Beau—there to use them faultlessly. And Perfect Pamela would have been shamed and exiled.

All right, Pip admitted. Maybe not that last part, although the imagery was very satisfying. The rest wouldn't even be close to the frustration and challenge she did face.

In the real world, she had a staff of six she had to get safely away from the Dower House. She had Beau to reach, and she had possible traitors in her cellars that she had to keep corralled until help could come.

First things first.

"Leave Macha and me off at the dower stables," she told Clancy as they turned their horses into the Dower House drive. She couldn't help watching for watchers. "Can you get to Beau at the Lion and Bandit? We shall need him and whoever he can gather. And we need weapons, Clancy. We need them quickly, and we need to get them without Lord Burke and Pamela Smythe-Smith realizing it. Without them realizing anything. You don't officially know this, but they are very possibly part of a plot to overthrow the throne."

Clancy gave a lazy shake of his head. "The things people get up to."

"There are also watchers out there between the Dower House and the manor. Can they be...er, shall we say, quietly put somewhere safe? Or at least watched to see what they do? So far, they look more like senior house staff than thugs or lords."

"What about you, Miss Pip?"

"I need to get my staff safely away. I'm hoping I can direct them to the Fairy Steps so they can get to the manor unseen. Then I need to see if there is a way to lock that second cellar from the house without being caught and secure the other end of that tunnel. I wish I could figure a way to collapse it in on itself. I imagine that would be more likely in a book, though, wouldn't it?"

"It would."

"And I need to find a way to protect Robbie Evans. The smugglers have him in that cellar."

For the first time she saw real emotion in Clancy's eyes. She would not want to be those smugglers when he met them.

"Fairy Steps ain't far from where the Dower tunnel should be," was all he said. "I can have men there to keep it watched all quietlike. Keep 'em bottled up 'til help arrives, if need be. They won't hurt the Evans boy. They need him for their bargaining chip."

She nodded, knowing that Clancy would never endanger the boy. Although that might be unavoidable. "And remember. No word about any plots. It's just strange smugglers."

"I shall inform mother," Lizzie said. "She is amazingly underhanded when she wants to be. And she knows who to trust."

"Make sure the girls are somewhere safe," Pip reminded her. "I wouldn't trust anyone involved in this."

"One more thing, Miss Pip," Clancy said. "There are a couple o' guns in the dower stables. You take one f'r yourself, now, and keep it with you. I'll get somebody to his lordship."

They parted at the Dower House stables, where Hawkins the groom came out to collect Macha. With off-handed wishes to see each other again soon, Lizzie and Clancy went trotting back along a side path to the manor house.

Left behind, Pip was suddenly beset with dread. What if she got this wrong? What if someone were hurt, or they couldn't prevent the guns going to their intended recipients? What if, through her own incompetence, she made things worse?

All she could do was shake her head and suck in a deep breath. Beau would be there soon.

"Two things, Hawkins," she told the groom loaned to the Dower House as she draped that blasted skirt back over her arm. "Once Macha is groomed, I need to see you in the kitchen for a few minutes. And bring the guns that are here. In a satchel, if you would."

The gruff, broad husband of Cook, Hawkins looked at Pip as if she had gone barmy, but he knuckled his cap and took hold of Macha. Pip turned for the house, hoping with all her heart that Clancy would get to Beau in good time. She had a lot to do in the meantime.

BEAU DIDN'T EXPECT Nate Adams to reveal what he was doing in Dorset. Nate was one of the most close-mouthed people Beau had ever known, all the way back to Eton when they had run an informal gambling ring together. Tall, dark, sinewy, Adams might be a Rake, but he was a law unto himself. No matter how imbedded Nate was in the aristocracy, third son of a marquess whose line ran straight back to the Conqueror, Nate could fit in at any level of society like a chameleon. Right now, he sat across from Beau nursing a glass of ale, obviously acting the fisherman who might just be supplanting his income out across the Channel, his attire homespun and wool, his black hair disreputably long and his face just that unshaven.

But then, Beau didn't look much better. The Lion and Bandit wasn't a place to wear a morning suit and a shave. Tucked in along a cove on the coast near Chesil Beach, which had its share of clandestine trade, the inn had the look of an old man on shaky pins. The top floor where unnamed men slept and unnamed women didn't, listed to the east from centuries of wind and creaked in protest with every footstep. There was never enough light, and the air was redolent with the smell of hops, tobacco, fish, and unwashed bodies. Beau and Nate sat in the darkest corner of a dark room.

"Old Burke, huh?" Nate asked, gazing into his glass like scrying water. "One of the Pater's chums. That will set him on his heels."

"Are you surprised?"

"Actually?" He looked up, offered a world-weary smile. "No. Lives quite well, does Burke. Not sure his estates support it."

"Have you heard anything else? I was detoured to Ripton Hall at the last minute. There seems to have been some suspicious characters visiting recently."

Nate's smile was grim. "Oh, aye," he said, sounding like a Dorset fisherman. "Quite a parade of queer folk seen in these parts lately. Especially up to Ripton Hall. I'm afraid the old duke might have been involved in a bit of hugger mugger that's still playin' out."

"The duke?!"

Nate nodded. "Had some shipping interests, and I've suspected they weren't always on the correct side of the revenue. I'm afraid I wouldn't put it past him to have had some fingers in this pie."

Beau was already instinctively shaking his head. "Could someone have been taking advantage of his...instability?"

Nate shrugged. "Don't know, do I? I'd be careful all the same."

Beau finished his ale. "I mean to be out of this nonsense in another week and back in London. In the meantime, if you learn anything, can you share it with me? I'm at the Ripton Hall Dower House."

"Oh, that's right," Nate said, brightening considerably. "I'd heard there were some surprise wedding bells up there. She finally caught you, huh?"

Beau scowled. "I gave my all for king and country, lad. Show some respect."

That earned him a delighted laugh. "Well, at least she isn't hard to look at."

Beau motioned to the barmaid for another round.

Just then a familiar face appeared at the door. Short, bow-legged as a jockey, with a shock of bright red hair and a face wrinkled and creased by the sun. Now, what was he doing here?

Whipping off his battered low-crowned hat, the Ripton Hall stablemaster caught sight of Beau and strode over, rolling like a sailor on a high sea.

"There you be, lad," he said, as if talking to his own grooms. Well, at least he respected an attempt at deception. "Been lookin' f'r ya. Need to get back. Doin's at the house need my full staff."

"You came all this way for me?"

"Lookin' over a likely pair o' plowhorses for the home farm, wasn't I?"

Beau nodded, suddenly beset by fear. Something was very wrong.

"Well, come on then," he said, standing and dropping some

coins on the table before gathering his own cap. "Sorry, luv," he called over to the waitress. "Work callin'."

"Walk you out," Nate drawled, following suit.

They had barely made it out to the dusty, rutted street before Clancy broke the news. He didn't even turn around or stop, which made Beau realize that this was not information for witnesses.

"Queer goings-on," the stablemaster quietly said. "Miss Pip sent me quick as could be. She said to say that smugglers have a shipment of guns in your cellar, and she thinks it's all tied in. Make sense?"

Beau was afraid so. That quickly his fear solidified. *Oh, God. Pip.*

"I don't suppose she ran away."

Clancy chortled. "Our Pip? You know better, milord. Settin' up camp, but said she'd wait for you."

"She'd better," he growled, shoving his cap on his head and heading for the stables. "Or I'll hurt her worse than they could. Now, fill me in."

Clancy did as the three of them walked over to pick up horses.

"I'll get word to Drake," Nate said. "He might prefer we just follow that lot, see who the guns are for."

"Not sure I'll be able to wait," Beau retorted, terrified he was already too late.

Damn her, he thought. How does she always manage to winkle her way right into the middle of disasters? Damn him, if he didn't get to her in time.

He walked faster.

COME BACK, *Beau,* Pip kept thinking as she gathered her staff in the kitchen. Her palms were sweating, and she wanted to vomit up the tea she had never gotten to. She kept listening through the open cellar door, struggling to hear any noise of invaders. She couldn't hear anything but her own breathing.

"Do you know where the Fairy Steps are?" she asked the assembled staff as they all crowded around her.

"I do," young Sam said with a grin. "Mighta used 'em to sneak back in late like
a time or two."

Mrs. Webb gave him a smack on the shoulder. "I should report you."

His grin was bright as noon. "But you won't. What's this about, milady?"

Pip still had to get used to that address. "I need you all to use the Fairy Steps to sneak back into the Hall," she said. "As quickly and unobtrusively as you can. I'm afraid we have a problem."

Every person in her kitchen straightened. "What kind of problem?" Joyful asked.

Pip sighed. "There seems to be a new—and unfriendly—group of smugglers who found a tunnel to the Dower House and a second cellar where they are even now storing crates of guns, which I fear they intend to use very soon. I do not want any of you to be in danger, so I am asking you to very quietly sneak out. There are watchers up by the hall as well, which is why I want you to use the tunnel."

"Tell you how careful we'll be," Billings retorted, on his feet like a new recruit. "We're stayin' here. You was gonna do this alone, wasn't you?"

She shrugged, heartened by the nods she saw at Billings' declaration. "I have sent for Lord Drummond. He will know what to do. Hopefully, in the meantime, we need to keep them in the tunnel. *Does* anybody know anything about that second cellar?"

She was answered by shaken heads. She nodded back,

assessing the staff's response. Billings and Hawkins looked determined. Joyful simply stood like a hipshot horse, her hand on her hip. It was very difficult to excite Joyful. Mrs. Webb and the maids looked nervous. And poor Mr. Sullins, Beau's very precise and nervous valet, looked as if he were about to weep.

"Mr. Sullins," she said. "May I ask you to follow Sam to the Fairy Steps and help guide everyone through the tunnel to the Hall's chapel? They will need a steady leader."

She saw Mrs. Webb stiffen in outrage and gave her a pointed look. The undercook took a quick look at the relief in Mr. Sullins' posture and huffed once before stepping back.

"Thank you, Milady," she said, folding her arms. "We'll all do fine."

"Thank you all for making this easy."

"I'm not going," Joyful interrupted, her laconic voice belying the steel suddenly in her spine.

"Joyful..."

She just shook her head. "Missy, I been in way worse places than this. I'm not goin' anywhere. You got guns? I can do guns. You got somethin' else? I can fight with it. I'm not goin'."

Pip intended to fight her. One look at the implacable look in Joyful's eyes convinced her otherwise. "Then everyone else, please. There are too many people here right now. If something happens, all we would do is provide a massed target, and I would never forgive myself if I had to tell her grace I got her favorite staff shot."

The staff left by dribs and drabs, so it didn't look like an organized movement. Pip accepted a gun from Hawkins and loaded it. Hawkins kept the other one and refused to budge, taking up a position by the front window where he could see the willow at the other end of the Dower House tunnel. Pip tried to figure out what Beau would want her to do. Find that second cellar and expose the fact that they knew what was going on? Attack the other end of the tunnel and box the smugglers in?

But if they did that, then Burke and Pamela would know. The watching man would know. And even riding back to the house would put Beau in danger, not to mention everyone up at the Hall.

After consulting with her stalwarts, Pip chose the option of looking for the second cellar as stealthily as they could. Leaving Hawkins upstairs to stand watch, Pip, Joyful and Billings crept down the stairs into what had obviously begun as a limestone cave, dry and cool and the perfect place for a small wine cellar and storage. Every wall that did not boast wine racks, had shelving crammed higgledy-piggledy with old dishes, linens, small furniture, and trunks that just cried out to be searched.

"We need to start with the wall to the tunnel," Pip whispered.

Joyful and Hawkins turned around as if it would set direction in their heads. They finally pointed to the front wall. As silently as they could, they moved the detritus of generations of dower lives away and searched the shelving for any hint of opening. Any way to let invaders in or lock them out. They had been down there at least a couple of hours when suddenly the door to the kitchen opened above them.

"Miss Pip," young Sam whispered down.

She ran over to see him leaning through the kitchen doorway. "You were supposed to be gone."

"I was. Her Grace sent me back till Lord Drummond got back. Says they have help up at the Hall, but that she thought we should all wait on his lordship before doin' anything."

"Thank you. Yes." She checked the little watch she had attached to her dress. "He should be here soon. Everyone upstairs, now. We can at least lock the kitchen door into the cellars."

She would leave it to Beau to figure out what to do about

the second cellar, Pip decided. Waiting until everybody else had climbed the stairs, she turned to make one last quick scan of the cellar. They deserved a little treat, she decided, heading for the wine racks. For their nerves. For *her* nerves. She was realizing that she didn't like adventures nearly as much as she thought she would.

She had taken no more than two steps when she heard the oddest sound behind her. From the front wall, almost a rustling, like mice scampering across the floor. She turned to see one of the shelves move. A crack opened between the uprights and she felt the whisper of cooler air.

St. Sophia's seashells, she thought, her stomach dropping to her shoes. Shoving her glasses up her nose, she pulled the loaded pistol from her pocket and took a careful step forward. The door—it was obviously a door, she could see—slid open without so much as a creak.

How did it do that? She wondered even as she positioned herself before the opening. She raised her gun, took hold with both hands, wondering what she could possibly accomplish with only one shot.

She came so very close to firing. But then she saw that the shoulder and arm that snaked through the door was at a child's height. The hair was towheaded and cowlicked. The face, tearstained, was freckled.

It was Robbie Evans.

She ran forward, but he quickly waved her away. She stopped just far enough away to see into the flickering light of what had to be the second cellar, where she could just make out the geometrics of large, long crates.

There was an adult back there. Pip could see his shadow. She lifted the gun.

"No, Miss," Robbie hissed. "Not him."

Which was when she stopped cold in place. He had taken a

step forward, that shadow man who was watching Robbie escape the second cellar. He lifted a hand and turned.

She knew that shadow. She knew that gait, that gesture. She swore she did.

For a moment she couldn't breathe. Her heart was pounding so loudly she swore Robbie could hear it. She couldn't take her eyes off that shadow that was already slipping back into the darkness beyond the door.

Instinctively she reached for the door. Robbie grabbed her arm. "No, miss. We have to go. He said so."

"Who said so, Robbie?"

Taking the time to push the wall closed, Robbie took a deep breath. "Said his name was Barnaby, miss. Said as how if I wanted to keep myself safe, I should say I found my way out all by myself. Nobody was to know he was there. Gave me a message, though. Said to tell somebody name o' Drake 'north of the Royal Arsenal.'"

Pip was still watching the wall. Her heart was thundering, and she thought somebody had robbed her of her balance. She couldn't even think. But that last sentence caught her attention. "North of the Royal Arsenal? What does that mean?"

Robbie shrugged. "Didn't say. C'n I see me mum now, miss?"

Pip did her best to pull herself together. No, of course she'd been wrong. There was no other answer. Without another thought, she ran over to Robbie and gave him the hug of a life-time. "I'm so glad to see you, Robbie. Do you think the men know you're gone?"

His grin was brash and bright. "Aw, they're too busy to notice. Sides. Barnaby says he's a magician. Says they won't notice."

She gave him another quick hug. Then, because she knew Beau would never forgive her if she didn't at least look, she walked up to the very well-hidden door Robbie had slipped through to see if there was some kind of locking mechanism, and by St. Thomas's Thumbnails, there it was, a tongue of sturdy wood that slid right into a recess in the stone wall. Tucking the gun into her apron pocket, she slid the lock home and took hold of Robbie's arm.

"Let's get out of here, Rob."

Just as they were walking by the wine rack, she finally heard a beloved voice up in the kitchen. "Is my wife here?"

All she could think to do was grab a couple of bottles of wine. She needed to get upstairs to Beau. She needed to tell him what she saw. Or whom she'd seen.

"Barnaby said not to tell nobody he's there," Robbie said.

She paused for a moment, a bottle in her hand. No, she thought, Robbie was right. She wouldn't tell anybody. It would be far too embarrassing to admit her obvious mistake. Especially to Beau.

Grabbing one more bottle for good luck, she laid that one in Robbie's arms. "Here," she said. "I believe we're going to need this."

She would keep silent. If she didn't, people would think she had lost her mind. After all, how could she possibly think that the person she saw in the second cellar edging Robbie to freedom was Theo Drummond?

12

Pip wanted nothing more than to throw herself into Beau's arms. She didn't, of course, not with the kitchen full of people and her arms full of wine bottles as she guided Robbie up the stairs. Especially not when she was still fighting the surprise of seeing that man in the basement. The last thing she or Beau needed was for her to blurt out her brief suspicion.

Of course she knew the man she saw wasn't Theo. It hadn't been any other time she'd sworn to have seen or heard him over the last year either. She had so badly wanted him not to be dead she kept imagining him alive.

But he had never been there. He never would be. So just like always, she would swallow that brief joy and subsequent grief and move on.

"I found something I think we misplaced," she greeted everyone brightly as she topped the stairs behind Robbie.

"Crikey," Sam whispered, eyes huge.

Billings just strode forward and gave the boy a convulsive hug. "You all right, then, lad?"

Robbie nodded with a huge grin. "Yes'r. They was all too busy with those big boxes to bother with me."

"How many big boxes?" Beau asked quietly from his spot near the back door, surreptitiously setting his own pistol on a counter behind him.

"Dozen or so, milord," Robbie was saying. "Long ones and short ones."

"Do you know about how many men?"

"'Bout seven or so. More gone back to the ship, they said. C'n I see me mum now?"

Beau laid a hand on his shoulder. "Good lad. I wish we could let you go home right now, Robbie, but I think it's better nobody but us knows you're safe. Do we have some chocolate for a brave lad, wife?"

Pip looked up to see a storm brewing in his eyes. Now what was he going to accuse her of?

"Of course, we do," she said, setting her wine bottles on the table with barely a tremble. "And could somebody open the wine for the brave adults?"

That was when she noticed that in the time she'd been in the cellar the sun had

gone down. At this time of year, darkness had dropped like a curtain. It would have made the kitchen cozier if Beau hadn't still been glaring at her.

He might not have looked so fierce if he had been wearing his regular attire. But he looked like a fisherman just walking off the wharf in homespun pants and a ragged gray sweater.

"I'll get the chocolate," Joyful offered, pointing young Robbie to the bench.

"I'll get the wine," Billings said, stepping into his pantry.

Beau turned to Pip. "Can I speak with you in the parlor, wife?"

Pip sighed. "Back to the parlor, is it?"

And without another word he took Pip by the elbow and

led her out of the kitchen. She walked alongside him with everyone watching them go. That did not increase her confidence.

The room was cold and lit only by the old fire in the fireplace. Pip couldn't help wrapping her arms around herself as she turned to suffer his judgement. But just when she was opening her mouth to defend herself, Beau grabbed her to him, crushing her against his chest, his head over hers. He was trembling!

"Beau?"

"How do you always land yourself in the middle of a crisis?" he demanded, his voice rough.

Pip wrapped her arms around his back, still feeling completely upended. "I certainly did not go looking for trouble," she said, resting her ear against Beau's chest just to hear his heartbeat. His fast, frantic heartbeat.

"You never do," he growled.

"It was the village," she explained, not moving. Not wanting to move. "We could tell there was something wrong. How could we know that what was wrong was right under our honeymoon retreat?"

For the longest moment Beau didn't say a word. He just enveloped her in his strength, his warmth. He just made her dream that he would always be there just like this if she needed him.

If only she could simply stay here and pretend everything would be all right.

She couldn't. Not yet.

"There's more," she said. "There was a man down there who helped Robbie out. Said that Robbie shouldn't tell anyone he was there. But he gave Robbie a message."

Beau pulled back enough to look down at her.

"He said to tell Drake 'north of the Royal Arsenal," she said.

Beau frowned. "North of the Royal Arsenal? That's it?"

Pip nodded.

Beau kept frowning. "In Woolwich? But that's up by London. And north of Woolwich is the river."

"Maybe they're taking the guns up there," Pip offered.

"But why?" Beau asked. "They already have guns."

"Maybe Drake knows."

He nodded again, his attention straying to that new puzzle.

"Tell me what you've done about the guns," he said.

So, she did, everything but her moment of wishful thinking. Before he would have appreciated it. After all, this would have been just the kind of adventure Theo would have loved. But not now. Not anymore.

It hurt so much all over again, but she would need to wait for that.

"Do you want to see the door to the second cellar?" she asked. "Maybe you can figure a way to reinforce it."

"In a minute."

For just a moment, he just looked down at her, his brow furrowed. Pip held her breath, not sure of what she wanted to happen next.

And then, just as suddenly, he lifted her chin and kissed her. It wasn't like the other kisses, incendiary, overwhelming. She didn't lose her sense of where she was or what she was doing. But she could not pull away, even if she wanted to. Beau had one hand at her waist and the other at the nape of her neck, but comforting. Reassuring, although Pip wasn't certain exactly which one of them he was reassuring.

All Pip knew was that in his arms, in this embrace, she felt safe and cherished and comforted. His mouth was so soft, so insistent, edging hers open so he could meet her tongue-to-tongue, as if just lips weren't nearly close enough. She pulled him closer, flush against her so her breasts could abrade against his chest and her hips could seek the strength in his. So she could feel the unmistakable hunger in him, the heat and hard length of him, the urgency and relief. So, she could self-ishly relish the hunger sparking to life in her own body, shoulder to toe.

"Don't ever scare me like that again," he rasped, pulling back enough to kiss the top of her head.

There were things to do. Suddenly she couldn't think what. She wasn't even sure her knees would hold her up long enough to do them.

She once again rested her head against his heart instead and closed her eyes, at least for that moment. "I didn't mean to scare you this time."

"I doubt you meant to scare me last time."

She couldn't help it. She grinned and knew he felt it. "What should we do?" she asked, holding on tight. "All we have here is a pistol and a long gun. Mrs. Martin in the village said the same thing Robbie did, that there are at least seven men. We saw at least three of them at the inn."

"Nothing," he said. "We are to do nothing. If we try to inter-fere now, we'll never know who they're supposed to contact and where they're supposed to go. The guns aren't enough. The destination is what we need."

"You're sure? What if they get away?"

"They won't. I brought help back."

"From the Lion and Bandit?!" She couldn't help envisioning an eyepatch-wearing smuggler, maybe with a peg leg. A hook for a hand.

"Don't you worry about from where. Just for once stay where you can be protected. We'll take care of the rest."

And darn if she didn't want to believe him. Still, she didn't move. But then, neither did he.

"Would you like to see where all that wine came from?" she asked. "Also, a rather clever door cut into the wall downstairs that seems to go into the next cellar none of us knew about—well, except for every person in the village and Lizzie's Aunt

Eleanor, evidently. I threw the bolt before coming up. I figure the smugglers cannot know that it was open before...well. I hope they don't know."

"I don't want you down there," he rasped, ruining what was left of the fantasy.

"If I am not, you'll have a difficult time finding that door. And if you cannot find it, how do you protect it?"

Beau pulled away, finally, which Pip knew was inevitable and necessary, but still hated. "All right, then. Show me. And then we need to figure out what to do with you."

There went her heart again, scudding down to her toes. "Oh, Beau, you do know how to say the most romantic things."

The concern in his eyes chilled to determination. "This is not the place for an amateur."

She pulled completely out of his arms and crossed her arms. "How inconvenient for you, then. Because with Burke and Pamela up at the hall and watchers meandering about, any surprise moves on our part would raise a red flag, now. Wouldn't they?"

Once again, Beau was dragging his hand through his hair. "I want you out of this, Pip. I can't focus if I'm worrying about you."

Well, she thought. *At least he's worrying about me. I suppose that's better than being inconvenienced by me.*

Not knowing what else to do, she dragged in a calming breath and reached up to straighten his hair. "Let's take one thing at a time, shall we? And I was always taught that the first step is reconnaissance. So, let us go downstairs."

Beau was frowning again. "Just who taught you about reconnaissance?"

Giving him nothing but a bright grin, she opened the door and walked out of the parlor. The house was awfully quiet. Pip couldn't help imagining that everyone was holding their breath to see what kind of explosion she and Beau would ignite. Wouldn't they be disappointed?

IN THE END, their visit to the cellar was rather anticlimactic. Pip showed Beau the lock, and Beau grabbed yet another bottle of claret that bore no tax stamp before they returned upstairs.

Half a bottle in, with Joyful cooking dinner, Robbie drinking his chocolate at the kitchen table, and Billings uncorking the second bottle, there was a soft knock on the kitchen door. Beau was on his feet before Pip could even react. She was so tired of her heart pounding for no reason. It could be anyone at the door. Why should it be someone dangerous? She put her hand on her gun anyway.

Blessed Barbara's beads, Pip thought when the door opened. It *was* someone dangerous. Exactly the man she had imagined from the Lion and Bandit, except for the eyepatch and peg leg. Dark, saturnine, scowling, silent. Clad in clothing even more disreputable than Beau's. He slipped in from the dark and stepped away from the windows.

"You need to give them the house, Drummond," he said, his accent just as precise as Beau's.

One of the Rakes? The man Beau was to meet? Pip stepped a bit closer.

"We don't get an introduction?" she asked.

"No," both Beau and the intruder answered without looking at her.

"Would you like some wine?" she asked. "We brought up some particularly nice vintages set down when the good smugglers used to visit my friend's aunt here."

The man grinned, and that quickly his entire visage changed, white teeth and mischievous eyes and a posture that went from threatening to easy. Pip found herself blinking, wondering at the sudden change. She came so close to demanding to know if he was a Rake. There was just an insouciance about him that she had long noticed in many of the others.

"Are you certain we are not allowed to know your name?" she asked.

Suddenly she had Beau's attention. "He is sure," he said, sounding a bit petulant. "You are not."

Pip just nodded and poured a glass of wine for the newcomer. "I assume that you do know my husband, however," she said, handing over the glass.

"Thank you," he said, accepting. "I do. And congratulations."

She nodded. "You might as well save the energy until we know whether it will take or not."

She got a quirked eyebrow from him. "I didn't think marriages worked like that."

Her own grin was far too wide. "Neither did I. Now, what is it we are supposed to be doing about our unexpected guests?"

The newcomer took a sip. "Leaving."

She blinked. "We just got here."

Beau motioned his friend to the servants' table and sat down. Robbie scooted over. When Pip joined them, Beau frowned. When she flashed him as big a smile as she'd flashed his friend, he absolutely scowled.

"If I am to play a part," she said, plopping down next to Robbie, "even only sneaking away in the dark, I must have the script. Now then, er...."

"Call me Nate," the newcomer said, folding himself onto the bench opposite her. "We need to make a point of emptying out the house. What about saying you were only staying here a night and going on to Delamere."

Pip topped up wine for the adults. "Not Delamere. Anywhere but Delamere."

"His aunt and uncle are still there?" Nate asked her as if Beau weren't sitting directly in front of him.

"They are. We do not get along."

Nate nodded and took a sip of his wine. "Nobody does. That is quite nice," he admitted, checking the bottle.

"Evidently, a tithe from the local gentlemen for use of that cellar. These, evidently, are not those gentlemen."

"No," Nate said. "They are not."

"You know?" Beau asked.

"Even the lot down at the Lion and Bandit don't know who they are."

"They told the townspeople they would be leaving tomorrow or the next day," Pip offered.

For a long few moments the only sounds to be heard in the kitchen were the soup bubbling over the fire and Joyful slicing bread. Suddenly Pip thought how hungry she was. It had been a long few days, and a long while since she had enjoyed her food.

"Can you provide us a messenger?" Beau asked his friend. "Tomorrow. Something urgent. Something not connected to the government."

"Miss Knight—er, I mean, Lady Drummond's father is home," Nate said far too easily. "Would that suffice?"

Pip came to attention like a bird dog hearing wings. "My father? Not my mother?"

"And how do you know?" Beau demanded. "I don't."

Nate shrugged. "I have connections in shipping. And no, Miss Knight. Your mother was not with him."

"Where would he go, Pip?" Beau asked.

"If he is here without mother that would mean it is government business, although why he could not simply send a messenger, I'm sure I don't know." She shook her head, completely distracted. "But I would be the last one to be notified. Especially if my brother Alex is in town."

Suddenly, though, she wanted to be there as well.

Nate spent a moment thinking. "I believe it to be our best option. A messenger will arrive tomorrow morning with the message that your father is home and ill. That should be excuse enough."

Pip blinked. "Is he?" she demanded.

Nate shrugged. "I have no idea. But that message would provide urgency."

"C'n I go home, too?" Robbie asked all of a sudden.

Everyone stopped.

"No, lad," Beau answered.

"But me mum will be that worried."

Beau reached out to lay a hand over Robbie's on the table. "I know, and I'm sorry for it. But if we even tell her all is well, she might give you away and put herself in danger. Do you understand?"

Pip saw the tears well in the boy's eyes and wanted to hug him. "It won't be long," she assured him. "Until then..."

"Would you like to hide in the stables with Hawkins?" Beau asked.

Robbie's grin reappeared. "I like the horses."

"Robbie also brought us a message," Beau told Nate, and then explained. "Bring anything to mind?"

Nate just shook his head.

"Well, now that we've figured all that out," Joyful suddenly spoke up, hands on broad hips, wooden spoon in one, "what about some dinner? Cook said it was mulligatawny. Who knew y'all had curry?"

"Are you staying, Nate?" Beau asked as Joyful began ladling soup into bowls.

The man cast a longing look at the thick soup and shook his head. "I have preparations to make." Standing, he drained his wine and picked up the rest of the bottle to take with him.

"Lock the cellar door. At least for tonight. I won't see you again."

Beau was getting to his feet, but Nate waved him down, gave a general wave to the room and slipped back out the door as Joyful set out bowls, spoons and bread.

"Kinda spooky, ain't he?" Robbie offered, looking to the door.

"A good word for him," Beau agreed, accepting a bowl from Joyful and passing it down the table. "Now then, lad. Eat up. You'll stay here tonight and then sneak over to the stables in the morning."

Pip was just about to dip her spoon into her soup when Beau's words registered. She couldn't help it. They made her smile.

"That's right, Robbie," she said, suddenly feeling better. "We already have some blankets on the sofa in the library for you."

That quickly Beau's head came up and he commenced to glare again.

Pip smiled. "Good thing my bed has lots of room, husband."

She decided not to mention the dressing room. Even so, poor Joyful, who was being ejected from her little bed there, flashed her own prized scowl.

"I'll stay up to watch for any problems," Beau snapped.

"If you don't mind, milord," Billings retorted, suddenly looking older. "I'd like to stand the first watch. Was in the navy before the duchess, she hired me. Won't let anything happened to her or hers."

It took Beau a minute, but Pip hoped he could see the devotion in Billing's eyes and allow him the responsibility. Finally, Beau nodded. "Thank you. It has been a long few days. I will relieve you after four hours."

"Yessir."

Four hours. It would give Pip enough time. With one quick

glance at Joyful, she went back to her dinner. Joyful gave her a miniscule nod. Pip would have hot water to clean up, and she would have help to quickly change. And she would have Beau in her bed.

And Pip planned on taking advantage of it all, because she knew in her heart that after tonight, she would lose her chance to show her husband how she felt about him and the idea that they would have a white marriage.

And oh, Blessed Bernard's buttons, she couldn't wait.

13

Beau had meant to spend the night in the front salon, no matter what Billings offered. It had to be better than trying to sleep next to Pip. But one look at the change in Billings' posture after Beau had accepted the boy's offer, and he knew he couldn't be anywhere in evidence during the boy's shift. It would destroy Billing's fledgling dignity. If he had been in the navy, he'd know perfectly well how to watch for trouble, to notice what did not belong even if it wasn't a sail on the horizon. And with Nate's men outside doing the same, Beau could get a bit of sleep.

He waited for everyone else to retire before officially handing off the duty to Billings and climbing the stairs. He had no idea where Pip was. She had disappeared some time earlier along with her lady's maid. He guessed she had gotten young Robbie bedded down in the library, because there he was sprawled out on the sofa under the blankets Beau had used the night before.

Which left Pip's bedroom. *The* bedroom. With the lady's maid in the dressing room to glower at him. Climbing the stairs, he pulled at the knot in his cravat. It was going to be a long night.

This was definitely not how he'd ever envisioned his marriage to be. Good thing he was planning to end it as soon as possible.

A lone sconce burned in the hallway, casting feeble shadows across the walls and floor, only the window at the end of the hall providing more faint light. Beau blew out his night candle and set it on the hall table before reaching for the door handle.

Someone had built up the bedroom fire, which threw out more warmth than Beau had expected. More light as well. He stepped inside, already pulling at the sweater he had borrowed from one of the stable hands.

"Pip?"

"I'm here," she said from behind the privacy screen.

Just the soft sound of her voice raised gooseflesh. What was it about her that so roused his body? Her voice, her smile, her sharp tongue. Her lithe horsewoman's legs and athlete's form. He couldn't help it. Every time he was with her, he saw her underneath him, her arms out, waiting. Wanting. And there was nothing that would drive him mad quicker.

Sitting on the chair by the fire, he tugged off his boots and rolled down his stockings. Even his toes were warm.

What did he say to her? How could he make this seem normal?

"Is Joyful in the dressing room?"

Pip chuckled. "No. She refused to feel like an interloper. I believe she is in the housekeeper's room by the kitchen."

He nodded. "Oh, good. I did not need her sneaking across the room in the dead of night."

Pip let go another chuckle. "Joyful does not sneak."

"Then I do not want her passing judgment without a word."

Pip chuckled. "That she most definitely *does* do."

Stuffing his stockings into his boots, he lined them up like toy soldiers. He didn't know how he was to relax, and he was so tired. Extortion and surprise brides did that to him.

Still, he didn't have to take it out on Pip. "Thank you, by the way."

Pulling his shirt over his head, he laid it over the other chair until he could return it to its owner.

"For what?" she asked.

"For keeping your head today. Most women wouldn't have."

She laughed. "Actually, most women probably would have, if they had grown up learning what I did. We women are involved in a lot more dangerous activities than men give us credit for."

He couldn't help but grin. "Like what?"

The answer was stark. "Childbirth."

Well, she had him there. He walked over to where the gold-colored covers were turned down on the old four poster. He was reaching for the buttons at his falls when he stopped. He was used to sleeping in the nude. That would not be a good idea tonight. His cock had been acting unruly enough lately. It did not need more freedom to further its mischief. Instead, he climbed into bed and pulled the covers up and thought how he was the image of a new bride waiting for her groom.

At least that made him smile.

"Are you coming to bed?" he asked, wondering what was taking her so long.

"I am."

And then, nothing. No sound, not clothing or water or hairbrush.

"Pip?"

It happened before he was ready. No, he would *never* be ready. But suddenly there was Pip, standing to the side of the fireplace, positioned in the exact spot on the floor where the firelight would limn every curve and sweep of her body.

Her body. Her *naked* body.

No nightdress. No robe. No slippers. Just. Pip.

Sweet suffering...

He sat straight up. "What are you doing?" he demanded, knowing his voice rose with each word.

Her breasts were so firm and high, the nipples the color of peaches, already tightening into nubs he swore he could feel against his teeth, against the back of his mouth. Against his tongue. Her skin was pearlescent, her eyes huge and so dark. Her shape was so sweet, from throat to shoulders to waist to hips to toes, a symphony of light and shadow punctuated by a blonde triangle at the juncture of her thighs.

"What," he demanded again, barely able to breathe, "are you *doing?*"

She didn't even look away, just faced him with the same expression of challenge she had worn when walking up the aisle to their wedding. It was all he could do to hold his position. He was rock hard and ready for pillaging just with just the sight of her, and he couldn't move.

"Well," she said matter-of-factly, only the smallest of tremors in her voice giving her away. "I imagine I am making a statement."

"Unless it is I've lost my bloody mind, I can't imagine what it is," he rasped.

Still, she didn't move. "It is this." She pulled in an unsteady breath, which just brought his gaze back to her breasts as they rose and fell to taunt him. "When I took my vows," she said, "I meant them. All of them, even the 'til death do us part' part. If you cannot tolerate that, I perfectly understand. I will not even stand in your way. But I will never marry again. Which means that it does not matter whether I am a virgin or not after this adventure. So..." She looked away finally. Swallowed. Blinked. Faced him again. "I would rather not be a virgin. If it's all the same to you."

Beau was out of the bed and on his feet before he knew it. Yanking the cover off, he stalked up to her, ready to wrap her in it, to shut her away from his eyes, from his desperately hungry body.

"That is not an option," he said, beginning to lift the cover.

Too late he realized that she was stepping toward him. Before he could make good his threat with the cover, she had stepped right into his arms, her own around his neck so that her sweet, naked body pressed flush against his, her breasts pressed against his naked chest, and he forgot to think at all.

"It won't do you any good," he protested, dropping the blanket.

"I don't care," she whispered against his chest, the warm sweep of air tightening his own nipples.

Sweet God, a man could only stand so much.

"I *do* care," he insisted.

And then, because he wasn't suffering nearly enough, she lifted her face to him, and he fell into the depths of her eyes, her beautiful night-sky blue eyes. Her heartbreaking eyes that those owlish spectacles so effectively kept hidden. Spectacles that she had conveniently left somewhere else.

"I should push you away," he rasped, bringing his arms around her so that he couldn't escape the delicious softness of her breasts. So they were close enough that he might simply bend his head and take one in his mouth, take that nub of a nipple into his mouth and taunt it with his teeth.

"Please don't," she answered, smiling. "If you push me away, I won't be able to see you. I left my glasses on the bedside table."

He slipped one hand down to cup her bottom, and God, if he didn't get even harder until he thought his bedamned pants would strangle him.

"This doesn't change anything."

She nodded. "I know. I don't care. Please, Beau. Just this once."

She broke him at *please*.

The funny thing was that after the last two kisses that had been incendiary, this one wasn't. This one was a communion, a consecration. This one, his hand on the nape of her neck, her lips softer than morning, her scent of wildflowers and sunshine, shattered his heart and left it at her feet. He tilted his head to get a better purchase, nudged her lips open so that he might enter to lay claim to every secret depth, met her tongue with his to instruct her on the dance that would follow. He pulled her head back and rained kisses down on her eyelids, her forehead, her cheeks, her throat, dipping his tongue into that compelling little hollow at the base, that hollow that was so very close to her straining breasts.

She was on her toes, reaching up as far as she could. Beau had to admit he loved the feel of it, but he knew there were easier ways of going about this. Which was when he realized that he had surrendered before she had ever spoken.

Grabbing the cover in one hand, he lifted her into his arms and walked her over to the bed. He was about to lay her down, when she pulled herself to her feet right by the bed. Lifting up for one final kiss, she reached down for the buttons on is falls.

"No..." he protested, taking hold of her wrists.

Her grin was pure, eternal woman. "Yes," she retorted, popping the first button free. And then the next and the next after that until she could reach in and take him in her hand and almost cause a reaction he hadn't suffered since he was twelve. Suddenly, he was panting like a mountain climber.

"You are quite sure this fits?" she asked, stroking it, giggling when it leapt in her hand.

Quickly shucking his pants, he took her face in his hands and kissed her again. "I have it on the best of authority."

And then, before she could get into any more mischief, he

lifted her onto the bed and followed after. She looked so glorious, her bright yellow curls framing her face like sunshine, her lips plumped with his kisses, her breasts swollen and her body lifting to his.

"After this I'll still be mad at you," he warned, kissing his way back down her throat.

She ran her hands down his back, setting up a shower of chills straight to his poor, aching balls. "After this," she murmured, the smile in her voice, "I won't care."

Finally, finally, he could bend his head and take one of those tempting nipples into his mouth and suck. And delight in her body as it bowed right up off the bed, and she mewled in the back of her throat and clung to his arms as if afraid of falling. He caressed one breast and then the other, unable to get enough of the taste of her, the texture of her. He feasted on her scent and traced the sweep of her hips right down to that beckoning triangle of hair.

"Open your legs for me," he begged, reaching underneath to the slick center of her sex where he could torment that swollen nub into madness.

"Can I touch you?" she panted, trying to reach down.

He avoided her questing hand. "Next time."

"Oh, good." Her voice was breathless, sensual as sin.

"Oh, good what?"

She grinned and kissed his nose. "There will be a next time."

He scowled and went back to stroking the slick lips of her sex. "Why don't we concentrate on this time first. Do you like this?"

She was writhing now, her head thrown back, her hands scrabbling at him, her voice almost a growl. He quickened his strokes, dipped his finger into her, returned to the feast of her breasts and sipped. He was ready to burst, his body thrumming with need. But he held back until he readied her for him, until he could feel her seize around his fingers. He slid his cock up and down her thigh, tormenting himself, tormenting her, urging her on.

"Come, Pip, you can do it....let go....I'll catch you..."

And with a startled cry, she did, bowed back, whimpering, desperately seeking purchase, her body rewarding them both. And as she climaxed, Beau gently pushed her thighs a little wider and moved over her.

She was gasping and frantic. "Now?"

He smiled and slid into her. "Now."

Of course, it wasn't as easy as he'd hoped with Pip. Her body resisted as he pushed bit by bit, trying so hard not to hurt her, knowing it was inevitable. He returned his finger to that nub and stroked, pushed into her a bit harder until finally he felt the resistance give and Pip cry out.

"That's it," he promised. "That's all. Come on, my Pip. Let me please you again."

Stroking, kissing her, he pumped into her deeper, deeper, gathering her whimpers and surviving her caresses, until her eyes flew open, and she opened her mouth and he felt her climax around him, milk him until he barely pulled out in time, wishing with all his heart he could have filled her with his seed and given them a future together. The minute he pulled out, he had the worst sensation that he had just been driven from home.

For very long moments, there was nothing in that shadowy room but the wash of frantic breathing, the sharp scent of love-making, the taste of sweat-dampened skin. There was only satiation and, finally, silence.

"Oh, my," was all she said, wrapping her arms around him to keep him next to her.

He found that he was relieved. He didn't really want to move anyway. He was still too busy reveling in the unbearable softness of her skin against his callused fingers, the silken dance of her flaxen curls against his cheek. He wanted to soak in the sound of her breathing and the scent of her soap, that garden she had brought into this uninspired room with her. He wanted, just for those moments, to pretend when he knew he had no right. The only way he gave in to reality was to roll off her and tuck her up under his arm, smiling when she laid her leg over his.

"Are you all right?" he asked, pulling up the cover against the deepening night.

She thought about that for a minute as she stroked his chest. "I'm not certain all right is a proper descriptor. At least I finally understand what all the fuss is about."

"I didn't hurt you?"

"Oh, you hurt me. But as odd as it sounds, it was a good hurt. It's good to have it over with. Next time I can enjoy it even more."

He lifted his head from where it had been lying on her breasts. "Next time?"

"That is what you said." Her grin was pure seduction. "We have at least three more hours."

He dropped his head back down again. "If I live that long."

She stroked his damp hair. "I'll be sure of it."

SHE KNEW she had no business feeling so cherished. When morning came, Beau would leave her behind. She couldn't deny that. She couldn't avoid it. But he was here now; he might have even fulfilled every woman's fantasy for her, leaving her replete and limp, still wondering how in the world they had fit together so well.

Just to be certain, she decided with an impish grin, they would have to replicate the experiment. In the meantime, she kept stroking his chest, surprised for some reason that he had hair there that curled across and then down like an arrow directing one's attention to her new favorite attribute. The attribute that was even now beginning to stir again.

Without waiting for permission, she reached down to gather it up.

"I'm not going to be much use for a while," Beau protested, winnowing his own hands through her hair, his eyes closed.

"That's all right," she murmured against his chest. "I am content to keep you present while we wait."

She was content to test the width and scope of him as she wallowed in the waning ecstasy that still warmed and periodically electrified disparate parts of her body. Her toes. Who would ever imagine toes tingling from such activity? She had expected to revel in his touch, to survive cascades of shivers in places she didn't even know how to name. And she had survived, even though she felt as if those places had melted entirely, even as her body began to wake again to nothing more than the touch of his skin and tickle of the hair on chest and legs and arms. It was something so new, a sensation she had never expected, even with the lessons her mother had given on the basics of procreation. She knew it was supposed to feel wonderful with the right person. She hadn't expected it to feel at once so alien and so very, very right.

Just when she thought Beau couldn't have proven a better, more thoughtful lover, he gave her a quick kiss on her nose, and climbed past her out of bed.

"Beau..."

He smiled. "Hush. If I know your Joyful, she left us prepared...ah, here."

And before she knew it he was carrying back a flannel he had wetted in the warm water. Climbing back into bed, before he pulled the covers back up, he nudged her legs back open and attended to her with the wet rag. Pip knew how bright her blush was. How could you feel mortified and beloved at once?

"Better?" he asked, disposing of the rag and covering them up.

It took all her courage to face him, which an hour earlier she never would have imagined. "Does this mean we have leave to begin again?"

She could think of nothing in her life more precious to her than the smile on Beau's face as he bent to kiss her, long and thoroughly, his hand cupping her cheek and his body cupping hers. She had imagined him loving her like this, although even with her mother's instructions, she had never truly envisioned the particulars. She couldn't have known how truly intimate and urgent this was. She had experience with hunger. She had hungered for Beau almost as long as she had loved him. She had had no experience with the triumph of completion. Of the unbearably intimate act of welcoming him inside her.

Blessed Bernard's benediction, she could still feel him stretching her, filling her, surrounding her until she didn't know where she began and he ended. Until she felt unpardonably integral to him. And worse, he to her.

He would never accept that; she had known it the minute he had pulled out to spill his seed where nothing would grow. But just for these few moments, she decided that it was an act of courage to pretend he would. Without another word, she curled up against his body and reached down to once again wrap her hand around him. And reveled in the fact that just her touch caused him to swell.

If only she had more time. If only she had forever.

But she didn't. So, she made do with what she had, and relished every sensation they unleashed.

14

She would have wished for more time. More time loving, more time simply sleeping wrapped about each other. She wished she could have convinced Beau to leave her with the chance of a child. When Beau climbed out of bed and reclaimed his clothing, though, she knew she would have to consider what they'd had to be enough. So she watched him in the bare flickering light from the fireplace and memorized every shadow and plane, the flex and flow of muscle and tendon as he moved.

She greedily ingested the sight of his body, his broad shoulders and taut chest and belly, that devilish nest of hair from which delight sprang. Literally. And those horseman's thighs, oh, those thighs. She even cherished the sight of his feet, long and lean and precise.

She took special care to stay quiet as he turned to slip on his unmentionables, because she didn't want him to catch her ogling him. But how could she not smile at the sight of that deliciously tight bottom? How could she not want to reach out and cup it in her hands?

She knew what a good person she was when she closed her

eyes long enough to pretend she hadn't been watching and let him kiss her good night before he left to relieve Billings at his watch. She knew she was a lost woman when she spent the next hour silently weeping for what she had just lost. She knew she was a survivor when she woke to hear a horse clattering to a halt in front of the Dower House door even before the sun topped the hills and rose to prepare for what she knew would be a very long day. A longer life with only a night to sustain her.

She made it downstairs to find Beau in the library reading a dispatch.

"Your friend was more efficient than I'd anticipated," she said. "I didn't expect anything 'til noon."

"It isn't from Nate," he said, walking over to tug on the bellpull.

Billings came almost at a run.

"Ask the Hall if we might borrow a carriage," he said. "And tell Hawkins to ready Ares for me. It seems we are going to be releasing you all back to your positions, Billings. I am needed at Delamere. As soon as we are gone, go ahead and close up the house. And I will be writing a glowing report to the duchess about everyone's service here."

Billings gave a bow worthy of obeisance to a minor prince. "It has been our pleasure, milord. Glad we satisfied. What about...?"

Beau flashed him a quick grin. "Our apprentice groom? Put him under Hawkins' wing as soon as possible and reinforce the sad fact that his mother may not know until we tell her. Oh, and is the messenger still downstairs?"

"He is. Said as how he was to return an answer."

Beau nodded. "Then feed him up and I'll have something for him to take back as soon as may be. Please close the door on the way out."

Billings had no more than shut the door before Beau turned concerned eyes on Pip. "Are you all right?"

Pip lifted up on her toes and dropped a kiss on his mouth. "Is it too trite to say I feel like a new woman?"

It might not have been trite, but it definitely crossed the line of intimate, certainly in the daylight hours. Beau did her the service of returning her kiss and then moved to put the desk between them, leaving Pip to feel as if he had run as far as he could from what they had shared. It was all she could do not to chase after him, just like she'd always done.

"If the message isn't from your friend," she said instead, "who is it from?"

"Drake," he said, pulling out paper and pen. "I am needed in London immediately."

She frowned. "I thought you said Delamere."

He didn't look up. "I am going to London. You are going to Delamere. I will leave immediately on horseback as if I am responding to an emergency at the estate, but I will be going on. You will support the fiction that we were needed at Delamere by proceeding to the estate in the carriage with your woman and Sullins."

Pip sank into the armchair across from the desk. "Does it have to be Delamere? Couldn't there be an emergency in, say, Bath? Paris? The Antipodes?"

Beau didn't stop scratching his message. "The excuse must be believable. We cannot give away the fact that we know anything. Drake has decoded our message. The guns are meant for riots that are to be blamed on luddites and protests against the corn laws, but are organized for the sole purpose of destabilizing the government."

"You're certain it isn't because I convinced you to be intimate last night?"

Beau looked up and she could see the distress in his eyes. After what they had shared she couldn't bear it. So, she focused on the business at hand.

"And the assassinations?" she asked.

Beau dropped his attention to whatever he was writing. "Will happen, I imagine while the population is being distracted by the civil unrest."

"And will be blamed on that as well?"

Beau briefly looked up. "Smart girl. We need to vacate as quickly as possible so the guns can be moved, and Nate's people find out where exactly. We still don't know."

Pip got to her feet. "I shall let Joyful and Sullins know to prepare our things. I will also need to bid farewell to the duchess. Do I also say goodbye to your aunt and uncle, or are they hopefully already gone if we are to support this fiction?"

Beau looked up, looking disconcerted. "If you see them tell them instead that it is your grandmother's property across the road that has the crisis. A fire in the house, perhaps. Which is why you must stay at Delamere."

She took a moment to look out onto the fields that swept away up towards the hall. "Will Robbie be safe in the stables? For that matter, will Hawkins? I hope to take Macha with me."

"Once we get away they can both go up to the hall." He looked up, thinking. "As a matter of act, why not tuck the boy in the carriage when it comes and drop him off when you see the duchess. One stable is as good as the other."

Pip climbed to her feet. "Are you sure it has to be Delamere?"

Pip met with an implacable gaze. "I don't want you in London, Pip. There will be nothing there for you to do."

"I could visit my father."

"He is undoubtedly busy with government affairs. You can see him when this is finished."

She wished she could rail at Beau for his assessment, but she couldn't. He was right. If her father was there on government business, the last person he would be anxious to see would be her. Even so, she thought dourly as she turned to leave, it was a good thing she hadn't promised Beau to obey. Because she suspected she wasn't about to. Again.

She had her hand on the door handle when she heard Beau stand. "Pip."

Why did she keep hoping? She turned, ready for at least a word of affection. "Yes?"

"Leave the gun here. Someone might have need of it."

"I'm not allowed to defend myself on the post road?"

"You'll have a guard up with the driver."

For a long moment she just stood there, waiting. What for, she wasn't certain. Maybe a promise, a smile, a reminder of what they had shared no more than five hours ago. But he simply stood there.

"We don't have any time, Pip," was all he finally said.

So, she left.

IF SHE HAD STAYED, she might have seen Beau's control break and his eyes close in pain. He couldn't do this. Especially now, after he had cradled her against him, after she had not simply been trusting but open and generous. When she had shared her lovely body with a selflessness that humbled him. His own body still hummed in satisfaction from not only their lovemaking, but their silence, wrapped in each other's arms in the darkness. His cock stirred again, quite without his permission at the mere thought.

Why did he have to sacrifice so much? Why couldn't he simply give in to inevitability and spend the next sixty years or so making sure Pip was a smiling, satisfied woman with babes in her arms? Would Theo never leave him alone? Would the grief and guilt ever ease enough to feel as if the both of them deserved everything they wanted?

He didn't have time for this, he told himself, sitting back down and returning to his note to Drake. Pip had known what she was asking for last night. She knew the cost as well as he. There should be nothing to think about but preventing the unfolding treason they had stumbled over.

Even so, it took him precious long moments before he could resume his writing.

THERE WERE times Pip wished the duchess's staff weren't quite so efficient and kind. She didn't want to leave her and Beau's little sanctuary, no matter who was lurking in the cellar. She didn't want to leave the duchess or Lizzie, who felt rather like her last lifelines in a world gone stark raving mad. She didn't want to leave Beau, although, to be specific, he left her standing out in the drive, his Ares restlessly pulling at the reins as Beau said a final goodbye before jumping on.

"I need your promise, Pip," he said, his head bent over hers as if this were a private moment. "You'll go straight to Delamere."

She couldn't look away from him, his eyes soft as earth in the early morning light. She couldn't move, even though the wind was brisk and clouds steel gray. She so wanted to tousle his hair, to pull him just a bit off balance to remind him that it was her decision to let him go, even though she didn't want him to. She wanted to wrap her arms around him and lay her head against his chest, as if that would be enough to keep her fresh in his memory.

Instead, she reached up to stroke Ares's nose. She smiled for Beau, grateful she had used up her tears where he wouldn't see them. "Of course, I shall go straight to Delamere," she said. "Since you asked so sweetly."

Beau huffed with impatience. "Pip. This is vital."

"Beau," she retorted, still smiling. "I believe I figured that out all on my own. Now go. I have carriages to pack and duchesses to part from."

"You'll give her my notes?"

No, she thought sourly. *I shall have them for breakfast with my toast and tea.*

"Exactly how many times," she asked, "must I remind you that I am no longer twelve? I have lived out in the world, Beau. I have survived my time in foreign countries as the daughter of a high-level diplomat. I understand urgent matters. Now go before I must wallop you with those selfsame notes for under-estimating me yet again."

Finally, that smile came out, the one that had felled Pip for the first time when she was six. Whimsical, self-deprecating, conspiratorial. "I am being a bit top-lofty, aren't I?"

So, she smiled back, a real one. "I'm glad you can admit it. Now be off. Your poor Ares is frantic to be moving."

"And you're frantic to be rid of me?"

Her smile faltered, even knowing that he was trying to leave on a light note. "Frantic for my goodbye kiss, maybe."

She hadn't really expected her plea to work. He had been so brittle this morning, as if he were even more anxious than Ares to be gone from her. Even so, she held her breath, held his gaze, held perfectly still. And bless him and all the angels, he reached for her and gathered her to him, wrapping her like a precious gift in his arms. She didn't even realize he'd dropped Ares's reins. She was too intent on his face lowering to hers, on the scent of him, horse and leather and something citrus. And Beau. The scent she could identify in a downpour, in a snow-fall, after years apart.

She was too overwhelmed by his kiss, gentle at first, quick dips across her lips. Deepening, darkening, developing like a symphony, his mouth soft, his cheek and chin smooth, his breath warm in the chilly morning. She opened to him before he even asked, and he entered. He met her, tongue and teeth and lips, plundering the soft recesses of her mouth as if collecting a memory to carry with him. For just a moment she lost herself. For just a moment, she let herself hope when she knew better. Too soon he pulled back, dropped a quick kiss on the tip of her nose, and grinned.

"Behave yourself now."

Which was when they realized he had dropped the reins. Ares had made it to the side of the house where Hawkins held him, his own face directed to the dormant bushes.

"Thank you, Hawkins," Beau said, stepping away completely without Pip's permission. "I think I can safely take possession again."

And so, still tingling, her heart racing and her throat tight with more tears, she was left there in front of the little Dower House as Beau rode off without so much as a look back. And blast it if she didn't suddenly suspect he did so to make sure Pip was left with no illusions. And no desire to follow him.

She would go to Delamere. And then she would decide what she would do next, Beau or not.

"You can retrieve the coach now, Hawkins," she said, wrapping her arms around herself against the cold that seemed suddenly so much sharper. "It is time I parted from the duchess."

Hawkins was the one who told her that Beau's aunt and uncle had set off as he was retrieving her coach. *Oh, excellent,* Pip thought, making sure Macha was safely tied to the back of the coach. *I'm quite certain we shall all be quite convivial.*

Even so, she let Hawkins help her into the crested coach the duchess had lent them drawn by four of her prettiest bays. Joyful and Sullins sat across from her, the luggage was strapped to the top, and Robbie was tucked on the floor, grinning with the adventure of it all.

"You promise her gracefulness will tell my ma as soon as can be," he begged Pip.

"I promise."

"I don' suppose we could camp at your grandma's instead," Joyful asked very quietly. "Mr. Beau's people don' like people of my color and have never made no bones about it."

Pip straightened, outraged on Joyful's behalf. "They have said so?"

Joyful gave her a look as if she were as credulous as a child. "Now, Miss Pip. You know they'd never talk to me except for, "move aside" and "why are you here?" while checking out the room to make sure nothin's missin'."

"Well," Pip retorted with steely determination, "since I now outrank them both, and since you are my personal servant and beholden only to me, I would say that if it comes to that, I would be more than happy to show them exactly where my priorities lie. And since Beau has decided he would rather be in London, I would say that gives me the complete authority, wouldn't you?"

She might be feeling a little better. Especially when Joyful grinned.

That lasted until they reached the hall to find the duchess waiting for her out on the shell drive. Pip immediately wanted to cry. She wanted to lay her head on the duchess's shoulder and tell her all the travails of the day.

"Off leader's not walkin' right," coachie suddenly announced as Pip was being handed down. "Need to take 'em to the stables."

The duchess looked surprised. Reaching the drive, her hand in Billings', Pip just smiled. "We do have a way to travel today. Please make sure all is well."

And Robbie is tucked away in the stables with Hawkins and Clancy to watch over him.

"Well then," the duchess said, her arms wide, "That gives us some time for tea before you go. I am sorry to have missed Drummond."

"He was too, ma'am," Pip said, winding her arm around the duchess's and turning for the front door. "He asked me to pass his thanks along with mine for your generosity, and especially the staff you sent to help us. They have been wonderful."

And resourceful, she almost added.

Pip and the duchess had a lovely tea, joined by Lizzie and her two younger sisters, saying nothing at all to the point about the goings-on at the Dower House. Maybe someday Pip would be able to share the absurdity of a seventy-year-old widow becoming the local contact for smugglers. Maybe someday she would be able to tell the story of what had happened in that Dower House this week. It would make a cracking good story.

She had just shared her hope of being able to accept the duchess's invitation for Christmas when Billings stepped into the room. "Excuse me, Your Grace. Lady Drummond's coach is ready."

"Thank you, Billings," Pip said, climbing to her feet.

One did not hug duchesses. Pip did hug this one and was hugged back.

"I will miss you all," she said, wrapped in those gentle arms.

"Nonsense," the duchess said with a pat on the head. "You'll be back for the holidays and steal your room back from Margaret." Wrapping her arm around Pip's shoulder, she guided her toward the front hall. "And don't worry about our little friend," she murmured for Pip's ears alone. "Billings filled me in. He shall be quite fine."

"Thank you." Pip smiled. "Did *you* know about Aunt Eleanor's...er, research activities?"

The duchess's smile was delighted. "How do you think she wrote those wonderful gothic romances about smugglers?"

Pip laughed. "That is what I thought."

Reaching the front portico, Pip stepped back and gave the duchess one last kiss on her cheek. "You have been so good to me," she said, her voice perilously close to breaking.

The duchess cupped her cheek. "It was an easy thing to do, Pip. Now step into your new life."

Pip almost told her. She *almost* confessed the devil's bargain she had made. But in the end, that was between Beau and her, no one else. So, with one more hug for the duchess, Lizzie, and the girls, she climbed up into the coach to leave the closest thing she had ever had to a home. The duchess was right, though. It was time to step into her new world.

She just wished her new world didn't have to begin at Delamere.

15

It didn't occur to Pip until they were halfway to Delamere that Beau had never told her exactly what to tell his Aunt and Uncle Drummond. Perhaps she was being overly suspicious, but she wasn't sure she trusted the couple who had come into Delamere and replaced the comfortable décor Beau's parents and grandparents had preferred, plump jade green couches and chairs little boys could curl up in, long galleries made for footraces, libraries for reading rather than ostentation. Instead, the last time Pip had been inside, it had been to find gilt lion's feet on the table legs, Pharoahs on the wallpaper, and sterile square gilt and velvet furniture set at such a distance that one could barely hear the other people in the room much less easily converse with them. Sterile and uncomfortable, all of it.

Delamere had always seemed to her to have a friendly face, with soft golden stone and rows of windows and gables and chimneys arranged in no particular order. Hallways lifted and fell with the additions of from various generations, and the nursery had been blessed with the kind of windows from which you could see the world. Well-worn rugs on hardwood floors,

children's art on the walls alongside masters like Canaletto and
Reynolds, banisters worn by little boys sliding down them.

The children's art was gone now along with the fat pillows
on the sofas and the comfort of footstools. But Beau's aunt and
uncle remained. Once this business with assassins was done
with, Pip decided, she would do what a gentleman like Beau
wouldn't. She would see the Drummonds to the door and their
furniture with them. And then she would hunt the attics for the
old sofas.

At least she would gain that from marrying Beau, even if he
never talked to her again. Delamere itself. The coach turned
into the Delamere drive just as the setting sun lit rows of
mullioned windows with scarlet and gold. She could reclaim
Beau's home for him. She would make an actual home for
herself.

"I always forget how pretty this place is," Joyful said,
looking out the coach window. "Much nicer than your
grandma's."

Her grandmother's estate had come down her mother's line,
a square, precise, grim-natured kind of place her grandmother
had survived rather than enjoyed. It had been the land she had
loved, not the house that crouched on it. Pip felt the same way.

"It will be even prettier when we get through with it," Pip
promised.

Sullins, Beau's valet, didn't say anything, only nodded.

Pip knew that Beau's aunt and uncle couldn't have reached
Delamere much before she did, but when the coach pulled up
to the front, there was no one to meet it. Billings, who had
insisted on accompanying them as guard, let the steps down
and assisted Pip out. The house and grounds looked tidy. But
something felt wrong. Soulless, perhaps. Empty, even with the
precisely sculpted evergreens that marched across the front
façade like riflemen keeping watch at the windows.

She would change that, too, she decided, shaking the wrinkles from her emerald circassian travelling suit. She would introduce a bit of whimsy, some disorder and surprise and color to exorcise the control of the couple who had tried to strip Beau of his joy and Theo of his dreams.

"Should I knock?" Billings asked, helping Joyful down.

"You should not," Pip declared and climbed the few stairs to the great carved wooden door that had been there since Elizabeth had stopped by for a visit.

Without announcing her arrival, Pip pushed the door open onto the entryway and looked around. At least Aunt Maude hadn't been able to rid the entryway of its black and white marble floor or the warm wood paneling and great staircase that swept up from the left of the entryway. Pip wrinkled her nose at the Egyptian entry table holding something that looked like a gold cat statue and the chair against the wall that had lion heads on the arms.

"That's awful," Joyful whispered behind her.

"Awful is a good word for it."

She was about to head off in search of staff when a very starchy young man with ruthlessly groomed blond hair and precise black and white attire stepped into the entry and faced her, one eyebrow raised. Pip waited for him to speak.

"May I help you?" he finally asked, sounding affronted.

"Where is Gibbs?" she asked of Beau's old butler.

"Why should you want to know?"

She raised her own eyebrow. Suddenly her elevation in rank became real to her. "Because I am the new Lady Drummond, and the staff is now my concern. Do you have questions?"

She almost felt sorry for the young man, who visibly paled as he dropped a belated bow. "My lady, we had no notice of your arrival. Gibbs is pensioned, milady. I am Foster." He waved an arm toward the interior. "Please, please come in. May I tell Mr. and Mrs. Drummond you are here?"

Pip untied her bonnet and pulled it off. "No need. Just tell me where they are."

"The dining room, ma'am. Should...should I ask chef to add another setting?"

She was hungry, but she was in no mood to make small talk with those two. So, she smiled at him.

"No, no. Do not discommode the chef. If I could have a tray in my room. Cold meats and cheese would suffice if necessary. If you would show my lady's maid Joyful the way, I will go see my new relatives."

He obviously hadn't noticed Joyful before the introduction. His hands out to receive Pip's bonnet and cloak, he almost let them fall to the floor. His eyes grew impossibly big and his mouth dropped. Pip ignored him.

"And you can show Lord Drummond's man Sullins to his room, please. My husband does not join me on this trip."

He blinked. "Er, milady...uh, which room would be yours, exactly?"

That stopped her cold in her tracks. "I assume the viscount sleeps in the master suite?"

The young man couldn't seem to look at her. "Um, not exactly."

"Then exactly where does he sleep?"

"His old room, ma'am. He never, uh, moved."

He had been viscount since his twelfth birthday. Pip was becoming glad she had made the trek. "Indeed. The master suite is empty then?"

He made a little chuffing noise, as if the words were caught in his throat. "Um, no, milady. Not exactly."

She straightened, nodded to herself. "Well, then. I will use the viscount's room tonight, Foster. Tomorrow after I consult with my husband's relatives and the housekeeper, we will begin preparing the master suite for the viscount's return. Please apprise the staff. I would appreciate a meeting in the morning with you and the housekeeper so we can evaluate needs, and then I will travel up to London for whatever I need to redecorate. I'm certain we can get a few local men in to work on it. As for now, I will speak to the Drummonds."

Foster clutched her cloak to his chest, his hands trembling just a bit. "I'll, uh, have someone air out your room, milady."

With a nod of her head as if she were Princess Charlotte on tour, Pip stepped past the trembling butler and wound her way back to where the dining room was.

Pip could not imagine anyone looking so much like they were not enjoying food. From the smells coming from the chafing dishes, it seemed to be some lovely fowl and beef, and the wine glasses were half full, with one of the footmen standing against the wall waiting to refill. And yet Uncle Edward and Aunt Maude looked as if their dinner were a punishment instead of nourishment.

Their expressions grew immediately dourer when they noticed her in the doorway.

"What are you doing here?" Uncle Edward demanded, jumping to his feet.

Oh, Pip thought, she was going to have some fun. Taking a quick look around, she lifted that selfsame eyebrow. "I live here. Foster is preparing Beau's room for me for tonight. I will be touring the house tomorrow to get an idea for Beau of what needs to be done before he joins me here. I will need some time with both of you, if you don't mind. And then I imagine I will spend a few days in London to do a bit of shopping for wallpaper and the like." She smiled. "I'm certain I might want to redecorate the master suite."

Pip wasn't certain which of them was more outraged. Aunt Maude turned the darkest red, but Pip thought Uncle Edward actually made a gobbling noise.

"What happened to your wedding trip?" Aunt Maude asked, her voice acid.

Pip smiled. "Beau had an emergency in London. Some kind of diplomatic crisis, I believe. I wanted to touch base here before I joined him. I can't tell you how grateful I am that Beau and I will be sharing our lives here at Delamere. It has always been a special place to me."

There was really nothing they could say to that.

"I shall leave you to your dinner," Pip said with another bright smile. "I'll be taking a tray in my room for tonight. It was a long journey, as I'm sure you well know. May we talk tomorrow about our schedule for transition? After all the time you have sacrificed for Beau and Theo, I know you're anxious to return home yourselves."

"How dare you bring up Theo?" Aunt Maude demanded, climbing to her feet. "If it weren't for you---"

But before she could finish that sentence, Uncle Edward stayed her with an upraised hand.

"Why should we simply take your word that this is what Beau wants?" he asked Pip.

"Because, as I just said to Foster, I am now Lady Drummond." She let her smile widen in delight, as if she really were glad the next sentence was true. "Which you know more than anyone. You were there. And thank you for that, too, by the way. I'm so glad Beau had family with him."

Beau's uncle said nothing. Pip suspected she knew exactly how delighted they were to see her. They now knew that she expected to take charge. Nodding her head, Pip turned for the door, amazed at the courage it took to turn her back on those two.

"Fortune hunter," Aunt Maude growled.

That made Pip laugh. She turned, now really smiling. "I know how uncomfortable it must be that my inheritance from my grandmother is twice the size of Delamere," she said, then shook her head. "I would never consider Beau a fortune hunter, though. That would be such a mean accusation, wouldn't it?"

And finally, she left.

Pip was not looking forward to the various confrontations she was expecting the next day. At least, though, tonight she could salve a bit of curiosity about Beau's room. It was the first time she had ever crossed the threshold.

She suspected the room hadn't been painted since his mother had decorated. The walls were a hunter green, the curtains and covers cream, the walls hung with a few horse portraits and the plain oak desk cluttered with paperwork and journals. He still had his collection of books on the shelves, everything from the Iliad to Robinson Crusoe to treatises by Townshend and Coke on farming, which made her smile. An old cricket bat leaned against the wall alongside fishing rods and a faded globe, and the clothes press held a range of brightly embroidered vests she remembered with great fondness.

The only real color in the room besides those vests was, amazingly, the pillow covered with rather lopsided peacocks and daisies she had embroidered for Theo when she was seven which now rested on Beau's bed. Walking over, she picked it up and held it to her, as if it carried its memories with it.

She could smell Beau's special scent in the room, which was more comforting than the featherbed she climbed into a few hours later. She took a peek through the small telescope he had trained up to the heavens through his window and picked out Orion in the eastern sky, a constellation her friend Fiona Ferguson had taught her to love. She went to sleep on the pillow he used clutching Theo's pillow and woke to the sun streaming through the windows he looked out. And she missed him all the more.

He had better forgive her for what she was about to do. Not the redecoration. One of the benefits of knowing Beau all these years was also being familiar with his taste. And the very last thing he would want in his house were Egyptian cats and snakes.

But she knew that the redecoration was just an excuse to see him in London. To have his back as he waded into this treasonous plot with the Rakes. Ever since she had seen that shadow in the basement she had had the worst itch between her shoulder blades that Beau's investigation was a lot more complicated than he thought. Worse, she had the most irrational suspicion that if she weren't there to keep him grounded, he would make this mission all about the fact that he hadn't been able to protect Theo.

He needed her up there in London. He just didn't know it yet. And she didn't know why.

Quite amazing what one imagined when the man she loved beyond reason or sense was out of one's sight.

When she woke to have Joyful tell her that the maids were moving the Drummonds to different rooms, she knew it was time to go. She had what she wanted. There was no good reason to rub their noses in it.

She wished they would leave, but she suspected they would hang on until they laid eyes on Beau. At least, though, she was reclaiming his place in his own home.

"I have a tour to take," she told Joyful as she stood from her toilette. "I suspect I will have nightmares from the master suite. After that we will be moving along to London."

"Mr. Beau isn't gonna like it," Joyful warned.

"I would be very surprised if you don't feel the same suspicion I do, Joyful," Pip said. "We need to be there."

Joyful gave a lugubrious sigh. "We do. I'll get ready. Billings said as how the duchess asked him to stay with us for the time bein'. I'll tell him to find a coach, since he already sent back the duchess's. Do we know where we're stayin'?"

Pip paused, letting the early morning sunlight warm her face and the sweeping lawns outside calm her spirit.

"Why, I'm not certain," she admitted. "I know Beau has a house on Charles Street. I imagine if Papa is in town, he'll resort to his club. He so hates making a fuss." Even so, she gave a bright smile that challenged failure. "I have certainly removed dust covers from more than one habitation in my life, Joyful. I say we sneak into our house on Bruton to see what the word is on father."

Joyful didn't look up from the clothing she was repacking into Pip's portmanteau. "Coward."

Pip's smile just broadened. "Yes, indeed. News will get to Beau soon enough. Then I can remove the dust covers in *his* house."

Before that, though, she had to face the challenge of the master suite. Slipping into an oversized apron she'd borrowed from a housemaid, she slipped paper and pencil into the pocket and straightened to take a purposeful breath.

"All right, my friend. Let us wreak some havoc."

BEAU HADN'T REALLY NEEDED to ride his Ares up to town. The note Drake had sent had set a time for a meeting a couple of days hence. He could have dropped Pip off at Delamere up on the Salisbury plain and then continued on alone. It would probably have been more sensible, since now he was without Sullins. But he had no illusions about how well he would do closed into such tight proximity with his wife. He needed these days to clear his head. He needed to be alone again where he couldn't smell her scent or hear the music of her laughter. Where he couldn't imagine her without all those clothes.

He wished he could say he was successful. But by the time he walked into Whites, the known haunt of Drake's Rakes, he was irritable and short-tempered. Drake had better have had a good reason for the summons.

Of course, Drake had a good reason for the summons. Beau just hoped it was definite news. He needed occupation. He needed something to focus on. So he assumed his personae of the man about town and sauntered through the door as if he had nothing more on his mind than a congenial card game.

Nodding to the perennials in the bow window who always joined Alvanley, he wandered on to the card room where the Rakes usually gathered, using desultory play to cover more serious conversations. The message Drake had sent had set a time of one in the afternoon to meet. The room, however, was empty.

Beau looked around as if he'd find them hiding. Well, this was odd. As he stood there, one of the waiters came up for his order.

"Have you seen any of my usual compatriots?" Beau asked.

"Sorry, milord. Would you like some food?"

Beau felt distinctly uneasy. "Brandy, I think. I'll wait for food until Drake gets here."

Beau accepted his drink and wandered over to the betting book, just for something to do. It was obvious that word of his marriage had preceded him. There were already bets on how long he'd remained married, how long before he set up a mistress, and how long before Pip did him an injury. Pip's name wasn't used, of course. Just *a petite blonde elfin figure.* For a moment Beau was tempted to put in his own bet. How long before Pip did injury to the person who had labeled her thus if she ever found out about it. He almost couldn't wait to find out.

"Well, my lad, so you've returned from the hinterlands."

Beau whipped around to see Kit Braxton approach. Tall, trim, tidy in a post-military way, Kit had a smile for him and his left hand outstretched. His right hand was missing, his empty sleeve tucked up to his shoulder. Beau gladly took his hand.

"A little thin of company today."

Kit nodded. "My thoughts exactly. Drake said he would meet me here, but I've been cooling my heels with some recent Cambridge graduates." Shaking his head, he grinned. "Is it me, or does every one of them seem like an unlicked cub?"

Beau matched his smile. "We do have mileage on us, old son. Share some brandy?"

"An excellent idea. And you can tell me all about that house party you were at....oh, yes. And the marriage you got yourself mixed up in. Some would say it's a bit soon to be escaping to the club."

"Pip had to go to Delamere, so I'm holing up here for a bit. You haven't seen anybody? Knight? Hilliard? Chuffy?"

"Just got in from the hinterlands myself."

They had just dealt the cards for whist, half-filled glasses of brandy at their elbows, when the note came, and they were forced to leave everything behind.

To Pip's surprise, when she reached her family's London house at mid-afternoon it was to find that she wouldn't have to remove dust covers after all. The house was staffed, clean and, evidently, occupied.

"Miss Pip," the butler greeted her with a solemn face and a bow. But then, for Soames that was his expression of delight.

Pip untied her bonnet. "I did not expect you here, Soames. I was all prepared to set the house to rights so I could hide here for a few days."

"Your father and brother just arrived back, miss, although they are out for the moment." He accepted her outerwear and gave Joyful her own nod before turning back to Pip. "Your father looks that much better."

Pip stopped in place. "Better? Better how, Soames?"

His face went very still. Pip felt her stomach drop.

"Better how?" she repeated.

He took a breath. "Sweet would know more about it, miss. Should I get him?"

"Not until you answer my question. Better how? And where is he right now?"

The poor man looked like he wanted to dig a hole in the oak flooring and climb in.

"Miss..."

She just stood there.

"His heart, miss. He had an episode, which is why he came home from St. Petersburg

without her ladyship. Although she just got here as well." Which seemed to distress him most of all. "That will be a reunion I'd like to see for sure."

Pip looked around. "My mother is here?"

"Not *here* precisely, miss."

Pip couldn't remember the last time she had lost patience with Soames. He was a very proper butler, but one who always anticipated every need and eased every way. Except now.

His brow was furrowed like a potato patch. "Would you like some tea, maybe, miss?"

"I am not in the mood for guessing games, Soames," she said, hands on hips. "Which is why I am convinced you're about to tell me exactly where my parents are, and what the story is about my father's heart. I am not budging until you do."

He looked around, obviously hating to have this conversation in the entryway. "Maybe they would like to tell you, miss. I can tell you where they both are."

"That," Pip said with immense patience, "would be lovely. And just to keep all the information straight, Soames. I am no longer a miss. I am a ladyship. Lady Drummond to be precise."

Smiling, she held up her left hand to show him her ring. He

gaped. There had been a lot of that around her lately. "Our heartiest congratulations, mi...er, milady."

"And where can milady find her parents, Soames?"

"At Lord Drake's, milady."

Ah. Rake business. "My mother as well?" she asked. When he nodded, so did she. "I need a carriage, Soames," she said and reached for the hat she had just handed to him. "Joyful, are you coming along?"

"Wouldn't miss this f'r all the cotton in Georgia."

16

Pip's reunion with her family was chaotic to say the least. She had never been to Lord Drake's house on Brook Street but found it to be mostly a dignified and unspectacular townhouse, its façade white, its un-porticoed door topped with a fanlight, its steps fronted by a black wrought iron fence that matched the flower boxes on the windows across three bays. Perfectly respectful, nothing to take note of.

Which was an ingenious place to hide one of the most devious minds in Britain. It made Pip smile. Well, until she was greeted by the ever-so-proper butler who would have exactly matched the house's façade if not for the unusual cant to his nose and the disfiguration of his left ear. An ex-boxer, Pip would guess. Handy for discouraging the wrong kind of people from bothering a busy earl.

Pip was surprised when he took a good look at her and Joyful and then broke into a delighted smile. "I believe I must be addressing Lady Drummond," the butler said with a formal bow. "Please come in. May I offer our congratulations."

"Why, thank you. My parents are here?" she asked, stepping

into a perfectly sensible entryway decorated in Wedgewood and Chippendale chairs. Not a lion paw in sight, or even a ceiling muraled with frisky cupids. There was, however, a pile of her mother's luggage tucked over in the corner.

"They are," Wilkins said with a bit of a sigh, closing the door. "Along with your brother and his fiancé, her sister and *her* fiancé, Lord Hawes and *his* fiancé, and several young persons I have not yet identified. We have not seen such a to-do since the Prince Regent held a card party here."

Pip was caught on mention of her brother. "Alex?" she asked, then catching up with the rest of that clause. "*Fiancé?*"

He gave a slight grimace. "It has been a rather busy morning."

"I would imagine so. I would settle for my parents for the present, please...er..."

He gave a little bow. "Wilkins, milady."

Joyful was sent off to the kitchens with one of the footmen as Wilkins guided Pip into a salon where, surely enough, her father and mother were sitting over a pot of tea in a lovely eggshell and pale green room as if they were having a normal morning call. Except that Pip could see that her father's color was not good, and her mother had that preternaturally calm look she got when worrying over her husband. Pip was glad she had been forewarned about his new heart issue or she might have made their greeting uncomfortable. As it was her own heart seemed to shrink at this evidence of her papa's mortality.

Lord Drake was nowhere in sight.

"Lady Drummond," Wilkins announced behind her.

Both parents turned to her, offering matching smiles. Her mother even got to her feet, which put her at exactly the same height as Pip, although her mother had a pleasing matronly plumpness, mousy brown hair and soft brown eyes. Pip wanted to throw herself into her parents' arms. It had been months since she had seen them. Instead, like a proper young woman, she waited for her parents to make the move.

"What are you doing here?" her mother demanded, wrapping her in a hug.

Pip comforted herself with a whiff of her mother's neroli scent. It always made her feel safe. Especially reassuring after a greeting like that. "I was told you would be here. I went to the house first thinking I would be removing dust covers."

Her mother pulled back, bemused. "But we were told you had finally married Drummond. And without us, I might add. I want to know what that was all about, young lady. I thought I taught you better than to trap a good man into marriage or I never would have left you behind."

Don't be silly, Pip wanted to say. *You never once considered it.*

"I didn't...." She sighed. "It's a long story. But yes, mother. I did marry him. Now, can I stay with you, please?"

"Are dust covers on in his house?"

"I have no idea. I have not been there. I came to see Papa first. Hullo, Papa."

His smile was brighter than the weary sag to his face. "Hullo, mouse. Why didn't you wait for me to walk you down the aisle?"

He actually looked hurt, which made her feel even worse. "That is a long story as well, which I hope we can save until we're back home."

"Not your home anymore," her mother reminded her, pulling her over to take a seat on the cream settee alongside her. "Tea?"

"Yes, thank you. My home temporarily, if you will."

"Why?" her father demanded. "Where is your husband?"

Pip shrugged and let her mother pour for her, just as when she was a child. "I have no idea. I was rather hoping that, since so many people seem to have congregated here, he would be, too." She looked around, ignoring the concerned look her parents shared. "May I ask why you two are here?"

"In London?" her mother retorted. "Your father had dispatches to bring."

No one mentioned the fact that her mother had obviously taken a different ship.

"I hear you are looking better, Papa. The old trouble again?"

His smile was rueful. "An annoyance. A friend of your brother set me to rights. Foxglove, of all things."

Pip stared. "Foxglove? But that's a poison!"

Her father lifted a finger. "In big enough doses, yes. But I have learned that a strictly controlled amount actually makes the heart stronger. I feel immeasurably better." His smile fell into the kind of frown a father sends his daughter who has disappointed him. "Well enough, in fact, to have walked you down the aisle."

She lifted her own hands in surrender. "If I had known you were on your way here, I would have waited...well, no. I wouldn't. We had Princess Charlotte breathing down our necks, and she wasn't about to wait."

That resulted in raised eyebrows from both of her parents.

"A long story indeed," her mother mused. "Fortunately, we will soon have time."

"Speaking of which," Pip said, motioning to the house. "What are you doing *here?*"

"Your brother, of course," her father said, as if that should explain everything. "And Drake asked us to stay in case he couldn't track down Drummond in time."

She blinked, certain she was missing at least half that conversation, which was often how one felt with her parents. "Whatever for? And in time for what?"

She got a pair of shrugs. So, she tried a different tack. "Alex is here?" she asked. "And engaged? That was mighty quick since he was at the duchess's house party only a few days ago."

Her mother passed over the tea, two sugars, no cream. "No faster than yours, from what I hear. He is to marry a friend of yours from school."

Pip paused, the cup halfway to her mouth. "Who?"

"Lady Fiona Hawes."

The teacup ended up back on her saucer, untasted. "Fiona?! St Paula's pockets, how did that happen? Where are they? I need to see this for myself."

"Asked for a moment of privacy," she heard behind her and turned to see another of her brother's old friends, Chuffy Wilde, standing in the doorway, his hand in Fiona's...no, not Fiona's. Fiona's twin sister Mairead, who was smiling and for one of the first times Pip had ever seen it, leaning against another person, her exquisite features soft and happy. Pip couldn't ever remember Mairead looking so comfortable standing this close to another human. And plump, whimsical, bespectacled Chuffy, of all people. It was like a Scottish queen running off with a stuffed toy bear.

Pip was back on her feet. "Chuffy! Mae!" She looked down at the joined hands. "Not you, too."

Chuffy absolutely beamed as he let go of Mae long enough to give Pip a hug. "Us, too. Congrats! Hear you nabbed Drummond. Won me a monkey at White's. Where is he?"

She was getting tired of repeating herself. "I have no idea. I was hoping you all would know."

"A little soon to lose a brand-new husband, what?" Chuffy said with a grin. "Need to find him. Might cost me my monkey if he shabs off."

"Might cost him more than that," Pip assured him, dryly.

His grin widening, Chuffy shook his head, which sent his wire rim glasses sliding down his nose. Without hesitation, Mae reached over and pushed them back up, another thing Pip never would have imagined.

"Wish somebody would do that for me," she said with a grin.

Mae beamed and patted Chuffy on the arm like a cherished child. "I am watching over him now. He and I broke the code."

"One of the codes," Chuffy clarified.

Pip chuckled. "Of course, you did."

Which was when it finally sank in that Mairead, notorious for her glorious head of waist-length gold-red hair was suddenly a cropped brunette. "Mae? Where is your hair?"

Pip actually saw tears well where she had never seen them before, even when their school had separated her from her beloved twin. Even more astonishing, Chuffy immediately whipped out a handkerchief and dabbed at her eyes for her.

Pip offered her own wry smile. "*Another* long story?"

Mairead's smile was small. "We were back on the streets."

Well, that was certainly a story she wanted to hear. But Mae didn't look as if she could share yet. Besides, Pip had a mission.

"Where is Drake?" she asked. "Isn't this his party?"

"We all rather descended on him, I'm afraid," her mother said. "Which means we should be returning home soon, I think. And Mairead, I think your hair looks lovely, such as it is. Should we go look for Alex?"

Papa patted her hand. "I think not, my dear. He'll catch up with us."

Pip shook her head. "I can't wait to see them."

"Sarah's here, too," Mae said of another of their classmates. "She is engaged to *our* brother Ian."

Pip shook her head. "I go to one house party and miss everything."

"But you're the only one who got married," Mae accused. "You shouldn't have. Could have gotten married with all of us."

"I can always do it again. It would certainly be more fun than the last time."

"Part of the long story?" her mother asked in dust dry tones.

Pip just shrugged. "We'll have plenty of time to talk about it at home."

"You will not," she heard from the doorway. "You are going back to Delamere."

Pip's stomach plummeted.

"I think we found your husband," Pip's mother murmured.

"Lord Drummond," Wilkins intoned in a very patient voice before backing out of the way. Pip would bet Macha he didn't go far.

"Doesn't look very happy for a newlywed," Mae piped up. "You'd think he would."

Chuffy patted her hand. "I imagine that is a long story as well."

"There are a lot of stories I'm not hearing," she pouted.

"I believe we need to talk, wife," Beau said in one of his forbidding voices.

Pip straightened. "I believe we are, husband. And the first thing I suggest you do is greet your new family."

It took all Pip's nerve to face him standing in the doorway in his best government mien. He might be wearing his official camouflage, but just one look at him and Pip could see him naked again. She could feel the astonishing sensation of him filling her, of him gasping her name as he spent himself, the indescribable joy that suffused her lying beside him.

Her thoughts must have been obvious, because for just a moment his eyes darkened, and he took in a breath. It didn't last long. Pip knew it wouldn't. But at least for that moment he had been hers again.

Dipping his head a bit, he stepped into the room to give his new in-laws a bow. "Sir Charles, good to see you looking better. Lady Knight."

"Looking better?" Pip immediately retorted. "Did you see him here as well?"

Finally, he looked just a bit uncomfortable. "In passing only. Chuffy, good to see you. Got a note that you broke the code."

"With my Mae here," Chuffy said, beaming. "Mae, this is—"

"The missing husband," she said, looking down from her regal height that had not been dimmed a bit by her short, darkened hair.

Beau gave her another bow. "Not missing. Just misplaced. Is Drake here? He sent me a note to come. Looks like he sent everyone else in London the same note."

"Question of the hour," Chuffy said with a huff.

"Tea?" Pip's mother asked, lifting the pot a bit. "We can have a nice coze, Lord Drummond."

Pip almost burst out laughing. "Mama, you have known Beau since he was six. Getting all formal now will not intimidate him."

"Don't be too sure of that," Beau muttered.

More introductions were made, which made Pip's palms itch. Beau had that look on him that presaged rough weather, and she would far rather get through it. In private. She was just about to get to her feet when Wilkins returned leading another guest.

"Mr. Christopher Braxton."

A rail-thin gentleman with blonde hair and a military posture took a step into the room, which was when Pip noticed that his one sleeve was empty.

"Oh," she said with delight. "You're Kit."

He bowed. "Here as well because of a seemingly erroneous note. Drake isn't around?"

Every shoulder rose and fell.

"It hasn't been that long," Chuffy suggested.

"Have some tea," Pip's mother chirped. "Wilkins, another tray if you will."

Furniture was rearranged and a message was received that Sarah Ripton and Ian Ferguson, the twins' brother, were heading over to Hawes House with 'the boys', whoever that was. Pip decided not to ask. Her mother was in her element supervising tea, and everyone talked around her, which gave Pip the space and time to fret. And remember.

"You are not supposed to be here," Beau growled beneath the bright chatter.

Pip sipped at her tea, thinking she would prefer brandy right about now. Or whiskey. "Why not? Everyone else seems to be here...well, except for Drake. And actually, I wasn't here. I went to my parents, but then I found out they were here. What was I to do?"

"Never leave Delamere, as I instructed you."

She shrugged, struggling to convey ease. "I had to come to London. There is so much I need in order to redecorate the master suite, and the village simply does not have the variety I require."

He seemed to freeze. "The Master Suite? But I don't sleep in the Master Suite."

Now she looked at him. She caught his gaze and refused to look away no matter what her own body did. "I know you do not. Which made it extremely difficult to establish myself as the new viscountess when your aunt and uncle had claimed the position of authority. Especially when you weren't there."

"They saw you marry."

"They saw you inherit your title at twelve. It didn't seem to disabuse them of the notion that they were still in charge."

He stared at her as if she'd turned around and bitten him. "What did you do?"

She gave him a bright smile. "I moved them."

He actually sputtered. "What do you mean, you moved them?"

"They have now taken over the Gold Suite, which they can clutter up with all the Egyptian atrocities they want, and I am here to buy paper, paint and a brand new bed for the master suite. Would you prefer your bedroom to be the same green as your last one? For my room I was thinking peach and green so that it would be harmonious."

She held her breath for his answer, although it was the last thing she would allow him to see. Or anyone else, since she could sense the attention they were paying, no matter the conversation. So, she returned to her cup of tea and pretended to sip.

There were tea cakes on the tray, but right now she didn't think she could manage a bite. Come to think of it, she hadn't had very much at all to eat since she'd had Joyful's mulligatawny soup. Too bad she didn't need to lose some weight.

Beau just stood there looking flummoxed. He didn't even comment when a footman appeared with a tea tray followed by Wilkins, his tray bearing a decanter and glasses that he poured for Beau and Kit.

"Thank you, Wilkins," Pip offered with a smile.

Wilkins bowed, his eyes smiling back, and turned for the door. Pip was hoping for some general conversation, but Mae and Chuffy had tucked themselves away in a corner, and her parents were holding hands and smiling at each other, a sure sign that no intruders were invited into their silent communication.

"I would like to speak to you privately," Beau informed her.

She didn't get up. "As soon as we find out what this is all about."

His scowl grew thunderous. "What this is all about has nothing to do with you. It's too late to return to Delamere today, but you can go to Drummond House. Pull off dust covers to your heart's content."

She smiled up at him as if he had offered her more tea. "No, thank you. I have not seen my parents in months, and Mairead even longer. And I am hoping for a chance to see Fiona, her sister. Oh, and Mama, did Cissy come with you?"

Her mother had the oddest half-smile on her face, as if this was all amusing her. "No. I suspected this would not be a discussion for a fourteen-year-old. We dropped her off at Cousin Ruth's house today. Are you certain you don't wish some privacy with your brand-new husband?"

How did she say, *dear heavens no* without sounding churlish. "Well, wife?"

Pip turned her attention to her half-empty teacup. He was spoiling for a fight, wasn't he? She wanted to once again remind him that she had not promised to obey him, but it wasn't something one did before witnesses.

"I would much rather wait until we are home before we rip at each other, if you don't mind."

His answer was to down the brandy as if it were water on the desert and then pick up the decanter Wilkins left to pour some more.

"Oh, good," Pip heard and turned. "Everyone is here. Even a few extras."

Of course, it was Lord Drake. Or, Pip thought, it should be, *finally* it was Lord Drake.

Everyone offered their greetings as he detoured to the brandy decanter and filled his own glass.

"My apologies for not being here earlier," he drawled, "but something has come up. Something rather important."

"Everyone here is allowed to be informed?" Pip's father asked in his quiet, calm way that usually deescalated any situation. Too bad that didn't seem to work with Beau. He didn't even sit down.

Drake looked around and smiled. "You are already involved. Except for Lady Knight. And of course, I trust her discretion. But if you don't mind, I need to speak with Drummond and his new wife alone first. So, if you'll excuse us."

"My wife?" Beau retorted. "Why would you ever need her?"

Standing and shaking out her skirts, Pip sighed. "Why, thank you, Beau. You do know how to make a girl feel special."

Beau scowled. "You know I didn't mean..."

Pip would have felt worse if, on the way past, she didn't intercept a wink from her mother, as if to say that it could be a trial putting up with these bumbling dolts. Yes, she thought, it certainly could.

And then, drink in hand, Drake gave Beau the kind of look bred into centuries of noblemen that let his friend know there would be no dissension, and led them both across the hall into another parlor.

"Ah, we're to be intimidated by all this splendor," Pip offered with a look around to the eighteenth-century art from the likes of Boucher and Watteau that circled the royal blue and gold room. And yes, there it was, the ceiling mural full of cavorting *putti*.

Ah, she thought with an unconscious nod. *So, this is where they keep the excess.* Boucher and Watteau art was awash in sensibility and emotion. Unlike their host.

"They had to put it somewhere," Drake said as if he had heard her. "All those grand tours couldn't go to waste, and the Pater wouldn't stand for it at the Abbey."

Leading the way to a grouping of ornate gilt chairs and settees, he sat himself down, his drink in hand, his legs crossed, as if he were sitting in his club ready to discuss politics. It took one look towards the door for it to silently close. Pip still bet Wilkins could hear somehow. She sat next to Beau on a delicate looking settee.

"We have a conundrum," Drake announced, focusing on the lint he was picking off his knee. "And a very tight deadline."

"Is this about the guns?" Beau asked.

Drake looked up and nodded. "In fact, yes. Clever work there, by the way. It turns out these were rifles stolen from the Royal Arsenal."

"What is north of the arsenal?" Beau asked.

Drake's smile was dry as dust. "North is one of the senior officers. He has been taken into custody."

"Well, that makes more sense," Pip muttered.

"What are the guns doing all the way down in Dorset?" Beau asked.

"Planned disturbances in Portsmouth, Plymouth, and Bristol. At least that is what we believe. We're still following the movement of the shipment, not to mention the persons of interest from the house party who have also moved on. The problem is that we don't know the exact details of the disturbances. Will they be together or separate? Will there be a general signal of some kind? Will it be while an important personage is in the area who might make an excellent hostage or political statement?"

"As in a royal personage?" Beau asked.

"We have several of the princes due to wander about on good will visits."

"And Princess Charlotte?" Pip asked. "Is she back in Weymouth? They wouldn't kidnap her, would they?"

"We doubt it. They need to be in her good graces. After all, she is who they are hoping to put on the throne so they can control her."

Pip couldn't help but laugh. "Have they *met* her?"

"And the conundrum?" Beau asked.

Something about that question notched up the tension in the room. For a long moment Drake was silent. He studied Pip as if she were alien to him.

"Well," he finally said. "It seems that one person knows the details. And that one person is missing."

"Who?" Pip asked.

Drake looked up at her. "Your Miss Schroeder."

Pip found herself blinking. "Miss Schroeder? Missing? She is not at the Academy?"

"Not for a while. In fact, a little while ago she helped someone escape from a place called Richmond Hill Asylum, another woman with vital information. To do that, Miss Schroeder took her place, so the escape went unnoticed."

"Not very observant, are they?" Beau muttered.

Drake continued. "You see, we have found that certain high-ranking husbands who are involved in the plot to overthrow the government...."

"Lions," Pip said.

Drake's eyebrows rose. "Yes. It seems that they needed to keep certain wives somewhere...er, safe, somewhere the women wouldn't be heard from. At least until the plot succeeds. And I am afraid it is far too easy to commit one's wife to a mental institution if she becomes...shall we say, a disturbance."

"Women know that," Pip dryly assured him.

Drake shrugged. "Evidently these wives were not as enthusiastic about the plan as their husbands and threatened to peach on them."

"And Miss Schroeder?"

"Recently let us know that she has been in contact with a woman whose husband is the one coordinating the attacks. But we cannot seem to locate Miss Schroeder. And we're running out of time."

Pip sat up straighter. "You can't just go in and get her?"

Drake shook his head. "We're trying not to give away our game yet."

"No," Beau said, abruptly standing.

Pip looked up at him, but he was focused on Drake, his expression murderous.

"No," he repeated.

Setting down his drink, Drake stood as well.

Pip looked between them and understood. She wasn't quite certain whether she was more horrified or thrilled. "I know what Miss Schroeder looks like. If she is still in there, I can get to her and get the information."

Beau turned on her. "I said no!"

Pip would have been angry at him if she hadn't heard the pain in his voice, the raw terror. But she couldn't let him give in to his fear.

"I don't understand," she said to Drake. "How did you know I would be here? I am supposed to be at Delamere."

Drake gave Beau quite a look. "You were supposed to be here. I especially asked for you."

"Well then," Pip said with quite a look of her own at Beau, "It is a very good thing that I am disobedient. Is that why you wanted my parents here, Drake? In case Beau refused to commit me to this place, my father could?"

"If we decided to go that route."

Finally Pip got to her feet. "Beau. This is too important. It is something I can do." Then she turned back to Lord Drake. "I just need to know the particulars. Especially how I am getting back out, for instance."

He shrugged, his smile rueful. "We're still working on that."

"I. Said. *No!*" Beau all but roared.

Drake didn't look at him right away. Instead, he drew a breath. Only then did he speak. "There is one more piece of information she has we need to get. Badly."

"What?" Beau snapped.

Finally, Drake looked up. "The location of your brother, Theo."

17

Beau swore he heard a roaring in his ears. "That isn't funny, Drake."

"It's not meant to be."

"Theo is dead." Beau dragged the words past the constriction in his throat. "You told me yourself."

Drake didn't so much as look away. "I lied."

Without even thinking, Beau drove a punch into Drake's jaw that sent him crashing over the sofa. Drake ended up sprawled against a curio filled with jade figurines that trembled with the impact. Pip instinctively moved toward Drake and then stopped, looking over at Beau with stricken eyes. But Beau couldn't afford to take his eyes off that perfidious bastard on the floor.

The door opened to reveal Wilkins.

"Out," was all Drake said as he picked himself up, gave his jaw a rub, and straightened out his clothing.

The door closed. Beau didn't take his eyes off his unofficial superior. The roaring hadn't stopped. It was joined by the damnest fire in his chest, a conflagration that threatened to simply turn him to ashes. And yet, he couldn't move. He couldn't even figure out how to talk.

Theo. Sweet God, Theo.

Pip was still standing next to him, her accusing stare on Drake. "You're serious."

Drake walked around the sofa to once again face them. It was all Beau could do to hold himself still, his hands clenched so tightly his knuckles were white.

"Let's sit down," Drake said, softly, as if facing a fractious horse.

Beau glared at him. "Let's not. Let's hear your explanation."

Drake considered him for a moment, then, finally, sighed. "Theo has been working for the home office," he said, and his gaze faltered. "But right now, we don't know where he is."

It was nothing short of a miracle that Beau didn't knock him down again.

Which was when Pip moved, an erratic step forward. "I do," she said.

Beau and Drake both whipped around on her to find her ashen, her hand to her chest as if holding in her heart. Beau knew exactly how she felt.

"What do you mean?" Drake asked her very quietly.

"Yes," Beau said, knowing how deadly he sounded. "What do you mean?"

Pip had never looked so flummoxed. "The boy Robbie, who was released from the cellar," she said. "He had help. A man. I saw him...."

Beau honestly felt capable of murder. "You *saw* him. You saw Theo."

"Well..." she looked back and forth to the men, suddenly frantic. "It looked like him. But I thought, how could it be? We all knew he had been lost in France. We all *knew*."

"What do you mean he was in the cellar?" Drake asked, suddenly very alert. "With the smugglers?!"

Pip shrugged. "It looked like him. I mean, I only saw a shadow, but his...his movements. They made me think of Theo. He told young Robbie his name was...." Her face crumpled into distress, and she turned to Beau. "Oh, sweet God. He told him he was called Barnaby. That was the name of Theo's dog, wasn't it? The mutt he rescued from the lake when we were ten. I didn't think."

Beau swore his heart was going to explode. Rage poured through him, taking his breath. Outrage. Betrayal. After all this time...all this *time*...they were telling him Theo was alive? Had been alive since that horrific day when that bedamned dragoon showed up at his door?

"That's not possible," he whispered, rubbing hard at his own chest, as if he could pull things into order. "It. Is. Not. Possible."

Alongside him, Pip shifted. He was terrified she would touch him, try to comfort or support him. If she did, he very much feared she would let loose the cataclysm that roiled inside of him and she would go sprawling, too.

She didn't. In a disconnected way, Beau was glad. The pressure was building inexorably inside of him, and he didn't want to take it out on her.

"Drake? What do you have to say?"

And Drake, who was igniting this explosion, didn't look particularly agitated. He sighed and motioned to the facing settees. "Sit down."

But Beau shook his head. "No. Explain this."

When he didn't sit, neither did the others, leaving them in an uncomfortable tableau.

"I told them they should tell you," Drake said, unnaturally stiff, as if at attention. "They promised Theo they would. But they were afraid that if you knew, you would give the game away. And his position was far too delicate."

There was a moment of fraught silence, and then Pip straightened.

"We just made the same decision about Robbie and his mother," she said to him. "For the same reason."

Which was when, oddly, the explosion came. "Not for a *year!*" he yelled. "Not after watching his family hold a fucking *funeral!* There's a plaque in the goddamn *church!* And now you tell me he's been alive all this time?!"

Drake never flinched. "That is what I'm telling you."

He was so close to simply howling. "And now you don't know where he is again, is that right?"

Drake didn't answer.

"Fuck you," Beau snarled, walking away. "Fuck all of you."

"His position was—"

Beau whipped back around. "I don't care if you say his position was under the goddamn queen! You had no right!"

"No," Drake said simply. "I did not. But it wasn't my decision to make."

Beau succumbed to the fury again. Instead of knocking Drake out, this time he put his fist right through the paneling within inches of the Watteau.

That was going to hurt, he thought vaguely. *Good.*

Pip ran over to him. Drake didn't move. Beau just stared at the fist-sized hole in the wall as if he didn't know where it came from. "You can bill me for that," he said, his voice just as suddenly exhausted.

"Don't be absurd," Drake drawled. I'll bill the Home Office. It is their fault."

Pip didn't say a word, just pulled a handkerchief from her reticule and reached for Beau's bleeding hand. He hoped he hadn't broken anything, but suspected he'd feel better if he had.

It didn't mean he should have let her wrap the handkerchief around his knuckles. He couldn't seem to pull away. Her hands felt so soothing. So warm against his suddenly cold skin. They were almost enough to let loose the tears that choked him, those hands. Good thing he was so disciplined. They merely choked him, acid in his chest, unbearable with her so close.

"What do we do now?" Pip asked, looking up at them both.

"Not *we*," he grated, glaring at her.

How could such a little thing contain such purpose? She looked up at him, and Beau saw implacability and felt the ground slip away.

"Exactly how will you pose as a madwoman, Beau?" she quietly challenged him.

"Not mad," Drake quietly said. "Just...."

Pip frowned. "Inconvenient?"

Drake shrugged. "Possibly intransigent. Angry. What we could easily label hysterical."

"Men can label sneezing hysterics if it suits them," Pip retorted.

Beau glared at them both. "Is no one going to listen to me?"

Pip refused to back down. She put her hand on his arm, this time, which made it worse. "Do you want to know where Theo is?" she asked. "Do you want him back?"

He flinched. He was having such trouble breathing.

"We know where he is," he snarled. "At least if we can trust Pip's impression. He's with the smugglers we're trying to wipe out. Was that part of the plan or did he decide to improvise?"

Drake dropped his head, rubbing at his temple. "He's been out of touch for about four weeks now."

"And you think Miss Schroeder might know where to find him. When she's been in that place for how long?"

"The wife with the information has only been in about six days."

Beau knew Pip was facing him. He didn't have the courage to look her in the eye. He was afraid again. He was so afraid. He didn't know how much more he could stand.

She squeezed his arm. "We have to do this, Beau."

"Why can't I go in?" he asked, not looking at anyone.

Drake walked over to the drinks table. "It is a women's ward," he said, splashing brandy into two glasses. "And Lady Drummond knows what Miss Schroeder looks like. We can either send her in as a patient or as staff. I believe she would have more mobility as staff. More reason to poke around."

"I think I prefer that," she said. "What do I need to do?"

"Wear a drab dress and look as if this is the best job you will ever get. You'll be presented as someone new to this who is committed enough to good health that you take a walk every morning so we can contact you if need be." He approached, handing off her glass. "I don't suppose you can manage a less refined accent."

She managed a smile. "Theo and I practiced nonsense like that when we were going to spy for the king. Would you rather I be from Dorset, Hampshire, or Seven Dials?"

Drake offered another wry smile.

"You've thought this through," Beau accused his friend, accepting his glass.

Drake didn't retreat. "They did. We're talking about the destabilization of the country, Drummond. Assassination of royal princes, politicians, and the most beloved general in the history of the country. Do you really want to be responsible for that?"

Beau knew that Drake had the answer long before he asked the question. There was really nothing else Beau could do. He had to find Theo. He had to protect his little brother....

Closing his eyes, he tipped his head back and emptied his glass, focusing on the fire as it washed down his throat and into his stomach. His little brother. His little brother he had finally given up for dead. His little brother who had planned to marry Pip.

No matter what happened, Beau knew he would somehow lose.

He had to do it anyway.

THEY WERE GOING to put the plan into motion the next day. Pip was fine with that. It was better than being left with too much time on her hands to wade through the stew of emotions the news had produced.

Theo. Alive. It was impossible to comprehend. She had mourned him. She had stood by the monument they had erected in the village church to one of their honored military dead. She had grieved as much as Beau. No, she reconsidered. She had grieved more. She had also grieved for Beau.

And it was all a lie.

She would kill him. She would pummel him like bread dough until he cried like a toddler. She would...

She would do whatever she needed to do to bring Theo back, if for no other reason than for Beau.

He wouldn't look at her. He wouldn't reach out to her. From the moment he'd learned that Theo was possibly alive, he had retreated into himself in a way Pip hadn't seen since those first awful weeks after the news of Theo's supposed death. He turned down Pip's parents' invitation to stay with them and took Pip back to his townhouse on Charles. He made sure Pip wouldn't leave the house and then disappeared into his study. And left Pip behind to fret alone.

Pip hurt for him. She knew how upended and chaotic she felt. She could only imagine how this was affecting Beau. To know that Theo had been alive just days ago. But not sure whether he still was. It was like being reprieved from the hangman's noose only to have them hold you at the edge of the scaffold while they decided whether to change their minds. To have no control over the outcome. Beau couldn't tolerate having no control.

She wanted so badly to simply walk into that study, wrap her arms around him and hold him. She wanted to reassure him that at least she would always be here. She didn't know that, though. She didn't even know whether he wanted that. Whether *she* wanted that. So, she did what she always did when she landed someplace where she felt like an intruder. She made herself busy.

Her peripatetic life once again came in handy, since it had taught her to be not only flexible, but to deal with all manner of servants and living situations. She was going to need that flexibility if she was to deal with the staff here. They were new to her, they were Beau's people, and it didn't take much effort to blame the wife when the minute a brand-new husband entered his home he hid away from her.

At least she could communicate with Sullins who she sent into the study to tend to Beau's hand before she introduced herself to the rest of the staff.

"We don't have the mistress's room opened up," the laconic Mrs. Waters announced, her hands clasped before her. The housekeepers' keys jingled just a bit at her belt, watery blue eyes wary in a jowly face topped by graying blond hair.

"I didn't expect you would," Pip answered equably. "So, while dust covers are being removed and Joyful sees to my wardrobe, why don't you and I take a tour?"

Mrs. Waters spared an arch look and a sniff for Joyful, who was standing behind Pip. Pip was not pleased.

"Is there a problem, Mrs. Waters?" she asked, straightening to her earl's daughter posture. She hoped that and her tone of voice carried every ounce of calm warning she could muster.

She also had her eye on Mrs. Waters' husband, the butler, another starchy sort with more precisely tailored clothing than

Beau and a head of hair that flamed red. At least he was casting nervous looks at his wife as if giving his own warning.

"How could there be?" Mrs. Waters finally answered, looking not a whit happier. "You are the new mistress. My sole goal is for the house to suit your needs."

Pip gave her a radiant smile. "Indeed I am. And thank you. Since you have so admirably suited my husband's needs— something Pip could not prove—I am certain we shall do fine together. Now, I cannot wait to tour this lovely house."

She got one sidelong look from Joyful that said volumes, and then was off for her tour.

When Pip could knowledgeably discuss Beau's favorite meals and accept suggestions in the way of housekeeping order and supplies, the housekeeper began to thaw. Pip knew it would be awhile before they developed an amicable relationship, if they ever did, but she could tolerate the interim as long as Beau was not inconvenienced.

The tour ended in her newly aired-out room that connected with Beau's through the respective dressing rooms. There was no question that Beau's Aunt Maude had had a hand in decorating this room as well. The paper was a dull gold that bordered on brown, the curtains and covers an odd pea green. At least the furniture had clean lines and no animal heads or feet. Pip imagined the lady had not had the chance to go shopping.

"When things settle down a bit," she said, "I shall want to do a bit of redecorating, I think. Till then, this will do fine. Thank you, Mrs. Waters. It is always a pleasure to enter a well-run house. I know you all will make Joyful welcome. I already feel so."

Stretching the truth a bit, perhaps, but Pip believed in calming roiled waters. It wasn't until she'd closed the door on the housekeeper that she finally let down. Dropping into a brighter gold armchair before the lit fireplace, she took off her glasses and rubbed at her eyes as she considered her new home.

Home.

Lord help her.

She so desperately wanted to belong here and at Delamere. She wanted to belong with Beau, to grow together like vines twining. She wanted to burrow in until she finally felt like she truly belonged somewhere.

Right now, though, she wasn't at all sure she would succeed. She wasn't sure Beau would let her. She couldn't even wholly commit herself to anything yet. She had to leave again almost as soon as she had gotten there, playing a part as a worker in an insane asylum. Mere weeks ago, she would have considered that the height of adventure. Everything she and Theo had played at when they were children.

Now, though, she knew the risks, the consequences, the uncertainties. The danger.

And not just physical danger.

Oddly enough, she wasn't worried so much for herself as she was for Beau. What if they were not able to find Theo? What if they were too late? Beau would never survive that. Worse, she suspected he would find a way to blame her.

Closing her eyes, she laid her head back against the chair. She was desperate to be with Beau, to hold him, to share the turmoil they both faced and find surcease in each other's arms. She suspected, though, that even as he feared for her safety, he would be relieved to have her somewhere else. And how was she supposed to begin to build a relationship when her husband couldn't stand to be near her?

She wanted a future with him. She wanted his children, she wanted to ease into old age by his side, enlivening his day and soothing his night. She wanted what every woman wanted for the man she loved. Right now, though, she couldn't quite see her way through. She was so terrified that this little adventure of theirs would end up leaving her once again the unwanted visitor in her own house. Which, she realized, would be even worse than not being in her own house at all.

Sighing, she climbed to her feet. There was nothing for it but to take the next step, and the one after that. She had made her decisions. She had taken her chance. There was no one else she would be able to blame if she never found a comfortable place in her own life. With her own husband or, if it came to that, without him. She could only do what she could and make sure that no one but Joyful saw her tears.

D rake sent over a packet of information which kept
Pip busy through the afternoon hours. Information
about the asylum, the patients they knew were there,
the conditions—which seemed to be better than most, if the
information was true. There was even information about
special rooms hidden away for those intransigent patients who
refused to conform. A 'quieting' room, they called it, and a map
as to where they were out back of the facility. Underground. It
gave Pip the chills.

Miss Schroeder was posing as a Mrs. Eloise Riordan, wife of
one of the mid-level members of the Lions, a man who helped
supervise the King's Bench. The real Mrs. Riordan was safely
tucked away with another of Drake's Rakes, Harry Lidge and
his wife Lady Kate.

The woman who had offered the new information to Miss
Schroeder was, to the best of their knowledge, a Mrs. Baxter,
whose husband was in a general in the Guards. Pip would have
to seek her out as well. And on her way to the asylum she
would be meeting another rake, Diccan Hilliard, who had put

together a team called Diccan's Household Army, since he would be the one supervising her foray into the asylum.

All the while she didn't hear a word from Beau. He came out to dinner, but the meal was no more comfortable than the rest of the day. Pip several times attempted to spark a conversation, but Beau couldn't seem to manage more than monosyllables.

Finally, she motioned the footman from the room.

"Is this the way it's going to be?" she asked, setting her fork and knife down.

He stared at her for a minute. "What?"

"Our life. Am I to meet you at dinner for stilted conversation and then watch you lock yourself back into the study?"

"I told you what my plans were, Pip. They have not changed."

She should not have asked. She knew it. And she got her answer. That was when she realized that she had been stupid enough after the other night to begin to hope. He had been so gentle, so considerate. So generous.

Only, it seemed, in the bedroom. In the bedroom, where you could escape everything else. You could pretend that you weren't crippled by guilt and grief and resentment. Those all waited outside the door. They lurked in the dining room over dinner.

Would she ever know what it was to find peace with this man? To fit herself into a comfortable place she knew she belonged and was wanted by the only man she wanted? Or was silence her future?

"What will you do while I'm gone?" she asked, hands clenched on her lap.

He shook his head. "Estate matters. Work with Drake on protecting the royal family. Decide what I shall say to Theo when he walks in the door."

It was on those last three words that his voice broke, and he surged to his feet.

"I need to check in at my club."

And before she could protest, he was finishing his glass of wine in one swallow. "Are you finished?" he asked.

She just nodded and set her serviette on the table. Beau helped her from her chair and guided her into the hallway where he dropped a quick kiss to her cheek before asking for his coat and hat.

And there she was left, standing in the echoing silence of her new home, alone again, aching for Beau to reach out to show her he shared her fear, her hope, her awful uncertainty. Knowing that it would be too much to hope for, that when he was struck by the most difficult revelation of his life, he would suddenly turn to her and beg for her support.

He didn't. That kiss was the closest he could come to her. And right after, he ran.

Sometimes she despaired of all men.

She watched him escape out the front door and then turned away. There was nothing for it but to retire upstairs to her room where Joyful waited for her.

"How is everything?" Pip asked as Joyful unlaced her.

"Not as bad as I feared. Havin' Mr. Sullins along sure helps. I think it was the surprise of things, not that they're bad people. I'm jus' not what they expect to see."

Pip nodded. As early as it was, she slipped into her night-clothes and robe and let Joyful go for the night. Her uniform for the next day hung in her clothes press, and the packet of information sat on a desk by the window. But Pip didn't bother with it anymore. She sat in a chair by the window watching carriages and cabs trundle by and wishing she had acquired a lady's accomplishments like stitching or piano to pass the time. A book was out of the question. She would never be able to concentrate. So, she sat in her armchair and waited to hear sounds from the adjoining bedroom. She waited for Beau.

She waited for three long hours. She'd almost given up and gotten into bed when

she heard his voice, then Sullins, and finally the door closing to the hallway. Sitting quite still, she drew in careful breaths, trying to calm the dread that crawled in her belly right alongside the anticipation. What if he said no? What if he simply left? This was the only way she could think that he would accept comfort, that she would be comforted. She had to take the chance.

Standing up, she slipped off her dressing gown, leaving her in a simple nightgown with no more embellishment than small roses embroidered at the neck and hem. She ran her fingers through her hair, wishing it were suddenly long and lustrous, and she walked to the connecting door and opened it.

He should have looked more surprised when she walked in. He was seated in a wingback chair wearing nothing but his breeches, even his feet bare. He was nursing another brandy.

"I hope you aren't becoming too fond of that," she said. "I hear it dulls your senses."

He tilted his head. "That is the idea."

She waited, but he kept silent. She waited until she grew angry.

"I'm as frightened as you are, Beau."

"You should be. You do not know what you're getting into."

She huffed. "I imagine not. But I'm worried more about you. I do know how you feel."

He just kept considering her. "Do you?"

She refused to back down. "Is there anything more painful than hope?"

When he didn't answer, she should have finally stalked off, given up. But she saw his eyes. She saw the devastating dread, the fear, the confusion. He rested on the same knife's edge that she did.

"I'd rather not be alone," was all she said.

And amazingly enough, it was all she needed to say.

Their coming together was cataclysmic. Before Pip could take a breath she and Beau were intertwined, his hands so tangled in her hair that pins pinged across the floor and his mouth on hers demanding entry. She gave it, knowing the feeling of desperation, the fear that everything would be lost. She knew that sometimes a port in a storm wasn't a quiet harbor.

They were nothing like quiet. They scrabbled at each other, desperate to be beyond clothing, to be skin-to-skin where nothing could wedge in between. Their kisses were frantic, deep, tongues dancing, lips bruised and mouths wide for invasion.

Pip felt tears gather at the back of her throat and tried to ignore them. Beau didn't

need tears. He needed solace. *She* needed solace. She needed mindless sensation and intense emotion. She needed Beau's skin under her hands, his beard chafing her cheek, his hands pulling off her gown as frantically as she fumbled with the buttons of his falls. She needed to explore his shoulders with her hands, tracing muscle and tendon and bone, sift her fingers through the curly hair that was sprinkled across his chest.

She needed to free him from his breeches so she could capture him, so she could torment him, so she could measure the length of him and cradle him, just as he was claiming her body with callused fingers and satin mouth, as they both met chest-to-chest so she could tease her breasts against the rough hair on his chest. She desperately wanted him inside her, so deep she couldn't lose him ever again.

By the time they tumbled onto the bed, they were both

naked and glistening with sweat. Beau had her breast in his mouth, worrying at it with lips and tongue and teeth. Pip arched up to him, desperate for more even as she did her own conquering of his shoulders and chest and belly, delighting with the unfamiliar texture of hair on a chest and legs, anxious to visit the delightful textures at his groin.

She still couldn't believe the size of his rigid length, iron sheathed in satin, so alive to her touch, so warm against her fingers. She reveled in the power of his thighs, the sensitive skin at the back of his knees, the growling sounds he made when she explored. For those few minutes, when she had him in her arms, she no longer felt alone. And for those moments, even knowing how tenuous the union was, it was enough.

And then, as if he heard her need for union, he nudged her legs open and reached down to tease her, his fingers just rough enough against her most sensitive core to incite fireworks. She found herself whimpering as he set loose unbearable pleasure, almost a pain that was desperate for a solution. For completion.

"Be about it, sir," she growled herself, reaching between them to take hold of him with authority.

She heard him chuckle, but he knew not to wait for her to complete the act for him. Brushing her hands aside, he positioned himself and drove into her body. Drove so deep he ignited her, drove her right into an explosion that consumed her, pulled cries from her, compelled her to use her own hands to claim him as her own, every inch of him, and then wrap her fingers into his hair, dragging him back to her so that she could brand him, mouth-to-mouth, cry to cry, meeting his thrusts and pushing back to drive him deeper, so deep she felt she might rend in two, except that instead of pain or fear, that meeting let in light, a light so blinding she wasn't sure she would survive it.

It wasn't until much later that she realized that when he climaxed, he was still inside her. All she knew at the time was that she wanted nothing more than to shelter his wounded soul and help him find surcease.

When he collapsed on top of her, weight and heat and ragged breathing, she knew nothing more than that with her arms tight around his heaving back, her legs wrapped around his and her heart beating against his, she had found her way home.

It was inevitable he would remember. Pip knew it the next morning when she woke warm and comforted in his arms, the covers pulled high and his arms tight around her. For one second to the next, he stiffened, and she knew.

He didn't say a word, thank heaven. But she could almost hear the turmoil roiling around in his brain, how he had taken advantage of her. How she had taken advantage of him. How maybe if he said nothing it wouldn't be real, and the chance of consequences would simply disappear.

Well, she wasn't going to bring it up. Especially since, in the cold light of day and the unescapable chill of reality, he was already pulling away, even though he didn't move. Even still wrapped tightly around her, he had begun to distance himself. She desperately wanted to tighten her own hold, imprison him in her arms so he couldn't run away. She had known him too long to believe she could.

"It's time to be up and about," he said, his voice curiously flat as he began to unwind from her.

Pip figured he would be back in his study within the hour. He was trying to tell her he was done, and this time, she was terrified that he just might be.

She should be glad it wouldn't happen again. She could only tolerate so much. She could only wake so often with her ear resting over his heart, her body tucked against his, her own heart filled with the sights, sounds, and scents of him, and suspect that he wasn't thinking how wonderful the night had been, how blissful it was to wake in the arms of his lover, but how soon he could get away.

"It's a good thing Drake is coming to get me at noon," she said, not lifting her head. "That way you can escape without seeming churlish."

"Pip—"

She rose, then, to look down at his sleep-tousled face, so indescribably dear to her that just the sight of him sent such a shaft of pain through her it stole her breath. She knew this time that the minute Theo was back, she would lose her home. And if Theo didn't come back after all, she would lose everything.

Silently she pulled herself away instead and climbed out of bed to retrieve her nightgown and return to her room.

Joyful was waiting for her, the battered little portmanteau Drake had provided for her already packed, her maid's uniform laid out on the bed.

"They have a way for you to get word out o' there if need be?" her maid demanded, her voice gruff with emotion.

Pip washed up. "They do. A special drop on the grounds. I'm also to leave a special marker twice a day so they know I am all right, and there will evidently be someone always watching if I need immediate help."

Joyful gave a brisk nod. "Then you let me know you all right. Hear?"

Pip smiled at her, even though they both knew she wasn't happy. But then, neither was Joyful.

After she dressed, Pip spent her time going over her instructions one more time. And then she sat and considered her future. Cycles of need and comfort and cold isolation. Hoping every time would be different even while she knew it wouldn't. Too much stood between them. Too much that would still be unresolved even if Theo did come back. Especially if Theo came back. And it would all continue unless she made a decision.

She did not wait for a messenger to come get her. She had two more tasks to do before the coach picked her up back by the mews to take her to whatever hideaway Drake had found to hide their activities. She had to say goodbye to Beau. And then she had to tell Joyful what that meant.

Clad in the drab gray merino wool that would become her uniform but saving the mobcap for later, she descended the stairs and made for Beau's study.

She knew she was making the right decision when Beau couldn't find a smile for her when she walked in. He rose from the chair behind his desk and considered her. "Would you like a seat?"

She shook her head. "I'd rather you didn't see me off," she said. A lie, but a valid excuse for the fact that he might not anyway.

And then she made the mistake of looking at him.

Blast him. *Blast* him. She knew he would be relieved when she said what she had to, and that hurt worst of all.

"Drake thinks this will only take a few days," she said and saw him withdraw even further. He was so frightened, and she suspected she was the only one who could see it.

"And yes," she said with a forced smile before he could say it, "I will be very careful. I have no desire to be a fond memory. But if you see Theo before I do, tell him I am extremely displeased that he has put us through this."

Beau smiled back, just as strained. "I will. And I do not care what Drake says. If you think you might be in danger, get out of there."

She nodded, even though both of them knew it wouldn't happen. "Happily. Will you stay in town?"

"Rather than face my aunt and uncle? Yes, I will. Besides, I have my own duties to carry out."

She nodded again, frozen in place by the memories of those harsh, hot kisses the night before, the frantic lovemaking. She desperately wanted him to kiss her, but it would make what she had to say worse. It certainly would for her.

Finally, hands clasped as if that would hold her together, she faced him with the inevitable truth. "I have been thinking," she said. "You might have been right after all. I am making you miserable here. And I am afraid I will keep doing it, because I cannot help but follow my own counsel, no matter how you feel." She took in a breath, feeling as if she were smothering. This was so difficult. "I shall go to the asylum today. But when I finish there, I think it would be best if I return to my parents. It will give you the peace you need in which to decide what you wish to do, especially when Theo comes back."

"What do you mean?" He truly looked flummoxed.

"I mean I think it is best that I am the one to leave. I can, now that my parents are home. When you're ready, let me know what your decision is to be."

"You won't wait until Theo comes home?"

She shook her head. "You two need time to be brothers again."

He swallowed. "Theo loves you, Pip."

Her smile was sad. "Of course, he does, Beau. Just as I love him. But I do not love him as I love you. I never have. But there are only so many times I can tell you that only to watch you try to escape from me before I get the message."

"Escape?"

She took one look around the room and then faced him until he couldn't look at her anymore. So, she finally told him the truth.

"I have been following you about my entire life. Time and again I have tried to make you see me. To see how much I love you. I cannot do it anymore. I can only have my hope destroyed so many times. I will not say you win, because I suspect that you haven't. But I will say that it is finally time for me to leave you alone. It's up to you, now. If you want me, it is your turn to come to me. If you do not, feel free to file the papers. You know where I shall be."

And without another word, she walked out.And as she had hoped, only Joyful saw her tears.

HE WAS A COWARD.

Beau stood there behind his desk like a headmaster who had just sent a student out to holiday. Except his heart was thundering and his chest was on fire with fear. She couldn't simply walk out as if she was going to the shops. She had no idea what danger she faced.

He couldn't let her go.

He couldn't prevent her.

He could see her off, though.

He was out the door before he knew it, scaring one of the maids into dropping a pile of linen on his way down the stairs.

"Pip!"

But she wasn't there. "Where did my wife go?" he demanded of his butler.

The man just shook his head and pointed to the green baize door. Beau slammed through it and terrorized every maid in the kitchen. He paid no attention. He had to get to the back door. He had to get to the mews.

He got to the mews. He got there just in time to see a rather shabby hackney turn onto Queen Street on its way to Piccadilly.

If only he could have told her that he wouldn't sleep, wouldn't eat, wouldn't move until she was safely returned. But he hadn't. So, he simply waited until the hackney disappeared into morning traffic and turned away, left with nothing but an empty house and reports to read.

Suddenly, after an adulthood steeped in silence and nothing more than the echoes of his own thoughts, he wasn't sure he could bear it. Because he hadn't had the courage to tell her that the reason he was afraid was because he loved her so much.

19

As she always did when she felt lost, Pip focused on a task to keep her busy. This time it was her role for the Rakes. It didn't ease the pain, but it allowed her to live with it, at least for a while. That way she could keep from thinking of the future until her job was ended and she returned to the wrong house.

It helped that what she was to do was more than simple housekeeping or socializing. She would be doing vital work, work that might not only impact the safety of her country, but her old headmistress. Not to mention Theo.

It was almost a relief, then, to enter an unpretentious rowhouse in Marleybone to be greeted by Diccan Hilliard. She knew him, of course, as a friend of her brother Alex, and had always suspected the elegant man about town to be a Rake. It was nice to have the validation. His instructions were simple, his precautions well-considered. Once he learned that among Pip's wide range of skills were the skills employed by the house staff she had haunted as a child, he made her feel as if she were the only person who could do the job. That confidence served her well when she entered the Richmond Hills Asylum as their new maid.

It took two entire days to find out that Miss Schroeder wasn't in any of the regular patient rooms or wards. To be fair, it took the first day to acclimate to the facility, an asylum for gentlewomen, they called it. A fairly inoffensive place on the surface, with clean rooms that had lace curtains, rugs, comfortable beds and chairs, tables with games, a piano that was usually locked in the public room, and three meals that contained more than just gruel.

The staff was mostly women, with a few men to provide extra force if needed, and one doctor who strode about the place like the ruler of a small principality. The patients, or residents as they were to be called, all wore identical limp blue dresses and had had their hair cut short. So it could not be pulled by other patients, the staff said. To Pip it seemed more so they forfeited their individual identities.

Calm, Pip was told repeatedly, was the motto. Calm staff, calm quarters, calm patients. And at first it seemed like that was the extent of it. The patients wandered about fairly freely, their feet shuffling, their meals eaten in silence, their calm undisturbed by visitors.

Even the staff followed the edict. Pip had expected to gather gossip at the dinner table, but meals were eaten in silence, and easy interaction among the staff missing except between Matron, two of the aides, and Dr. Whaley. They always seemed to be in conference.

It should have reassured Pip that this seemed a place like some of the new Quaker institutions that insisted on treating mental patients with compassion and dignity. But it didn't. It felt...wrong, somehow. Unnatural. She noticed that the patients never made eye contact and seemed to edge away from Dr. Whaley in the halls. And the few times a patient cried out or swung at a staff member, they were simply taken out a door at the back of the building. To the 'quieting' rooms, she was told. A place she didn't have access to yet.

All she knew was that she saw one woman return, held on either side by an aide. The woman shuffled more than the others, her head down, and retreated to her room where she sat in the chair not speaking to anyone.

Pip's own quarters were spartan, but no worse than she had seen in other servants' quarters, maybe better. She was alone in a two bed room. She had a bed, a hook for her clothes and a small bureau to hold her brush and comb. She was allowed a fair amount of freedom, which meant that when she got up in the morning no one protested her taking a constitutional around the grounds. They didn't see her leave a blue rock outside in the garden to the right of the front door to let Mr. Hilliard know she was all right. When she quit for the day after dinner, she left another. She also had yellow rocks if there was danger.

And when she readied for bed, she slid her knife out from the holder on her ankle and put it under her pillow along with the muff pistol she pulled out of her pocket and checked. She grinned, thinking of Diccan Hilliard's surprise when she had cleaned and loaded the gun in a matter of seconds. He had offered her a full-time job in his Household Army.

It was on the third day she made several vital discoveries, although not about Miss Schroeder. About how the inmates were kept so calm. In the pantry, she stumbled over several bottles of laudanum. Next to cones of sugar. Next to the tea.

Blessed Bertram's bicycle. The women were being drugged. Every one of them. Not only that, there was a way to dispatch them if they became problematic. Her chances of success had just dropped precipitously.

After finding the laudanum, she took a few minutes to see what other surprises were stored near the giant tea urn.

There was a treasure trove. Ginger for stomach upsets,

feverfew and willow bark for fevers, chamomile for anxiety, cowslip for catarrh.

Foxglove.

Did the staff here know of the herb's use for strengthening the heart, or was its presence more malicious? She vowed to keep an eye on it.

And then Pip was introduced to the treatment room. Her task was simply to clean and restock after its use. On that third morning she saw the evidence of its use, round red wheals on the backs of a patient who had just returned, shuffling and mumbling.

"Cupping," the Matron pronounced, nodding her scrupulously tidy head with what Pip thought was uncomfortable enthusiasm. "It draws out evil humors."

It caused pain when superheated air was caught in a glass cup and laid against bare skin creating a vacuum.

Then there were the ice baths. Nobody could actually say what those helped, except to torture the patients who misbehaved. The more Pip saw, the more determined she became find Miss Schroeder.

But her old headmistress wasn't to be seen. Which meant that if she was truly still here, she was in the 'quieting' rooms that existed somewhere beyond the main building. Somewhere underground, from what Diccan had said. Worse than that, Pip could find no mention or record of the Mrs. Baxter who had allegedly shared the information they needed.

The more Pip saw, the more she wanted to tell Diccan to just shut the whole place down.

And then she stumbled over the worst surprise. She was walking down the hall with an armload of towels when she needed to sidestep two aides guiding another shuffling, muttering woman down the hall.

"This is Mrs. Mary Meyers," one of the aides said with that

false, cloying smile that said to treat the patient like a slow child. "She is joining us for a bit. She had to visit the quieting room for a few days first to acclimate, but she's fine now."

Pip didn't recognize the woman at first, since her head was down. She wore the ubiquitous blue dress and kid slippers.

"Welcome, Mrs. Meyers," she said with a dip of the knee as she'd been instructed.

Mrs. Meyers never reacted. So the women led her into one of the better decorated rooms that almost looked like a personal bedroom, with the usual lace curtains, a pale yellow rug and a soft blue quilt. There was also a comfortable navy armchair faced to look out the window, although the view was compromised by the bars that gave lie to any comfort.

It was also near the linen closet, so that as she stacked towels, Pip could see how the patient was handled. The staff was calm and efficient helping Mrs. Meyers but didn't waste time on words or gestures of support as they left her lying under the covers staring at the ceiling. Pulling a red card from a pocket one of the aides slipped it into a holder by the door on her way out, leaving the door open.

Pip had seen those cards by a few other doors and was going to ask about it, when she took a look back at the patient.

Pip stopped cold, suddenly distracted. She recognized the woman. The woman whose breasts were impressive even under covers. The woman whose shorn hair was a rich chestnut color. The woman with empty green eyes. The woman she recognized. But not Miss Schroeder.

Pip instinctively made a move to the room but pulled herself up short. No one needed to see her interest. Her profound shock and suddenly sick stomach. She had wanted to make sure, but she didn't really need to. She knew her. In fact, she had seen her no more than a few days earlier at the duchess's house party.

For a long moment Pip could do no more than simply stand in the hallway staring into the room at the woman who was definitely not anyone named Mary Meyers. That woman's name was Lady Pamela Smythe-Smith.

Blessed Bernard's buns, how did that happen? Who put her in this awful place?

But Pip knew, of course. It had to have been Perfect Pamela's husband. Did that mean he was the real lion in the family? Would it also mean that Pamela had more information than Pip had thought? And what had she done to deserve this?

Then Pip saw something that made it all so much worse. Something she couldn't bear, even if it was Perfect Pamela. As soon as the aids left the room and turned back toward the quieting rooms, Pip saw Pamela lift a hand and drop it, nothing more, as if that was all the energy she could muster.

"Please," she whispered to the ceiling. "Don't do this."

There were tears trailing down her temples to dampen her pillow and a look of such despair in her eyes Pip caught herself just shy of running in to help. Even though there was no help she could offer. At least not then.

She so wished she could talk to her. She wished she could simply sit and hold her hand. But she couldn't risk being unmasked. Not until she found Miss Schroeder. After her run-ins with Perfect Pamela, though, it should have surprised her how hard it was to simply turn away.

"Cox," the Matron said, approaching at a brisk clip, her starched white apron rustling, "the usual maid is busy and Quieting Room number one needs cleaning. If you go to the back, you'll see the blue door. It leads to them. Here."

And she handed off a key.

Pip curtsied, her eyes down so she didn't betray her relief at not being caught, and walked on to the closet that held her cleaning supplies. Her heart had begun to gallop and her hands to sweat. This was her opportunity. She could at least assess the area. She desperately needed to find Miss Schroeder and get her out of here. She had to alert Diccan. She had to get Mrs. Baxter. She had to hope they were in the quieting rooms, or she feared they would never find them.

At first glance the quieting room looked to be fairly innocuous. Down a flight of wooden stairs, obviously dug from the earth just like the dower cellar, along a sterile-looking hallway that was unaccountably unattended. Five feet square, perhaps. Painted unrelieved white and empty.

Empty. How did that work? No bed? No Chairs? Not even a chamberpot?

She found the chamberpot down the hall, but it was obvious that Pamela had had trouble with it. The room reeked of urine. Pip couldn't imagine what that would have done to such a proud, vain woman. Blast if it didn't make her feel even worse for her.

But then Pip realized that in this empty white room there were no lights. The only lamps available were hanging in the hallway. No windows. Just a closed box where a person spent at least two days alone. Dark in the middle of the day, and as cold as any cave. She wasn't even sure the women were fed while they were in there. She had never seen any trays pass that way from the kitchen.

She stood in that stark, blank room for too long, just imagining what it would be like when they closed the door on you. She had been right to have had chills.

The need to find Miss Schroeder became much more acute.

There were five more doors in the hallway, two with those red cards, and no visible staff anywhere. Should she yell? Call out a name? Or just try the key in each lock to see what happened.

She quickly mopped down the empty room. Then, key in

hand, she tested the door across the hall, holding her breath, straining to hear any sounds, either from the cell or above her.

The door opened. To show nothing. The same empty stark white space. The same vague, pervasive scent of urine. Nothing more.

The same for the second cell. It was the third where she succeeded, one of the red card rooms. Tucked back in the far corner, knees to chest, head on knees, was another woman in dingy, wrinkled blue. It wasn't Miss Schroeder. She was far too small and her hair gray.

"Mrs. Baxter?" Pip quietly asked.

The woman's head snapped up. She winced at the light from Pip's lantern, and then stared as if trying to decide whether she was an apparition.

"Yes?"

Pip let out a sigh of relief. "I am here to help. I am a friend of Miss Schroeder. My name is Phillipa Knight, and I have been sent by the people who are trying to stop the Lions."

Pip could see no expression. "You want to know what I told her."

"I do. But, as I said, I want to help you. I can't do it alone, though. I need help. If we needed to move you fast, could you walk or run?"

She nodded. "I would crawl if I needed to. And then I want you to arrest my husband for treason."

"We'll try. Is Miss Schroeder down here?"

She pointed. "Next door. You are to get her out too?"

"I think we must. If you give me a minute, I need to see her."

Again, Pip listened for visitors. Again, she tried the key on a red card door, her hands shaking. Again, she opened the door to see a woman tucked back in a corner, knees at her chest, arms wrapped around them to maintain heat, her shorn hair blond. Miss Schroeder, though, had her head up and her eyes open. She too, winced, then lifted her hand to shade her eyes. When she realized who had just come through the door, though, she jumped to her feet like a teenager and rushed forward.

Pip wasn't prepared for the sudden, tight embrace.

"So, Miss Knight," Miss Schroeder said with a grin, pulling back. "You are to be my savior? I think that only appropriate since I was yours those years ago at school."

She had been, too, coming into their awful boarding school and cleaning it up, literally and figuratively. There was something different, though. It took Pip a moment to figure it out.

"Where is your accent?" German, to be exact. A precise accent the girls used to mimic sometimes.

Miss Schroeder looked and, unfortunately, smelled as if she had been in this room for quite a few days. But her answering grin was bright and rueful. "Ah well," she said. "That comes and goes as needed."

"You aren't German."

"I am not. Are we leaving?"

"Not just yet. I must notify Mr. Hilliard and ask what we need to do. My job was just to find you. It seems I have found two other ladies we need to rescue as well. Tell me. Is the red card significant?"

Miss Schroeder nodded. "They call us the Lion Admissions. If the officials come, we are to be quietly disposed of."

Pip shuddered. She suspected she knew for certain what that foxglove was for. "Can I ask how long you have been down here? Certainly, longer than the three days I have been working here. Did they catch you exchanging information with Mrs. Baxter?"

And if so, why didn't they kill her then?

It was as if Miss Schroeder had heard her. "They did catch us. But they are so certain they will prevail that they just needed us out of the way until their plan worked. In fact, they still believe I am Mrs. Riordan."

"They haven't hurt you?"

"Besides leaving me in absolute darkness on a hard floor with only a chamberpot for relief and gruel for meals?" She smiled again, that indomitable woman. "I don't wish to brag, but I have withstood worse. Mrs. Baxter has not, though. I do worry for her."

So did Pip. "I cannot do this by myself," she apologized. "I must inform Diccan Hilliard as soon as I can."

"Of course, you must. First, however, let me quickly give you the information Diccan needs. Can you remember it all?"

Pip grinned. "Are you saying you aren't certain whether you taught me well enough?"

That earned her another smile and the information about the planned attacks and assassination attempt scheduled to happen in just two days. Not on the Duke of Wellington, however. Their target was the Prince Regent himself. Thankful she had gotten to Miss Schroeder in time, Pip quickly repeated the information back and nodded.

"One more thing," she said. "Theo Drummond. You said you knew where he is."

"We think he embedded himself with the smugglers to follow their trail and possibly disrupt the plans. Although he'll need help to do it. He'll be with them at Bristol and wearing a blue knit cap. So, they need to watch out for him."

Pip nodded, and then realized something. "How did you escape the laudanum?"

Miss Schroeder's eyes twinkled as she pointed to her chamberpot. "Those are handy for more than relieving oneself of too much tea. Now, go, before someone catches you in here. We don't need any more souls in the quieting rooms."

Pip could think of nothing more to do than shake her head.

"Indeed. I hope we can have you out in the next day or two. Will you be able to move fast?"

"Do not worry about me," she said. "I have been playing this game a while now. I know how to protect myself."

Pip shook her head. "I wish I'd known this at school. Think of what you could have taught us."

They were both still smiling when she locked her old head-mistress back into the dark.

Her work was almost finished. She just needed to make her constitutional a bit longer tonight. In the meantime, she had a lot of work to do as the maid.

Diccan had made it easy for her to pass on her information. When she took her walk, she meandered over the modest-sized grounds of the asylum set at the edge of the city. Diccan had told her that if she needed to talk to someone, put a candle in her window—unlit—and they would have someone meet her at the corner.

And when she slipped out that evening, there he was. A man sat slumped against the brick wall of the building next door, a tin cup on the ground in front of him. Then she saw the empty sleeve and breathed her first sigh of relief. Blessed Brian's bottles, she thought, briefly closing her eyes. When this was over, she was traveling straight to the seaside and sit all alone for weeks just to watch the water. She had had quite enough of this unrelenting fear. She would say this task would have been easier with Beau, but he never would have let her into that asylum in the first place.

"Kit Braxton," she murmured to the beggar, reaching into her pocket as if reaching for a coin. "I'm afraid we have run out of time here. We need to get not only Miss Schroeder out, but Mrs. Baxter, and Lady Pamela Smythe-Smith."

Braxton, clad in a tattered Rifleman's uniform, raised his scruffy face. "Pamela? You're sure?"

Pip scowled at him. "I just spent two weeks with the woman, some of that time under her bed. I know what she looks like."

Although she didn't much look like that now. Pip shivered, wondering if she would end up in one of those cells if they caught her. Well, at least her hair was already short.

Kit grinned. "You were under her bed? I bet that's a story."

Pip grinned back. "It is. We'll save it for later. For now, here is Miss Schroeder's information. You need to get it to Diccan as soon as possible."

As quickly and concisely as she could, she repeated what she had been told. Especially about Theo and the assassination attempt on the Prince of Wales.

"Good work," he answered, lifting his cup and jingling it as if asking for more. "Look for me in the morning. Same street corner, same cup. But Miss Knight..."

Pip grinned. "Miss Cox, if you please."

He grinned back and suddenly looked younger. "Miss Cox. Drake might refuse to aid the women yet. It might be too dangerous to tip our hand at this moment, since the attacks are to happen in two days. If they think we've winkled them out, they might change the plans, and we'll lose them. Can the women wait?"

Pip's instinct was to say no. No matter what Miss Schroeder had said, she had suffered down in that awful cell. And that was when they simply thought her a gabby wife. What if they discovered her real purpose? What if they discovered Pip's?

But she knew that more was at stake than those three women, as desperate as their situation was.

She nodded. "As long as you're here the minute you can be. I would say bring a magistrate, but I suspect nothing is being done here that is illegal. At least to women."

Kit tapped her arm with his cup. "Good job, my girl. We'll not let you down. Be careful yourself. And one more thing…"

She looked down to see that his smile had disappeared. "Drummond will be with us when we move," he said. "Do us a favor and don't shoot the man. "He's been driving Hilliard mad to do something. I don't know what he did, but he's acting as if he's the greatest sinner in the world. Which we know he isn't. Drake is."

She knew he was trying to lighten her mood. He didn't. "He is safe from me," she said.

She was still reflecting on Braxton's odd request and battling unrealistic hope and dread at the same time as she walked back into the asylum kitchens.

"What were you doing out so long?" Matron asked, standing in the doorway like judgment herself. Around them the kitchen worked on, dishes clattering, pots steaming, the red-faced cook stirring.

Barely keeping herself from jumping straight in the air, Pip finished shutting the door, lifted her head and offered a tired smile. "There's an out-o'-work soldier. I give him pennies, sometimes."

Matron scowled. "You don't make so much you can give it away."

Pip shrugged, trying so hard to seem nonchalant when her heart was banging against her ribs. "It's sure I make more'n him bein' thrown out on the streets after defending our country so's he's only sportin' one arm. Can't hurt to be nice to such as him."

All Matron could do was huff at her. "Do you still have the key?" she demanded.

Pip nodded, desperate to figure a way to keep from giving it up. "If you'll pardon me saying, ma'am, that room needs a better cleaning than I could give it today. There's still a smell I couldn't quite get out. Can I have another go?"

Still scowling, the matron flapped a hand at her. "Might as

well. The numbers two and three rooms across the hall could probably use the same. The key works for both. Mind you don't neglect your other work."

Pip smiled. "Thank you, Matron. I just hate the idea of our ladies caught in with a bad smell. Doesn't seem quietin' at all, then, does it?"

IT WAS a good thing there was a pub with a view to the asylum, or he would have

lost his mind. If he was lucky, he saw her twice a day. It wasn't enough to ease his terror, but it helped. He knew he should be with Drake organizing to strike the minute they heard a timetable. But he couldn't just leave her alone, no matter what she thought. He needed to be close in case she needed him.

He might have to leave her when this was over. But until then, he was responsible for her.

He eased his conscience by eavesdropping on the conversations of the male hospital staff who stopped by for a wet on the way home from work. He might just pick up a valuable bit of gossip, even though he hadn't so far.

Lord, if she got out of this, he would never let her leave the house again.

Which, of course, was why he was here watching his wife instead of helping her. He was torturing himself with the truth that he could never be at ease with her. He would never be able to simply assume she would be safe. He would forbid her from doing something that might put her in danger, and she would pull herself up to her tiny five-foot height like a Russian Grand Duchess and just walk off to do whatever it was anyway. And he would be left to fret. Or grieve. And by God, he'd already done enough of that in his life.

He had just taken a sip of his ale when he saw movement across where Kit had set up shop posing as a down-on-his-luck veteran. He, of course, was also having fun. He insisted he might keep up the premise, since he'd already gained about a crown in donations. But when Kit looked up, it was to greet a young woman bent over him dropping a coin in his cup, a blonde woman whose glasses glinted in the fading light.

It took every ounce of control he had to keep from leaping to his feet. He could just see her in the twilight, smiling down at Kit as if she'd just discovered a new friend. He scanned the area, making sure no one took particular notice of them.

They were, but inside the pub.

"That the new maid?"

"Tasty morsel, ain't she? Thought I'd welcome her to Richmond, you know. Just bein' all friendly. She all but broke me finger."

There were generalized guffaws and back slapping.

"Worse," he said, "she's got the only key to her room. She might be a bit more of a challenge than Maisy before her."

"Maisy was no challenge. I'm waitin' 'til they give us leave to entertain the rich ones. We could be real comfortin', we could."

More laughter.

Beau memorized their faces for later. Then he turned back just in time to see her give Braxton a little wave and turn back into the asylum. He wanted to jump up and run after her, make sure she was all right. She had looked all right, even in that awful gray sack and oversized mobcap. She looked healthy and smiling.

Even so, it took all he had to remain in his seat until Kit wandered in the door ten minutes later, his cup clutched to his middle, his head down as if a supplicant.

"Can't ya dress a little better?" one of the asylum guards demanded. "Look like a scarecrow."

Braxton bobbed his head. "Just want a bite. No bother."

Beau raised his hand. "Soldier! Come on over here. I'll stand you to dinner."

"He's a beggar," one of the men complained.

"He's also a Rifleman, as was my brother who died at Busaco. Did you fight?"

That shut them up quickly enough. Braxton slid into a chair and set his cup down. Beau took a look inside. "Not a bad day, eh?"

"I've 'ad worse, for sure," Braxton said. "Thankee, milord, for 'elpin' out."

And that quickly, the others lost interest. It was no trouble then to order some stew and another pint and share desultory dialogue that hid the intelligence that had been shared.

"Pamela?!" he gasped, hearing that news.

Braxton just nodded.

Beau shook his head. "Not possible. Pip must be mistaken."

"She said that, as she'd been under the lady's bed for three hours, she should know what she looks like." Braxton considered his beer. "She was most definite about wanting to save her, Drummond. After what I've heard about Pamela's escapades, makes that wife of yours unnaturally kind."

Beau was still trying to digest the idea of Perfect Pamela in an asylum being drugged with laudanum. Pip was correct. It wasn't right, no matter how capriciously vile Pamela could be. But yes, he agreed. His Pip was truly inordinately kind.

Then he got the rest of the message.

"Two days?" he echoed, appalled. "It barely gives us time to get there."

"You need to get the information to Drake soonest," Kit said, sipping his beer.

"He's waiting to hear from me. You'll watch for Pip while I'm gone?"

"I will. Will you go to Bristol?"

Beau stared at him for a moment, his heart hitting his shoes.

Bloody hell. Bristol. Theo was supposed to be at Bristol. But Pip was here where she could be in imminent danger if those people learned of her connection to the government action. He could help either place. He wanted to help both.

He didn't know what to do. God, he did not know what to do.

20

H e stayed.

As Drake reminded him, while they sat in Drake's parlor being watched over by frisky angels, Theo would have the army to assist him at Bristol. There was no way they were going to leave the safety of the Prince of Wales to a handful of gentlemen spies, even if they had been successful in rooting out the conspiracy. As soon as he dispatched the flurry of messages to all parties involved, Drake would assist as well. After all. The Prince of Wales. Alex Knight could be dispatched to Portsmouth to oversee operations there with the home guard and revenue officers, and Ian Ferguson back to Plymouth as fast as possible.

"I would rather you not be involved at Bristol," Drake said, leaning back in his chair. "Might strain your patience too much. We'll send him up as soon as we separate him out. Why don't you maintain vigilance along with Braxton at the asylum and report to Hilliard, since that project is under his Household Army. If the Lions catch a whiff of our movements, they might try to cut their losses there."

And Beau had thought he couldn't feel any worse.

But before he could protest, Drake was on his feet. "In fact, why don't you head over to see him now? Organize the response if we find we need to go in. If there is a danger of losing any of the women, we won't be able to wait. Hilliard cannot afford to lose Schroeder."

Beau followed Drake to his feet. "And I cannot afford to lose my wife."

He almost stopped breathing. He hadn't exaggerated, he thought. He had survived believing that Theo had died. He doubted he would Pip. He might well lose her to Theo. He wouldn't even consider losing her to death.

IF PIP LEARNED nothing else changing beds and cleaning out chamberpots, it was that no matter what Beau paid his staff, it was not enough. She couldn't imagine being more exhausted. And then on top of her regular chores, she made it a point to claim the quieting rooms as part of her purview. Considering how much trouble she was having trying to eradicate that smell, she wasn't surprised that no one challenged her for them. Matron's only restriction for her was that she was only allowed into the rooms once they had been vacated.

She did not obey that directive. Along with her mop and bucket and scrub brush, she managed to smuggle in some food. Nothing fancy. Bread and cheese and a wrinkled apple or two. From the reaction she got, it could have been manna.

She hated this. She hated the fact that every time she opened those doors, their occupants would be huddled in the corner in the cold darkness. She hated that she could already see that Miss Schroeder was losing weight, and that Mrs. Baxter was beginning to look vacant and disconnected.

"How long has she been in here, Miss Schroeder?" she asked, since Mrs. Baxter just shook her head when asked.

Miss Schroeder lifted an eyebrow. "Considering the fact that I expect you to help me escape this hovel, do you not think you could see your way to calling me Barbara?"

To be truthful, Pip had never imagined it. But since Miss Schroeder—Barbara—was sitting on the floor tearing bread apart and gnawing on it like a badger, she supposed it wasn't too outlandish a request.

"How long, Barbara?"

She got a smile, even as her teacher kept chewing. And then, to show how far they had fallen, she spoke with her mouth full. "Well, I was put here some eight days ago, I believe. It is difficult to gage days in the dark. She came two days after."

"Have you heard anything from staff about the Lions?"

Barbara shook her head. "They only appear once a day to drop off food and empty the chamberpots, and they don't waste their time speaking to us. Although I get the strong impression that the good doctor works alongside Matron and the male guards to keep the Lion wives in control."

Pip's eyes widened. "The men?"

She shook her head. "They haven't bothered me. But there are others."

"I saw five red cards besides yours."

"In this I suspect they are egalitarian."

Pip kept thinking she couldn't be any angrier. She kept being wrong. Pip made a vow that she would be leaving this hellhole with them if she had to free every woman in the place.

Considering how every woman was being treated here, that might not be a bad idea. Although, since many of the families would just send their women to another facility, possibly futile.

After the first day with no contact from Diccan, no intervention, Pip took her walk around the campus, looking for a familiar face, wishing desperately for someone to talk to. No, she realized. Not someone. A particular one. She wanted a chance to sit with Beau and share everything. She wanted his opinion. More, she wanted his support. His comfort, even if he could only provide it in the dark.

She wasn't sure why. He had never given it easily.

Oh, she knew why. For so long he had seen her as a little girl. Certainly, her size and, blast it, *elfin* looks hadn't helped. And then, by the time he had realized his mistake, Pip had helped Theo to rebel enough to go to war. To go to war and disappear.

She couldn't even blame him. But it hurt. She knew the passion, the goodness, the need for love that roiled beneath his crust of skepticism. She knew that he had locked himself away where he couldn't feel the pain of loss. Where he didn't have to fear more. And now, he had to fear what Theo's return would mean, and would carry guilt for the question.

But oh, she wanted more. She wanted the chance to simply snuggle up against him and talk out everything she had faced and learned and overcome the last few days. She wanted him to help her dissect the conflicting feelings she had about Perfect Pamela, now one of the shuffling, muttering inmates. So lost in laudanum that when she had seen Pip pass by in her maid's uniform and mobcap, she hadn't even blinked.

And by St. Bertha's baskets, Pip wanted to lie in his arms and recreate the poignant sense of belonging she had so briefly felt when they were skin to skin, when he was inside her, changing her, wakening her, devastating her.

But she had sent him away. She had made him finally choose, because she couldn't crawl after him, begging him to see her anymore. And that hurt worst of all.

She got to the corner where she usually saw Kit Braxton, but the corner was empty. It was silly to feel bereft, but she was beginning to feel abandoned. She needed to know what was going on. Instead, she found herself turning away and wondering if she would get any sleep.

"Well there, missy. What are you doin' out here?"

Pip did not stop walking. This was the last thing she needed. "I am taking my walk as I do every evening, which you know since you stand at the guardhouse by the gate."

He was matching her steps. She gaged her distance from the kitchen door and was not encouraged. Why did men always do this? She almost found a grin, because her next thought was, why did the man she wanted to do this never do it?

"You don't have to be inside yet," the guard wheedled. "Why don't we visit in my guardhouse."

"No, thank you."

She could feel his breath on her neck.

"Not very friendly, are you?"

And then, between one breath and the next, his hands were on her arms, and he was spinning her around. Pip battled a flash of terror. No. This was *not* going to happen. She took in a breath just as his face came down to hers, and she drove her knee straight up into him.

His scream was most satisfying. Pip jumped back as he jackknifed onto the ground. "You...*bitch!*"

"Just be glad I did not use my knife," she rasped, straightening.

"You'll pay for..."

Pip was walking fast to the door. His sudden squeal made her turn. And there, as if called up by her wishful thinking stood Beau. Not the kind, smiling Beau she had been wishing for, though. This Beau was dark vengeance, his hands clasped around the guard's neck, the guard's feet dangling inches off the ground. Beau must have yanked him straight up. Pip saw it and found herself disconcerted that just as much as she was unsettled by his actions, she was elated. St. Steven's stones, she was *aroused*.

Well, that couldn't be allowed. Not when she was still trembling from the guard's attack. But there was Beau looking too much like the avenging angel.

Pip turned toward him. She came within inches of calling out his name and ruining everything.

"Don't...sir," she begged, hand out. The guard's face was turning purple, and he was scrabbling at Beau's hands. "He's not worth your being sent to prison. Please."

And then Beau finally looked at her, and time stopped. She swore her heart stopped. His dear chocolate eyes were so fierce, as cold as death. Until they met hers. Then, like lightning, they flared with such agony and relief she could barely stand it.

"You will apologize to the lady," he grated in the guard's ear, easing the pressure on his throat a bit. "And if I ever happen to see you molesting another woman, I will happily saw your cock off. Do. You. Understand?"

The guard rightly looked terrified. Pip felt terrified. She had the most horrible feeling Beau was balanced on a knife's edge of control.

But finally, the guard looked her way. "So...sorry. I thought...You..."

"You were wrong," Beau informed him and let go with a push that sent the man stumbling.

"Thank you," Pip spoke up and was horrified to hear that her voice was trembling as well. "I don't know what I would have done if you hadn't walked by."

And unbelievably, Beau grinned. "You would have used your knife, I imagine."

"Why, yes," she said, smiling back, trembly with reaction. "I imagine I would."

"Since this man works here, I hope you have a lock on your door."

She nodded. "And if that doesn't work, I have the knife, with which I am quite proficient."

"Then go in now," Beau said, "and I will wait here with this gentleman until you are safely inside. Then he and I shall have a bit of a talk."

Pip frowned. "Not too much of a talk."

"Just enough."

The last thing she saw before running for the kitchen door was the look of dread in the guard's dark eyes. She supposed she should have felt bad that it made her feel better.

BEAU WASN'T GOING to survive this. Walking back to the pub he had made his base, he rubbed at the scraped knuckles on his right hand and let loose the foulest curses he could think of. They needed to find another way of communicating. What if he hadn't been there tonight? What if she hadn't reacted so quickly?

He had to grin, though. By damn, she had a deadly knee. Hopefully in the future that guard would reconsider importuning young woman.

"Saw you was in a bit of a scuffle," the pub owner offered as Beau pushed open the door. "You took care of that pest?"

"You know him?"

"Only seen him around. One of the men works at the sanitarium. Don't like it. Don't like it at all, all those poor women and this jackal free on the grounds."

"Well, I don't think he'll be bothering her again. I got there just as she was disabling him with a pretty fierce knee."

The publican, a red-faced bear of a man, just nodded his head and picked up a stein to fill it. "This one's on me. We need more gentlemen in this neck of the woods."

Beau grinned, even though he hardly felt like it. "Why, thank you. So, that's an asylum? I wondered."

The man looked up and frowned. "For women. I could tell you stories."

Beau had been about to retreat to a table in the corner. Instead, he pulled up a barstool and sat.

"You're not from around here," the man mused.

Beau took a long draft of a surprisingly nice porter. "I'm not. Hope you don't mind. I'm supposed to meet a friend to do a bit of private work for me. He got delayed in Portsmouth and didn't know when he'd get here."

He got a slow nod. "Why not meet him at home?"

Beau's smile was wry. "'Cause my wife's at home, and she objects to me meetin' a man who soused me out of a monkey."

That got him honest laughter and eventually stories he didn't want to know about

Richmond Hills Asylum.

Beau wasn't sure anymore that he could wait until Drake gave the go ahead before getting Pip out. In fact, he should have kept going with her tonight, rather than let her remain anywhere near that bastard. Or the other bastards, from what he was hearing.

The problem was exactly what it would always be. She would never leave until she could get those women out with her.

It was time for another drink. Lord, by the end of this mess, he'd be drooling and singing sea chanties.

It was two days later in mid-morning when Pip realized something had changed. The atmosphere inside the asylum had suddenly gone tense and whispery, with the longer-term employees formed into clusters, and those clusters looking unsettled. Nervous. Angry. She tried to sidle up to listen to the whispered conversations, but they saw her and immediately dispersed.

Pip wanted to go check to see if Kit Braxton was at his post, but she was unaccountably afraid to leave the women alone. Patients were being led into their rooms and their doors locked.

Matron had disappeared into the pantry. Two of the guards entered from the back door and met with the matron, one the man who had assaulted her the night before. Pip couldn't take her eyes off them, even as she swept the floor in the dayroom.

She was afraid. She didn't know what to do or how to get a warning out. She couldn't get to her room to set the candle up. But she couldn't simply stand by. So she finished her sweeping and wandered into the kitchen for a glass of water. And did her best to listen to the conversation in the pantry.

"*All* of them? That's an awful lotta dead people. "

"You want them raising the alarm? The red cards first, though. And we'll need you inside to help or we'll never get out of here. Now start brewing tea. And give the laudanum a little help."

Pip kept her silence, unable to breathe. She had run out of time.

Carefully setting her glass down on the counter, she slipped out of the kitchen and made for the quieting rooms. She was already having trouble breathing and she hadn't even crossed the line yet. She was about to, though. She briefly closed her eyes and conjured up Beau to give her courage. Even though he wouldn't have wanted her to be anywhere near this. Would he be proud of her if she succeeded, or even more angry?

"Barbara," she murmured, opening her door. "It's time."

Miss Schroeder—Pip couldn't *not* think of her as Miss Schroeder—climbed to her feet and settled down her dress.

"The guards are inside right now. I have a terrible feeling they are preparing to poison the women with laudanum and foxglove. You and the other women with red cards first. I need you to run for help. There should be a one-armed soldier sitting at the corner with a tin cup. He is here to help."

Miss Schroeder brightened. "Braxton? Excellent."

"If he isn't there, I suppose you'll need to get to a magistrate."

"Don't worry. I know exactly how to get a quick message to Diccan. What will you do?"

Pip let go of a frustrated laugh. "I don't know. I have a knife and a small one-shot pistol to protect thirty ladies."

"Let Mrs. Baxter out. She can hide in an outbuilding."

Pip nodded. Miss Schroeder gave her a quick, hard hug and slipped out the door. "Be very careful. These are not good people."

Pip's smile was wry. "I already figured that out. Hurry."

The last Pip saw of Miss Schroeder, she was running up the steps and out into a cold, overcast late autumn day. Pip hoped with all her heart that Kit was on his street corner. They didn't have a moment to lose.

With that thought, she turned to Mrs. Baxter's door and unlocked it.

BEAU WAS the one who saw her first. He was bent over a bowl of soup when he spotted a familiar-looking woman step out of the asylum gate, her blond hair chopped-off and her attire a wrinkled, faded blue institutional dress and scuffed slippers. No coat, no bonnet, when the temperatures were barely above freezing.

"What's she doin' out there?" the publican demanded, stepping up to the window.

"Freezing herself, looks like."

Grabbing his coat, he ran out of the pub. Across the street, Braxton saw him and looked up. Beau discreetly pointed. Braxton was on his feet in a minute.

"Good heavens," Braxton said. "Barbara."

She was shivering. Beau reached them and slipped his coat over her shoulders. A few pedestrians noticed the activity and slowed, but nobody wanted to get involved with any of those women, so eyes were turned away and people moved on.

"Come into the shop," Braxton urged, and pulled them into the sweet shop that had been his backdrop.

She just nodded and followed. The proprietor inside took one look at the people who stepped through the door and disappeared into the back.

"A friend," Kit said. "How did you get out?"

She was shivering, so Beau grabbed the owner's stool and sat her out of sight of the window.

"Pippin Knight," she said. "Told me to get help. The staff is about to murder everyone incarcerated by the Lion, possibly the entire population. I suspect they got news from one of the attacks."

"They're certainly more efficient than we are," Kit retorted. "Haven't heard a thing yet. How long do you think we have?"

She shook her head, her hands clutching the coat closed. "I don't think very long. Especially if they come and find me gone. They know Pip has a key to the quieting room."

Beau frowned. "The what?"

"Isolation rooms. Pip emptied them out. She says the other women are locked in their rooms. The doors with the red cards are at most danger. Please. Hurry."

Kit stepped out of the sweet shop. "Thrasher!!"

Immediately a familiar teen clad in the most reprehensible of garments came trotting across the street. "Yeah, your worshipfulness?"

Now Beau recognized him. He was an unofficial page and spy for Lady Kate Lidge, who had long had a habit of taking in strays. Thrasher was also invaluable in ferreting out information in low places. Now he was grinning and bowing to Miss Schroeder.

"Reinforcements, Thrasher," Kit snapped. "Now. Here."

Without another word, Thrasher set off down the street to

hop on the back of a beer wagon that was heading towards Mayfair.

"I don't think I can wait," Beau protested. "How about I go in looking to tour a place for my sister."

"Wife," Schroeder said. "They like wives. Tell them she never got over losing the babe. And that you have an obscene amount of money. Oh. And here. I'm warm inside. I think you'll need the guns in these pockets."

Beau took her up on her offer.

"Go out the back," Braxton said, "and around the mews."

So, he did, picking up a hackney a few blocks over that could drop him off at the asylum gates.

Except that there was no one guarding the asylum gates to see him. He wasn't certain if that made him feel better or worse. It would be easier for him just to walk into the facility, but it also might mean they had already begun to carry out their plan inside.

Only one way to find out and calm his frantic heart. *Please let Pip be in there. Let her be safe.*

He at least got the answer to one of those questions when he blithely walked through the two separate doors that should have been locked and all the way into the patient area.

"Hello!" he called as he assessed the hallway beyond. It looked like a beehive had overturned in there. Staff were bouncing about in seemingly random ways. What he didn't see, was patients. "I rang, but nobody answered!"

The person who turned his way was a stern, gray-haired woman in a dress and apron so starched he could hear her rustling.

"Keep your voice down, sir," she said, striding up. "This is not Astley's. How did you get in here?

Beau pointed. "Door was open. Pardon me sayin', doesn't seem all that secure that way."

She stopped a few feet away and glowered. "What do you need, please?"

He looked around as if assessing the lay-out, when he was really looking for Pip. Hoping to draw her out, he spoke in a loud north-county voice.

"Well," he said, slipping his hands into his coat pockets to find the reassuring bulk of two pistols. "I come to see whether your place would be a good fit for my wife. Respectable, you know. Safe. Settled. 'As a very nervous disposition, she does, and needs quiet. Tried care at home, but she kept slippin' out, and what with me bein' at my mills all hours..."

The woman's posture didn't change as Beau thought it should. She should have looked far more interested. All those mills. All that money to spend on an inconvenient wife.

As if on cue, there was a monstrous crash toward the back of the building, and a too-familiar voice crying, "Oh, St. Simon's spectacles, look what I've done! I'm so sorry. Shall I mop it up?"

Of course, everyone turned that way to see a river of what looked like very strong tea flooding from an urn that had shattered all across the floor.

"You numbskull!" his greeter howled, spinning in that direction.

"I'm that sorry, ma'am," his Pip apologized, twisting her hands in her skirts like a prized ninny. "I'll clean it right up."

Beau wasn't certain whether he felt better or worse that when she caught sight of him her expression didn't change by an iota.

"Is this how this place is always run?" he demanded.

The matron turned on him as a middle-aged man in a suit skidded to a halt before Pip.

"Come back later," the matron snapped to him.

"You imbecile!" the man screamed at Pip, and before Beau could move swung on her like a longshoreman, knocking her right down into the mess on the floor.

"Here, now!" Beau protested, running around the matron to get to them. "There's no call for such as that!"

He came within an inch of serving the man his own punishment.

"Who are you?" the doctor demanded.

"Who are *you*?" Beau countered as he crouched to a wincing Pip. "Ta harm a wee soul such as this. You all right, miss?"

"I've 'ad worse, sir," she answered, a hand to the rising bruise on her jaw, and then in a tone so low no one but Beau could hear. "Don't drink the tea."

Even caught in such a mad tableau, he almost laughed. Winking at her, he helped her to her feet. One side of her uniform was soaking, and tea dripped from her hair.

"Clean up the floor or get out," the matron hissed. "We need another urn!" she called to one of the passing staff, somebody above Pip, if her tidier outfit and starched apron was any indication. Matron only got a nod on the way by before disappearing around the corner herself.

"Please, sir," Pip whispered when Beau didn't let go. "I need to clean..."

"Are ya sure?" he asked, peering down at her. "Ye're welcome to work in one o' me mills in Birming'am. Can always used a good strong girl there."

"No, sir," she said, pulling away. "I need to clean now. Wet floors is dangerous."

So, for the moment Beau turned to the gentleman. "Now, 'oo might you be again, a man who'd strike a wee girl. I have plenty o' girls in my mills, and ha'n't served one of them so in fifteen years."

"I am Dr. Whaley," the man said, leading Beau back toward the front door. "The administrator of Richmond Hills."

When the man gave a general wave of his hand to indicate the institution, Beau caught sight of a signet. A red ruby with some kind of carving. Beau remembered the sign out front. Tasteful, simple. The name and a red Tudor rose. Oh, hell. Why hadn't he noticed? The Lions used the Tudor rose as a signal.

Turning back to Whaley, he smiled. "Ye wouldna strike my missus, would ye?"

Whaley was just straightening and puffing out his chest to respond when he was interrupted again.

"Who has been in the pantry?!" the matron yelled, running back out. "It's gone! It's all gone, and we haven't any more!"

Every staff member stopped in their tracks and turned towards her, some looking frightened, some angry, some bemused. Pip was studiously mopping up the lake of tea that pooled over half the floor. She only looked up briefly, but in that time, Beau was certain she knew. What was gone? What exactly was enraging the matron?

One of the men pointed right at Pip. "Saw her in the pantry not an hour ago. Want I should find out?"

Not the guard Beau had chastised, but another that didn't look much more civilized. The other guard, though, was coming up behind him, and suddenly both looked far too avid.

Pip didn't even look at him. "The pantry?" she asked, blinking like a child. "o'course I was in there. Missed me lunch and 'ad some bread and cheese, didn't I?"

"Did you now?" the Matron said, her voice slithery as she approached. "And what else did you do? Let me smell your hands, girl."

Pip looked surprised. "My 'ands? There's naught there but lye soap and piss."

Beau rose on the balls of his feet, suddenly feeling the real threat. What did the matron want?

"Where is it?" she growled as she grabbed Pip's hands and lifted them to her own face to sniff. "You've taken to stealing laudanum now, girl?" she demanded, pushing them away again. "And foxglove? For what, I wonder?"

"You can smell that on somebody's hand?" the irrepressible Pip demanded, sniffing her own palms. "Not mine. Don't hold with the stuff."

"Laudanum?" Beau echoed. "*Foxglove*? What kind of place are you running here? That's poison, that is!"

Suddenly, a back door slammed open and yet another player entered the stage holding a teapot in one hand. "The quieting rooms are empty! Somebody's let them out!"

"Don't think I want ta leave my Myrtle here after all," Beau said, watching everyone freeze again and give him a pointed look. "Queer doin's, ya ask me."

He was just about to turn for the door when the doctor took hold of his arm.

"You won't have to worry about it," he said, sounding unperturbed. "Richmond Hills is about to shut down. Along with you."

Which was when Beau looked down to see that the gun suddenly resting in the doctor's hand was pointing right at Beau's chest. He was reaching into his coat pocket when the gun went off.

21

He should have felt something, was Beau's first thought. At least a punch to his chest. His second was that the doctor's eyes weren't focusing, and his hand had begun to drop. When the doctor began to topple, Beau realized that it hadn't been the man's gun that had fired at all.

His first reaction was to catch the doctor's dead weight before it took him down too. His next was to check on Pip, only to find her standing there beyond the Matron, a small smoking pistol in her hand that was still pointed his way. She looked almost as shocked as the matron. Not nearly as shocked as he was.

He thought to check the doctor. Just as he bent, the wall in front of him exploded. A gunshot echoed behind him. After that, all hell broke loose.

Beau spun around to check on Pip to see that more than the doctor were armed. Those two guards were running their way brandishing pistols.

Beau retrieved the doctor's gun. He saw the first man raise his gun toward Pip. He didn't hesitate. Stepping away from the doctor, he shot the man in the chest, just as he fired. The guard dropped to splash into the pond of tea. The shot slammed harmlessly into the ceiling.

"Run, Pip!" he yelled, ducking the plaster that rained down on him.

But it was too late. Damn him if the matron didn't pull her own gun. Before Beau could get to her, Pip grabbed hold of that gun with one hand and slammed the heel of her other hand straight up against the woman's nose.

The matron screeched, but she held on. So did Pip, even though the matron was at least two heads taller and two stone heavier.

Beau tried to get a bead on the woman, but Pip was in the way. Staff were scattering, most fleeing down the hallway to the back. *Where were the patients?* Beau wondered briefly, hearing screams and wails somewhere. Then he realized that the second guard hadn't stopped. And two armed women followed him.

Beau knew he was running out of time and ammunition. And who knew who else was tucked back there waiting for their turn?

"Pip!" he yelled, still unable to get a good shot. "Your knife!"

He thought she would dispatch the matron. Instead, unbelievably, in a move Beau would recount innumerable times over the ensuing years, without letting go of the gun she was struggling over, in one smooth move, Pip lifted her knee to draw a fair-sized knife from an ankle strap and sent it winging hard to embed itself in the other guard's throat just as he and Beau were both lifting their guns. The guard went crashing to the floor next to the other one, pumping blood over the sterile tiles and into the tea.

Even still struggling, Pip shot Beau a look of astonishment. "Would you look at that."

He couldn't help it. He laughed. The women kept coming.

He had two shots. What did he do?

He had two more weapons headed his way and the matron who had just grabbed Pip by the throat. He ran towards them, but he couldn't fire without hitting Pip. Then Pip gave him a brief look and spun around until the matron's back was toward him. Damn. She'd given him a clean shot. He fired. The woman screamed and dropped her gun. Her right shoulder exploded in scarlet, and she went down by the others. She wasn't dead. But she was impotent. The floor was getting to be an obstacle course, littered with bodies and various fluids Beau was going to have to step over to get to Pip.

So, he raised his last gun and pointed it at the oncoming women. Pip did the same.

"Now, really," he said. "Wouldn't you rather turn state's evidence? Your other choices are to be shot or hung."

Both of them, tall women with broad shoulders, skidded to a halt. Looking at each other, they dropped their weapons. Before Beau could do it himself Pip trotted around the growing pool of blood and tea on the floor to pick them up.

"Why didn't I know you had to have a gun to work here?" she demanded with a sloppy grin.

"They made us," one of the women said, looking mournful. "Said it was good protection."

Pip smiled. "I'm glad we didn't have to shoot you. You're good people." Then, turning, she caught sight of the floor. "And who's going to clean all this up, I'd like to know?"

"You're not a maid," one of the women asked. "Are you?"

Pip beamed at them. Beau fought a hot tide of rage. It was normal, he knew. But he wanted to kick somebody. He wanted to...

He looked at Pip and thought how he would have been furious at her before. His heart was still racing, not for fear for himself, but for her. Once, he would have scooped her up and run, chastising her all the way. And yet, he couldn't. His Pip was amazing.

"No," a voice behind him said. "She is definitely not a maid. I might not let you two out together again. Look at the mess you made."

And there walking in the front door with soldiers pouring in behind him, was Diccan Hilliard, dressed for a stroll through Hyde Park, leaning on a silver-tipped cane.

"Thrasher got to you?" Beau asked as soldiers filed down the sides of the room.

"We were already on our way. Miss Schroeder warned me this would happen."

Pip looked around. "That there would be a terrible scene?"

His smile was immeasurably dry. "That you would take care of the problem before we got here."

"Well," Pip said, grinning like an urchin. "I had some help."

And then two things happened at once. It seemed that Pip's adventure finally caught up with her and her knees quite suddenly failed her, leaving her sitting in an untidy lump right next to the epic puddle. And Beau heard a voice he never thought he never would hear again in his lifetime.

"Leave it to you two to create a stir."

Theo.

Beau froze. Then he turned, his heart in his throat, stricken silent. He was there. Theo. Dressed like a dockworker in a blue knit cap. Healthy. Whole. Impossibly, grinning, hands on hips as if he were a father surveying an unruly child. Beau thought his heart might explode.

But he didn't even have to think about what happened next. "Hold there a minute," he told Theo and turned instead to collect Pip.

❧

BEAU HAD his chance to hug his brother. Pip had her chance as well, since Theo sat himself down in one of the day room's comfortable chairs as the mess in the hallway was cleared up and Pip and Barbara Schroeder and Diccan and the aides Claire and Edna sorted out who went where and how to contact families.

It turned out, Pip was relieved to see, that Claire and Edna had thought they were protecting their patients. They had known, of course, that some of the women were here for reasons that had nothing to do with their mental health. They had tried, it seemed, to ease their way. To ease all the women's way. Other staff who wandered back in, corroborated their assertion. They asked that if possible they be allowed to stay, at least until the families came, and went off to settle all the patients, including Lady Pamela, who still didn't have the clarity to recognize anyone. And yes, they helped separate the sheep and the goats as Pip and three other maids cleaned up the floor.

Pip couldn't just leave it there, after all, no matter how much the Drummond brothers objected. Not only because the blood would stain her dreams for the rest of her life, but because of the large quantities of laudanum and foxglove she had poured into the tea urn before she sent it crashing onto the floor. It wouldn't take much at all to kill a horse.

And, as she reminded Beau, when she was overset, she needed occupation.

But all of that happened long after Theo walked in the door. Or maybe not so long. It just felt long, as epiphanies should.

At least it happened a good while after Beau picked her up and cradled her in his arms. After he turned to both Theo and Diccan to say, "Welcome home, you reprehensible urchin. Does this mean we have successfully interfered with the attacks?"

Diccan grinned, as if he wasn't standing five feet away from where soldiers were collecting bodies, and the floor looked like the first plague of Egypt. "We did indeed. The Prince sends his heartfelt thanks and wonders if you would like a title."

Beau frowned. "I have a title."

Diccan's grin widened. "He wasn't talking about you." Then he turned to Pip.

"We can gladly discuss this later, Diccan," Beau said. "But first, I must take my wife somewhere quiet to have an important talk."

"More important than me possibly being made a peer?" Pip asked, not making a move from her comfortable berth in Beau's arms.

He glared down at her. "Much."

Theo tilted his head like a bright bird. "We aren't going to have to summon a constable, are we?"

Beau actually smiled. "Not this time. Don't count out the possibility in the future, though."

And then he turned to the back of the asylum.

"What are you doing?!" Pip demanded, even as she settled deeper into the comfort of his arms. "That was your brother back there!"

Beau shoved open the door into the back garden. "And he will most certainly be there when we finish our talk. Not a very impressive garden, is it?"

Pip relaxed against his chest as they walked. "Nobody gets out here much."

Beau looked around. "That's because there's nowhere to sit."

"Try the greenhouse. We grow a lot of our produce."

And a greenhouse there was. With the bonus of a bench and a fire to keep the place hot and steamy, an oasis of greenery in an otherwise sterile place. Beau pushed his way in and along the path to the single white wrought Iron bench. And there he sat down, Pip still tucked close in his lap.

"I'm not so sure this is a good idea right now," she protested, hating that her voice was suddenly trembling. That her arms and legs were as well. St Bede's bed, she was about to have a reaction. "I can take care of myself, you know."

"I know you can," Beau responded gently, bending his head over hers so that she was completely surrounded. Completely nurtured and protected. "But just for this once, try to be a delicate flower and let me be the strong one."

She could never in her life remember a moment when she felt so safe, so whole. So cherished, blast it.

It wouldn't last. She knew that.

"I had no other choice, Beau," she said, her voice thickening uncomfortably, the sound of that gun loud again in her ears. "I had to do it."

And oddly, she trusted Beau to know what she meant.

He tightened his hold on her. "You saved my life, you unruly brat. Who taught you how to shoot like that?!"

Her laugh sounded a bit frantic. "You did, you clunch."

He pulled back. "Never. I cannot imagine encouraging such behavior."

She felt as if she were suddenly one giant smile. "It was the year we were all to become pirates."

"Ah." He nodded. "Yellowbeard and company."

"I even knitted a beard from yellow yarn." The trembling was worse, and she was afraid her stomach would disappoint her. "This, however, is not how I anticipated feeling after an action."

He wrapped even more tightly around her. "Like you'll fly apart? Like your breakfast will make an abrupt return? Like you want to cry and laugh and curl into a ball and disappear?"

She pulled back a bit, making certain he wasn't easing his grip. "Exactly. Does this happen every time?"

He looked down at her and his eyes were fathomless and dark. "I'm afraid so."

She nodded and tucked herself back in, her tears beginning

to soak Beau's coat. "Does this have something to do with why so many old soldiers drink?"

He tightened his hold again. "I imagine it does."

She nodded against the bulwark of his chest. "Have you felt it?"

For a moment, all she heard was silence. But when she lifted her head, it was to see the price of his service in his gentle brown eyes. "Yes, Pip. I have."

She tucked herself back into his embrace. "I don't like it, Beau. I don't like it at all."

His breath hitched. "I know, sweetheart. I'm sorry."

She just kept nodding, sad that he understood. "I am sorry for the state your coat after all this."

"Cry all you want. You earned it."

She shook her head. "I don't want to," she protested, crying. "It gives me a headache."

"We never did practice what to do for those when we were pirates, did we?"

She shook her head, burrowed deep into his coat as she sobbed. "We did not."

Beau was good enough to let her wear herself out a bit, tucked safely in his arm, his hand against her hair.

"There is something I must ask you, Pip."

She settled for a small nod. She was too deeply folded into her sanctuary to manage more.

"Is this likely to happen again?"

That brought her out like a badger from a set. "What do you mean?"

He used his thumb to gently wipe tears from her cheeks. "If someone asks you to put yourself at risk for, say, your country or your family or...well, me. Will you dive right in?"

Pip gave him the courtesy of thinking about it. She felt as if she had finally done something worthwhile. She also suspected that she would have nightmares featuring that moment when her knife had flown true. When that man, who hadn't really been a bad man, had looked right into her eyes, his own shocked and despairing and hollow, and she saw his life blink out like a night star.

She had killed a man. She had killed Matron. Oh, she had needed to do it. But their souls would weigh on hers for the rest of her life. Just how easily would they rest?

They certainly weren't now.

But would Beau be there to help her carry the load? Could she help carry his?

"Well," she retorted, desperately trying to keep the tone light, "I might not save you. You can be quite an annoyance."

Leaning over, he dropped a kiss on the shell of her ear, and her toes curled. "How about now? Am I an annoyance now?"

Pip held her breath against the chills that raced through her body. "Are you attempting to bribe a different answer out of me, sir?"

This time he kissed her eye. "I am."

She chuckled. "Well, you're not going to manage it here. We're about five minutes away from any of those louts out there barging in for more answers."

There was a rather long silence in response. "What if we continued this discussion back at home?"

That brought Pip straight up to stare at him. "Who's home? And I warn you. My parents are light sleepers."

Lifting his hand, he stroked the side of her face, her neck, her shoulder.

"*Our* home."

Now her heart thundered, and she was trembling for an entirely different reason. "And after tonight, what? Do I fill my days with housework and charitable endeavors while you hibernate in your study? Will you ignore me until I can coerce you into bed, and then punish me with silence for my presumption?"

"Theo would never let me."

"We are not speaking of Theo....." She hiccuped, a hair's breadth away from a sob. "Doesn't he look wonderful? Oh, Beau, he's alive!"

Finally, Beau sat her down alongside him. "And what does that mean, Pip?"

She shook her head, so out of patience with this thick-headed lump. "It means that my oldest friend and your beloved brother is safe. That we have been granted a miracle." She glared at him. "It means he will be godfather to our children. What did you think it meant?!"

For the first time, he looked away. Completely out of patience and frantic for a sign that she wasn't just wasting her time all over again, Pip took hold of his face and turned it to her.

"When in my life, Beauregard William Villiers Francis Drummond, have I expressed an undying wish to have Theo's babies? Teach me how to swordfight, perhaps. Help me decode enemy messages. Even engage in a horse race across Delamere. But never...*ever*...have I —nor has he, come to mention it— expressed an undying devotion or pledged to live with him till old age." She laughed. "By all that's holy, we would have murdered each other long since."

Beau tensed up again. "But he has expressed a desire to marry you. He said it to me."

Pip thought she might cry for him, wishing he had spoken to her years ago. Blast strong, silent viscounts. "Let me guess. 'If no one else marries good old Pip, I'll have to do it myself. She would be an asset following the drum.'"

Beau's horrified expression said it all.

Pip sighed and reached up to kiss him. "My darling boy, he only said that to comfort me in case you failed to come up to scratch. And I imagine he said it to you to goad you into doing it."

For the longest moments, there was nothing but absolute silence in the greenhouse. Even the rustle of autumn winds didn't reach inside where Pip struggled to hold herself perfectly still before Beau's ambivalence. She would *not* beg him again, even if it meant standing up from this bench and walking away from him forever. He had to know that the choice was his. That he hadn't been coerced by her.

But couldn't he see that she needed him to ease the nightmares and strengthen the light? Couldn't he see that he was her home?

Just when Pip was about to flee, Beau stunned her by getting up himself. She stopped breathing, certain he was about to do the walking away. Frantic with the fear of it. Frozen with the struggle of keeping her mouth shut.

And then, as if he were in the parlor of her parent's house, he simply dropped to one knee.

Pip actually gasped.

He grinned. "I know. Miracles can be overwhelming."

She couldn't even find a sharp retort.

"So tell me, Brat," he said, reaching up to take hold of her shaking hands. "You said I should come to you. You didn't say what your answer would be."

Pip pulled in a shaky breath. "There is only one way to find out." She hated that her voice shook, too.

"In that case," he said, clearing his throat, his hand cold in hers. Nervous? *Beau?*

"Phillipa Ellen Alexandra Trentham Knight, would you consent to be my wife?"

"Why?"

He all but reared back. "Why? Because I love you, you scrubby elf. Because I finally realized that what I love most about you is that you are fearless."

She shook her head. "I wouldn't be so confident about that."

He smiled. "Let me correct that. You are courageous,

because you fight for what you believe in. Even if that misbegotten clunch is me. You make me laugh, and you make me swear, and you make me impatient for what the rest of my life will become. Marry me, damn you, so I can get off the floor."

Her giggle echoed from the glass even as more tears slid down her cheeks. "You could have saved your knees. It might have slipped your mind, but we already are married. By a bishop, no less."

"That wasn't any fun, though. This time, let's have some fun."

Pip was already delighted with his proposal. But the next moment set the seal on it. He lost his smile. He tightened his hold on her hands. He faced her like a man scaling a great wall. And then he said it. "Please."

Pip did stop breathing then. She swore her heart stopped. How does one say no to *that*?

She didn't, of course. Pulling as hard as she could, she yanked him off the floor and back onto the bench, where her acceptance was punctuated with some of the most lovely kisses of her life.

"There is one more thing," Beau murmured a little later as he stroked a hand along her arm.

"What's that?"

He pulled back to look her in the eye, his own earth-brown eyes finally, thankfully, brimming with love. "An apology. I have been a coward, Pip. I've been too afraid to love you. It was too much, too..."

"Dangerous," she said with a smile. "Because if you loved me you might lose me like Theo. You might. I might lose you. But I think what Theo taught us wasn't to fear love, but to cherish it every moment we have it."

Lifting his hand, Beau ran a finger gently down the side of her face. "I'm not certain whether I am going to be more intimidated by your courage or your wisdom."

She grinned. "Kind of a surprise coming from an elf, isn't it?"

"Not from this one." And he rewarded her wisdom with more kisses of the very best kind.

It was quite a while after that they returned to the asylum to help the others sort things out.

EPILOGUE

"Are you sure this is what you want to do?"

The afternoon could have been nicer. A late autumn storm raged around the old walls of Delamere, rattling the windows and sending a hint of smoke from old fireplaces back into the rooms.

The rooms themselves were a bit bare, as their previous furnishings had been sent off to Hannick House, where Beau Drummond's aunt and uncle could enjoy the snarling gilt beasts wrapped around all their furniture and wallpaper. The staff, once assuring their loyalty to the Viscount and Viscountess Drummond, had happily remained and made the old house a comfortable place to plan a future.

The only two chairs situated in the breakfast room were currently occupied by Viscount Drummond and his brother the newly named Baron Drummond. It had been Prinny's compromise after Pip had graciously thanked him for the honor but let him know she preferred her own name. He had passed the title to Theo instead, another of the heroes who had saved him from assassination, and Pip had invited him to her wedding. Her third wedding.

The first had, of course, been at Ripton Hall. The second had been in London at St. George's, just as any good ton wedding should be. The third would be at Delamere so the neighborhood could enjoy feting their Miss Pip and Lord Beau. Also, so the duchess could help plan the festivities.

The best part for Pip would be that her friends would be joining her in front of the altar. It was not to be their first weddings either, but they all agreed that if you couldn't throw the weight of your title about in order to take advantage of the festive Yule season with special ceremonies, what was the thing worth anyway?

What was being discussed now in the Breakfast Room were the plans for after the wedding.

"I am perfectly happy with the idea of being Delamere's steward," Theo Drummond said, sipping at his coffee. No one at Delamere had been able to enjoy tea since that last day at Richmond Hills. The color of it could hide so many surprises. "But, America, Beau? Are you certain you are ready for the wilds of that continent?"

Taking a bite of one of Pip's newest hobbies, something called a flapjack slathered in butter and syrup she said she had discovered in Savannah, Georgia, Beau smiled. "Pip says I shall love it. She says the capitol is a fever swamp, but that the mountains are lovely, and Charleston cultured. And, as she has reminded me, having a diplomatic post in an English-speaking country gives me added time to brush up on my French and German before we accept posts there. But we won't accept if you would prefer to keep your freedom. And really, it won't be for another couple of months."

Leaning back in his chair, Theo gazed out the window where the bare tree limbs tortured themselves against the windows. "I can say with impunity, big brother, that I have had quite enough excitement and travel for a very long while. I will take great pleasure in playing nursemaid for Delamere while you go gallivanting about for the government. It will be good practice for my own estate." Another perk of a title. Taking another sip of coffee, he considered his brother over the rim. "And you? Will you be shedding your cover as a *bon vivant*?"

Beau grinned. "I do believe so. The last thing I wish is for Pip to be bothered by inconvenient rumors, so I have turned in my Rakes membership."

"You mean you don't want Pip to use her newfound knowledge of poison on you."

"I mean my services are no longer needed."

Theo lifted an eyebrow. "You don't mean that the Lions are vanquished?"

"Not at all, I'm afraid. It simply means our adversaries have gone to ground for the moment. But other younger lights can carry the torch. I am now an old married man."

"I hope not," he heard from the doorway and smiled. "I would hate to miss the kind of exercise we enjoyed last night. I understand it is good for your health."

Beau reached out and wrapped his arm around Pip's waist. "Cease, wife. You put me to blush."

Both she and Theo laughed. "These diplomats are so sensitive," she informed her brother-in-law with an arch smile before dropping a kiss on the top of her husband's head.

"Are you looking forward to your post?" Theo asked.

She nodded. "I am. When I was a little girl, I met a young gentleman of the Iroquois nation who promised to teach me the Iroquois language and to track, and his sister will show me their beadwork. I certainly think it would be a far nicer accent piece in our home than jackal's heads."

Theo's grin was delighted. "I expect at least a vest to wear with my formal attire."

Pip turned to Beau. "Did I hear that you are giving up the Rakes, husband?"

"Completely," Beau assured her.

"Too bad. I think my new tracking skills could come in handy."

He shook his head. "Exactly why I am leaving. I would never get a wink of sleep thinking of what trouble you could get into."

"No clandestine work at all?"

"None."

She sighed. "You do take all the fun out of life."

"You'll be busy enough with diplomatic dinners and abolition."

"I suppose. I will miss the excitement, though. I might go in search of the various people who have disappeared after our mission to help me ween myself."

Miss Schroeder, having finished her assignment at Richmond Hills, had faded away somewhere. There was a pool among Pip's friends as to whether she was now posing as an opera singer or royal gardener. Mrs. Baxter, now widowed, was living with her children, and Perfect Pamela had retreated to the estate she had brought into marriage, which turned out to be a good thing, since her husband had evidently run off somewhere with Gerta of all people. Drake assured them that measures were being taken to find out where.

Truthfully? Pip doubted she would do anything for the Rakes ever again. She was still having nightmares over the last excitement. She had also sworn never to pick up a gun again. America was looking better and better.

With her luck, that was where Pamela's husband and her lady's maid had eloped.

"No tracking the enemy," Beau told her. "No code breaking or impersonations or surveillance."

Pip sighed. "The quiet life for me."

"If it makes you feel any better," Theo said with an impish grin. "I have sworn off the fun stuff as well. I have resigned, retreated, retired. I shall settle myself into the bucolic life of a gentleman farmer and leave endangered people to others."

As if he had been called, Foster stepped into the doorway. "Milady, you have two guests."

Pip straightened. "We have no furniture, Foster. Where did you put them?"

"They wait in the front hall. One is a Miss Schroeder."

That brought everybody to their feet.

"Good heavens," Pip said. "Bring them in here."

Foster dropped another bow and left. He was gone only a few minutes when he returned followed by two women. Pip smiled to see Miss Schroeder, looking healthy and bright in a lovely Nile green round gown, her lovely blonde hair just about the same length as Pip's and looking much tidier.

"I know it is early," Miss Schroeder apologized, "but I believe I need some help. Are you still among the Rakes, Lord Drummond?"

That brought both men to their feet.

Beau frowned. "Not as such. What can we do?"

Miss Schroeder sighed. Shaking her head, she stepped aside to reveal what looked to be her exact twin, an elegant blond woman with a flawless face and sad eyes. "I'd like to present Lady Riordan. She needs some help."

Before Pip could say anything, Theo stepped up, his attention on their new guest. "I believe I could be in the Rakes if you want."

Mrs. Riordan's smile was beatific. Theo beamed right back at her.

Beau and Pip exchanged glances. Pip grinned. "I think we'll need to look for a new estate agent after all."

ALSO BY EILEEN DREYER

A Prince of a Guy

The Princess and the Pea

A Rose for Maggie

A Soldier's Heart

A Walk on the Wild Side

Perchance to Dream(RITA)

Timeless

The Kendalls

Jake's Way

Simple Gifts

Some Men's Dreams

A Stranger's Smile

Worth Any Risk

Edge of the World

Lightning Strikes

Playing the Game

Hotshot

Don't Fence Me In

The Road to Mandalay

Daughters of Myth

Dangerous Tempation

Dark Seduction

Deadly Redemption

ABOUT THE AUTHOR

New York Times bestselling author and RWA Hall of Fame member Eileen Dreyer and her evil twin Kathleen Korbel have published over forty novels and novellas, and ten short stories in genres ranging from medical suspense to paranormal to multiple sub-genres in romance. She is thrilled to bring her work, including the continuation of her Drake's Rakes series, which she considers historical romantic adventure, to Oliver-Heber Books.

A native of St. Louis, where she still lives with her husband Rick and family, Dreyer is an RN, BS with two decades experience, including sixteen in trauma medicine before retiring to write full time. She is also trained in in forensic nursing, death investigation and Tactical EMS (as in being a medic on a SWAT team) (yeah, it was that cool).

A seasoned conference speaker, Dreyer travels to research, and uses research as an excuse to travel, including an unforgettable participation in the 200th anniversary Duchess of Richmond Ball and Battle of Waterloo. She has animals but refuses to subject them to the limelight. And yes. She was on Jeopardy. The way she puts the results is that she won the silver medal.

Visit Eileen's website:
Www.eileendreyer.com